Praise for the Woodfalls Girls Novels

Contradictions

"Tiffany King pours her soul into each book. She captures the hearts and minds of her characters perfectly, weaving tales of angst, hope, and redemption." —M. Leighton, *New York Times* bestselling author

"I absolutely loved this book . . . With quirky, unforgettable characters that will make you laugh and swoon, *Contradictions* needs to be at the top of your must-reads!"

—A.L. Jackson, *New York Times* bestselling author of *Come to Me Softly*

"If you are looking for a New Adult filled with fun, fandom, romance, and the perfectly sweet kind of opposites attracting, then *Contradictions* is the book for you."

—Jay Crownover, *New York Times* bestselling author of the Marked Men novels

Misunderstandings

"A beautifully woven story of a love that can withstand anything."

—Molly McAdams, *New York Times* bestselling author

"Funny, real, moving, and passionate, *Misunderstandings* is a MUST-READ for New Adult contemporary romance fans."

—Samantha Young, *New York Times* bestselling author

continued . . .

"Sweet and sexy! Great characters and an intriguing romance . . . So good!" —Cora Carmack, *New York Times* bestselling author

No Attachments

"Super sweet and swoon-worthy!"
—Jennifer L. Armentrout, #1 *New York Times* bestselling author

"Allow me to summarize *No Attachments*: Great story. Amazing characters. Awesome read." —*Book Freak Book Reviews*

"Readers will spend the first half of this story on the edge of their seats and the last half hugging a box of tissues."
—Priscilla Glenn, bestselling author

"Sweet, beautiful, funny, and heartbreaking all rolled into one amazing story." —Tara Sivec, *USA Today* bestselling author

"The story itself is heartwarming, which really is a characteristic of a Tiffany King book. Her stories always turn struggles into strength and her characters always find the good. That's one of the reasons I love to read her books. They're real. They're emotional. They're heartwarming." —*Stuck in Books*

"*No Attachments* will leave you more than a little attached to Ashton and Nathan." —*Book Angel Booktopia*

"Absolutely heartbreakingly beautiful." —*Once Upon a Twilight*

Contradictions

A Woodfalls Girls Novel

TIFFANY KING

BERKLEY BOOKS, NEW YORK

THE BERKLEY PUBLISHING GROUP
Published by the Penguin Group
Penguin Group (USA) LLC
375 Hudson Street, New York, New York 10014

USA • Canada • UK • Ireland • Australia • New Zealand • India • South Africa • China

penguin.com

A Penguin Random House Company

This book is an original publication of The Berkley Publishing Group.

Library of Congress Cataloging-in-Publication Data

King, Tiffany.
Contradictions / Tiffany King.—Berkley trade paperback edition.
p. cm.—(A Woodfalls Girls novel)
ISBN 978-0-425-27480-4 (paperback)
1. Love stories. 2. College stories. I. Title.
PS3611.I5863C66 2014
813'.6—dc23
2014031340

PUBLISHING HISTORY
Berkley trade paperback edition / January 2015

PRINTED IN THE UNITED STATES OF AMERICA

10 9 8 7 6 5 4 3 2 1

Cover photo by Greg Daniels / ImageBrief.
Cover design by Lesley Worrell.
Interior text design by Tiffany Estreicher.

ACKNOWLEDGMENTS

To all the readers, for your overwhelming support. Thank you, Kevan and Kate, for your guidance. I truly adore working with you. To Jennifer, I may never be able to repay you for all the help and advice you have given me, but you have my gratitude forever. Finally, to my family, because there is nothing better.

1.

"Where's Chuck?" Cameo asked, handing me a beer she had snagged from the coolers that lined the floors in the kitchen of the frat house we were hanging out in. The house was Gamma Phi something or other. Honestly, I couldn't remember, and I didn't care. They were all the same to me anyway.

"Who knows? Playing darts with the guys, I think." Hopefully, they were using his head as the dartboard.

"You two make up?" she asked, raising her eyebrows.

"I think you misunderstood me, sweets. When I said, 'who knows,' I meant, who cares. I hope someone throws a dart that sticks right in his egotistical ass," I corrected her, not feeling very appreciative of the guy who was supposed to be my current boyfriend. Of course, after only two dates, it didn't seem right to fall into that trap, as far as I was concerned.

She laughed, taking a long drink from her beer before answering. "Another one bites the dust," she continued, holding up her bottle to toast.

"Cheers," I answered, clinking my bottle to hers without further comment. I twisted the cap off my beer as I surveyed the rowdy crowd around us. The decibel level at frat parties was always nothing less than near deafening. Not that I was complaining. I was in my element—the louder it got, the better. This was the kind of scene I didn't see when I still lived at home and went to community college near Woodfalls. Going to an actual university was like stepping into another world. A world that I took to immediately. I was loud and raucous, so what?

Cameo and I left the kitchen and headed outside to the patio, which gave us a front-row seat to all the action. The guys were entertaining the crowd by trying to one-up each other with one crazy stunt after the next. We'd already seen some idiot jump from the balcony on the second floor, hugging a mattress. Cheers erupted on the front lawn as people hooted and hollered, yelling scores for his landing. He stood up with his arms raised in victory before bowing at the waist and tossing his cookies splendidly on two unsuspecting girls who stood off to the side. Both girls shrieked with disgust, which only invited more cheers from the onlookers.

Not to be outdone, a group of girls decided to get in on the action when the guys initiated a girl-on-girl mud-wrestling tournament. Within minutes of being soaked by hoses spilling water at full blast, the front lawn of the fraternity house was a sopping mess. Judging by the steady line of participants that had quickly formed, the nominated contestants seemed to be too drunk to care about being subjected to male gawking, or the fact that it was too cold to be rolling around like pigs in shit.

"You going?" Cameo asked.

"Hell no," I answered, choosing to keep my seat on the sidelines.

I'd been there, done that, and I didn't relish taking an elbow in the nose or having a handful of my hair pulled out to entertain drunken college guys. Chuck, who had finally appeared from wherever he'd been hiding, couldn't seem to get it through his thick head that I didn't want to participate. It took me stomping on his foot and threatening to twist his junk into a knot before he finally stopped trying to pull me into the fray.

"Aw, you mean you don't want to give your boyfriend a show and roll around and get all wet with another girl?" Cameo teased, breaking into my thoughts. She looked halfway past tipsy as she smiled at me.

We had been at the party for an hour and were nursing our third beer each. I could hold my liquor better than Cameo, who was a bit of a lightweight. Chances were I'd be dragging her ass home later since she'd barely be able to walk. She and I had made a pact when we first became roommates that we would never leave the other behind, unless of course a hot guy was involved. Little did I realize when I made the pact that it would be me shouldering most of the load.

Honestly, I didn't mind. I loved Cameo to death. I had

completely lucked out when I found her as a roommate after being accepted into Maine State College's business program. I got in by the skin of my teeth since I wasn't exactly what you would call an "academic all-star." I had taken a full year off after high school because I didn't know what I wanted to do with my life. Finally, my mom talked me into at least trying community college, and somehow, I managed to drill into my stubborn head that if I wanted to transfer to a state university, I would have to work hard. Not that I wasn't still having fun at the same time. I wasn't dead, after all. My acceptance letter came at the perfect time. My best friend, Brittni, had moved to Seattle, and I was feeling lost without her. She was the voice of reason I didn't have myself that kept me in line for the most part. Without her, my antics in Woodfalls had hit an epic scale. After some of the shit I'd pulled over the years, I think the entire town let out a collective sigh of relief when I moved away for school. Even though MSC was only sixty miles away from Woodfalls, at least I was out of their hair. Now, in the almost two years that I've been on campus, I've managed to bring my reputation as a bit of a hell-raiser with me.

I pulled my thoughts back to Cameo, who was still waiting for my answer. "Please, you know I'd have no problem throwin' down in there. It's just too damn cold to roll around in the mud," I said confidently. "Besides, Chuck's been working to get in my pants. Little does he know, the Vagmart store is closed to his ass."

"Ha, your vag-store," Cameo snorted, setting her beer on an end table that was already overflowing with bottles. "Guys are so predictable. They think all chicks wanna get naked with each other and have pillow fights."

"Well, I know that's all I think about," I said, wagging my eyebrows suggestively.

"Gross. You perv." She slapped my arm and tried pushing me away.

"Oh come on. You know you want this," I teased, running my hands down my curvy figure. I had to sidestep a couple who were too busy sucking each other's faces as they walked to watch where they were going. "Hey, get a room," I called after them as they stumbled into the wall.

"Where the hell do you think we're going?" the guy asked, dislodging his lips long enough to answer.

"Sorry, shit, carry on then," I said, grinning at Cameo.

"See, that's why we will never have a party at our apartment," she stated.

"What, you don't want an orgy to break out on your bed?"

She held up her hand like a crossing guard. "Don't even finish wherever your perverted mind was headed with that."

I laughed loudly. Cameo was the perfect roommate in most aspects, but she did have a bit of an obsessive compulsive personality, much to my amusement. Not that I didn't agree with her. I didn't want drunken college peeps using my bed to get nasty in either.

"Could it be you're just bummed that your bed hasn't seen any action in how many days now?" I teased, wincing as I watched two girls in the mud pit go for each other's hair. Why did girls always do that? Why couldn't we fight like men? With fists and punching instead of hair pulling and scratching. I'd much rather take a punch to the gut than have a handful of my hair pulled out.

"Whatever, you whore. It's been four days," she answered, watching the fight with interest.

"Whoa, takes one to know one," I laughed.

"Bite me, bitch. I just like guys."

"And sex," I added.

"Yes, so what, Mother Teresa?" She grinned, throwing out her beloved nickname for me.

It wasn't like I didn't enjoy sex. She knew that. Lately, I was just more selective about who I fell into bed with. Take Jockstrap Chuck for example. A few months ago, I might have caved and given it up to him. But I was getting sick of the games and acting like someone I wasn't to keep a guy. I used to be a total boyfriend pleaser, especially back in high school, when I dated the same creep off and on for almost four years. I finally called it quits once and for all about a year ago. The relationship was toxic, to say the least. Years of scathing comments about how I looked or what I did, and then he would push to have sex, only to lay a major guilt trip on me when he felt remorse after we did it. Jackson suffered from a serious case of being a momma's boy. We'd no sooner done the dirty deed than he would whimper about premarital sex and how disappointed his mother would be. Even after years of putting up with his shit, actually committing to break up with Jackson was difficult. He was my first serious boyfriend. The one I gave my virginity to, or my V-card, as I liked to call it.

That was a big deal to me, despite my wild-child persona and the way people perceived me on the outside. It's not like you can ever get that back, even when the guy turns out to be a douche. Jackson definitely became that and more, telling me when we broke up that I was worthless and that no other guy would ever want me. His words cut me deeply and made me feel like I was lacking. His mom actually threw a party when we were officially over.

After leaving the Jackson mess behind me, I eventually found the confidence to try my luck with guys again, but after a string of disastrous first dates, I began to believe that maybe Jackson had been right. He was as good as I deserved. If not that, then maybe the dating gods were punishing me for all my past sins. Like the time in seventh grade I talked Braxton Fischer into switching the video we were supposed to watch in Mr. Morton's science class with a porno he had found hidden in his dad's nightstand. Mr. Morton made the mistake of leaving the room for almost ten minutes before he came back to see two topless, big-breasted girls washing cars on the TV.

"What the hell?" a shocked Mr. Morton yelled as he turned several different shades of red. The class erupted with laughter, and although none of my classmates ratted me out, Mr. Morton knew better and immediately sent me to the office. I could have argued. He had no proof it was me, but my reputation had already been established.

The principal, Mrs. Jameson, called my dad to pick me up, which I thought was odd considering she knew my mom.

I finally understood when he showed up and she handed over the video to my dad with a scornful look on her face, like she was repulsed to even be that close to something so unholy. She thought the video was his, but my dad didn't skip a beat. He didn't flush with embarrassment or stammer at being reprimanded. Instead, he thanked her and told her he was wondering where he had left it, leaving Mrs. Jameson looking utterly scandalized.

The only lecture I got on the way home was a reminder that some parents may not want their children to see movies about those kinds of car washes. That was the best thing about Dad. He always understood the person I was, never judging or scolding me. He would simply give reminders and pointers of what a better course of action may have been. I loved both my parents fiercely for their gentle restraints.

I wish I could tell you that was the last prank I ever pulled, but my reign of stunts continued into high school. I would pick a victim and execute my prank with the precision of a surgeon. Dad always said if I would learn to harness that power toward school, I would be a straight-A student. That would have been tragic and a complete waste of fun, in my opinion.

Eventually, I mellowed when I was dating Jackson. He reminded me countless times that his mom would never approve of me if I was always causing trouble. Little did he know, I didn't want or need his creepy mom's love.

For that reason more than any other, breaking up with Jackson had been necessary. Our relationship was like a runaway train headed for a brick wall. Unfortunately, none of my relationships after that turned out any better. My friends Brittni and Ashton said I had an uncanny gift of gravitating toward the only jerk in the crowd. I always shrugged off their comments. I dated guys who suited me, which usually meant they were as loud and wild as I was.

"Wow, did she seriously just push that girl's face into her boobs?" Cameo asked, pulling me back to the present. She stepped closer to get a better look at the two mud-covered girls, who had grabbed the attention of most of the male population at the party. As the crowd cheered the girls along, I noticed everyone watching had their cell phones out to record the wrestling match, so I pulled out mine too.

"You're not going to post that, are you?" Cameo asked as I moved in closer.

One of the girls shoved the other to the ground and straddled her. "Why the hell not? This is epic on a whole new level."

"Damn, that's hot," a warm male voice said behind me.

I grinned as I turned around, recognizing the voice of my friend Derek. "Really? I can score their numbers for you if you'd like," I joked.

"Honey, I'm talking about Tall, Dark, and Shirtless over there," he answered, pointing to a well-toned guy who had removed his shirt so it wouldn't get splattered with mud.

"Right, here I thought you had suddenly decided to bat for the other team," Cameo teased Derek, looping her arm through his.

"Sweetheart, you could only wish," he said, dropping a kiss on her forehead.

"Damn straight," she giggled. "No pun intended," she

added before frowning up at him. "Why do all the good ones turn out to be gay?"

"So we can have marvelous friends like you two without the mess of a romantic relationship. Just think, if I was straight, we wouldn't be friends."

"That's because we'd be lovers," I cooed, snuggling up to his free arm.

"I love you, Tressa baby, but you'd scare me in bed," Derek said, wrapping his arm around my waist.

"Oh come on, I'd go easy on you," I answered, grinding my hips against his leg.

"Don't believe her. I swear the wall looked like it was going to collapse the last time she had a guy over," Cameo teased, sticking out her tongue at me as I swiped at her with my free hand.

"Whatever, Wonder Woman," I said, reminding her of the last guy she slept with, who had a fondness for comic books. He showed up at our apartment one night with a costume from the Halloween store. Usually, I didn't mind sticking around when Cameo had a guy over, but I had to leave for that one. The truth was, it had been months since I'd even considered being with a guy.

"Hey, what about the dude with the camera? I'm surprised you didn't take him up on it," she returned, talking about the last guy who almost made it into my bed until he wanted to record us. He had to go collect his camera and clothes from the yard after I threw his belongings out the window and kicked his ass out.

"Unlike you, I only do high-class porn," I threw back.

"As stimulating as this conversation is, I'd rather be dancing," Derek said, indicating the open door of the frat house where the music had been turned up.

Cameo and I agreed, following Derek toward the music we could feel pumping through our chests. Joining a crowd that seemed to be flowing as one, we let loose and lost ourselves in the music. Dancing came naturally to our trio, and it was something we enjoyed doing together. As in, just the three of us. Being in a large crowd, we would occasionally have to put up with some drunken dude trying to grind against Cameo or me, but Derek was good at stepping in. At six foot five, he was an imposing figure who could maneuver his body wherever he wanted to shelter us from unwanted advances.

After an hour, we were dripping with sweat, despite the nip in the nighttime air that circulated through the open windows and doors. Pulling my damp hair off the back of my neck, I indicated with a nod of my head to Derek and Cameo that it was time for a break. It felt like we needed a shoehorn to squeeze through the jumbled bodies, but eventually we made it out of the room.

"Holy shit, talk about a cardio workout. I should be a twig after all that," I complained, snagging another drink. I glared at Cameo, who was practically a waif standing next to me. "I should effing hate you."

"Don't be an ass. I'd take your boobs any day over these." She cupped her smallish breasts in her hands. "At least you've got curves. I'm like a stick."

"Look, ladies, you can both be jealous of my perfect body," Derek interrupted, making a point of tossing his imaginary long hair. "Some of us got it, and some of us don't." Cameo and I laughed. Derek was a bit of a showboat, which made him perfect for our group. "I'm going to get a drink," he added, following Cameo, who was already headed in that direction.

I stayed behind, content with the beer I had pulled from a nearby cooler. It was nice to take a breather and observe the crowd a little. I became preoccupied watching a group playing a distorted version of Spin the Bottle when a pair of arms reached around my stomach, pulling me roughly against a hard chest.

"Are you ready to kiss and make up?" Chuck growled in my ear. He smelled like a distillery.

"Not really." I shrugged my shoulders, stepping out of his grasp.

"Come on, girl. You're gonna let a little fight ruin this?" He sounded as drunk as he smelled.

I wanted to laugh, but that would probably only egg him on further. I also wasn't in the mood for a messy scene tonight, so I went with a softer approach and a little more tact than he probably deserved.

As I spun around to face him, I couldn't for the life of me remember why I had gone out with him in the first place. He was a partier like I was and had seemed cool when I met him at Club Zero a couple weeks ago, but he was a meathead. I pretty much realized on our first date that we probably weren't going to make it. Mostly because he was a perpetual nut scratcher. I don't mean he would do the occasional subtle shift that some guys do with their junk. If that was all he did, I could have lived with it. He was an all-out ball scratcher, and didn't seem to care who saw him do it. It could be the waitress who looked disgusted as she handed over our pizza, or Cameo, or basically anyone who was having a conversation with him. If you stood next to Chuck, at some point you would see him scratch his balls.

"Chuck, it's not you, it's me," I said, cringing at my chosen cliché. How did you tell someone you would rather gouge out your eyes than see him play with his junk again?

"What the fuck? Who uses a bullshit line like that?" He grabbed my arm so I couldn't move. I looked down at his hand that was wrapped around my wrist. Seriously? Why did it always come down to this? Did I have the words *please manhandle me* tattooed on my forehead?

I noticed Derek approaching from the corner of my eye. He was hard to miss because of his size, and judging by the look on his face, Chuck would want no part of what was coming. I held out my free hand to stop him before he could get involved. I may have an uncanny knack for dating assholes, but I also knew how to take care of myself when I needed to. I stepped on Chuck's shoe and slowly rolled my weight so my platform heel sank down on the softness of his toes. "In case you're too stupid to notice, we're done." He grunted in pain, making me smile. Sometimes it paid not to be a lightweight.

"Get off me, you bish," he slurred. He wobbled to the point where I could have pushed him over.

Derek stepped between me and Chuck, pulling me snugly against his side. "Why don't you go sleep it off?" His insistent tone made it clear he wasn't merely asking. This was why Derek was the best kind of friend. He wasn't a fan of violence, but you would never know it when it came to Cameo and me. Back home, I had always been the protector when it came to my friends. It was kind of nice to have a knight in shining armor. Not necessary, but still sweet. I found it endearing that even though he'd only known me for a year, he acted like we were lifelong friends. Derek was a perk that came with Cameo picking me to be her roommate last year. When I had transferred to Maine State, I knew I didn't want to do the whole dorm thing. Living at home my first two years of college made me yearn for more independence. I wanted to let loose without so many restrictions. Living in an apartment with Cameo had provided the freedom I was looking for, and sharing her best friend, Derek, sweetened the deal.

Chuck looked like he wanted to retaliate, but in his drunken state, he was in no shape to attempt anything more. With a shake of his head and a look of bewilderment in my direction, he staggered off, scratching his junk the entire time.

"Honey, you sure can pick 'em," Derek said, shaking his head with amazement before turning away from the train wreck to Cameo, who'd returned with a drink.

"You're a fine one to talk," I pointed out, punching him in his bicep. If it seemed like I was being picky at the moment when it came to guys, Derek was even worse. He claimed he didn't feel like wasting time on meaningless relationships. I think he missed the memo on what college dating was supposed to be.

"I'm searching for someone who understands me," he said dramatically, making us laugh. "Speaking of which, hello, Clark Kent," he added, looking toward the front door. "He looks like he could understand everything I have to offer."

Cameo and I pivoted around to see who had managed to snag Derek's attention. He could be a bit of a snob when it came to man-candy. Anyone who caught his eye had to be worth seeing.

"Oh, hell no," I muttered under my breath. He was the last person I expected to see at a party like this.

2.

"I know him."

"What? You bitch, you've been holding out on me," Cameo said, giving a low whistle under her breath.

"Really? We're construction workers now?" I said.

"Honey, sometimes an appreciative whistle is necessary," Derek answered as he straightened his shirt and smoothed a hand over his hair.

"Hit the brakes, lollipop. That's Trent, a guy I know from Woodfalls. Trust me. He's as straight as they come."

"Woo-hoo!" Cameo shouted, adjusting her top so her small but perky breasts were more visible.

"Down, horndog. He's not your type either."

"What the hell does that mean?"

"She means maybe he doesn't know what he's missing on Team Derek."

"No, God, you freaking sluts. I'm saying look at him. He's straight out of *The Big Bang Theory*. Completely not our type."

"Speak for yourself. I like the whole glasses thing," Cameo said, making a move toward him. "Smart but sexy definitely works for me."

"Chill," I commanded her, grabbing the hem of her shirt. "Trust me. Trent isn't for you."

"Oh, now I get it. You have the hots for him." Her eyes practically lit up with fascination in the darkness. "Why didn't you just say so?"

I gritted my teeth in frustration. "Why don't you suck it?"

"Sounds like that's what you want to do," Cameo returned.

"Ha, you two really know how to speak my language," Derek chuckled.

Why was everyone so quick to push Trent and me together? I heard the same load of crap from my two best friends in Woodfalls, Brittni and Ashton. They were convinced Trent had some kind of thing for me. I never understood why they didn't see what I did. Trent and I were complete opposites. He and his parents moved to Woodfalls during our junior year in high school, causing quite the stir. Trent's grandfather was a respected town resident, having owned the local hardware store for nearly forty years, and Trent's dad was a Woodfalls native who had moved away many years prior to start college. I couldn't recall Trent and his family ever coming for visits during holidays or anything when we were kids, which was probably why everyone was so surprised when they suddenly moved to town. New people rarely moved to Woodfalls. Those who did were typically young couples looking for a small-town atmosphere in which to raise their families. Woodfalls was far enough from major cities to make you feel like you were part of a different lifestyle. I had just started dating Jackson when Trent's arrival caused a ripple of gossip to spread through the school. I was too wrapped up in the newness of my first real relationship to give Trent much thought. Jackson, for some reason, seemed to dislike him from day one. He was always harping on the fact that he thought Trent was watching me. I dismissed his paranoia, telling him Trent could probably just sense a fellow trouble-maker. One of the benefits of having Brittni as my best friend was that her mom was the first to get information. She was the town gossip queen and filled us in on the fact that Trent had gotten in some kind of trouble at his old school and his parents hoped a move to a small town would change things for him. After only a few months, I chalked up Trent's bad-boy rumor as total bullshit. Brittni's mom had to have gotten some bad info because Trent was boring with a capital B. He kept mostly to himself and was always either tinkering with some computer at school or reading graphic novels during class. And yet, he still managed to pull straight As. We all thought he was a shoo-in for valedictorian, but Suzy Braxton somehow got it. We speculated that whatever Trent had done at his old school must have affected his grades and trickled over.

"And he goes to Maine State. My, oh my, how the plot thickens," Derek said, rubbing his hands together.

"Shut it. I think he's in some graduate program. He's a total brain."

"I like my eye candy to have a little upstairs too. As long as he can match his abilities downstairs," Cameo interjected. She eyed him like he was an all-you-can-eat buffet.

I glared at her. "You're out of your league, honey," I said, taking a sip of my beer as I watched Trent make his way into the main part of the living room. He had yet to notice me, which was fine with me. I knew when I transferred to MSC there was a chance I would run into him. The previous summer in Woodfalls we had spoken for a few minutes and he made a point of telling me he would see me around campus. Thankfully, our paths had not crossed until now.

"You seem to know an awful lot about someone you have no interest in," Cameo pointed out.

"We live in a small town. People know when you take a piss in Woodfalls."

"Maybe, but you seem to have a little sparkle in your eye. Just sayin'."

Thankfully, Derek changed the subject to some reality show he and Cameo were completely obsessed with. I tried to watch it with them a couple of times, but it took lame-ass to a whole new level.

While they discussed the latest drama on the show—something about one of the girls getting it on with two guys in the hot tub on the same night—I watched Trent. He was stationed against one of the walls, surveying the crowd as if he was waiting for someone. Free to study him without detection, I tried to understand why Derek and Cameo seemed so fascinated with him. As far as Cameo was concerned, the fact that he was male was half the battle. Derek, though, was harder to please. Sure, if you removed his glasses and maybe messed up his hair a little, Trent wouldn't be half bad. He had been blessed with blue eyes that were so clear they seemed electrified. And I guess I couldn't deny he looked like he had a decent build, even though his nerdy Batman T-shirt made it hard to focus on anything beneath it. I was watching him so intently that I was caught off guard when he left his spot against the wall. Without thinking, I ducked behind Derek before Trent's eyes moved in my direction.

"Babes, your hottie friend is heading this way," Derek said blandly, turning to where I was huddled behind him.

"You can stop hiding. It looks like he found what he was searching for," Cameo said with disdain. "No way. Is he seriously hooking up with Panty Muncher?"

"What?" I stood up so quickly I felt slightly dizzy. Quick movements were not the best idea when you were on your third or fourth beer. Trent had stopped not ten feet from us to chat with Patty Jones, who we had dubbed "Panty Muncher" since she always seemed to have her panties all up in her junk. She was also notorious for giving half the male population at Maine State College an all-access pass. "Oh, hell no. She'll chew him up and spit him out," I muttered, not sure why I even cared. I should have been pleased that he was on someone else's radar. Maybe if it was anyone but twat-face Patty I wouldn't have felt the insane urge to rush in and rescue him.

I watched from my vantage point as Patty ran a finger up his arm and leaned in close to whisper into his ear. The need to protect Trent from her roared through me like an angry lion. I practically pounced away from my friends and within a few strides forward, I was standing in front of Nerd Boy and Camel Toe.

"Tressa, hey," Trent said, pushing his glasses back up the bridge of his nose. They only seemed to magnify the intense blue of his eyes, and I found myself momentarily distracted. "I didn't know you were here," he added, extracting his arm from Patty's.

"What are you doing here?" I cringed at how bitchy I sounded, but seeing him on my turf was more unsettling than I expected.

"Tristan Wilder wants me to take a look at his laptop," he answered, not breaking eye contact. This was one of the issues I had with Trent. He looked you right in the eyes, like he was studying you or something. The few conversations I'd had with him over the years made me feel like he was always digging for something more. It was like his mind needed to analyze everything that was said. Being more of a crowd-pleaser, I felt comfortable with lighter conversation and keeping things fun. I felt we didn't need to take life so seriously. We were only young once. The time would come when we could put on our adult faces, but not now.

"Oh, so you're not here for the party?" I asked, looking pointedly at Patty, who was still eyeing Trent like he was a hot Scottish man in a kilt.

"Why don't you mind your own business?" Patty said.

"Why don't you shut up, bitch, before I make you my business," I returned sternly. "I'll show you where Tristan is," I said to Trent, grabbing his wrist to pull him away from Patty before she could corrupt him. It took me a few minutes to stop fuming. Trent offered no resistance as I dragged him away like a dog on a leash. The surge of protectiveness I felt disappeared the instant we stepped outside. What the hell was I doing? I avoided him like the plague back home, and suddenly I felt the need to swoop in and save him. I would have blamed it on the liquor I had consumed, but I knew that was a crap excuse. Hell, I wasn't even tipsy. "You could have waited until morning to check out Tristan's laptop," I snapped at him.

"Why?" He put on the brakes, bringing us to a halt with my hand still wrapped around his wrist.

I dropped it like it was a poisonous snake. "Because this kind of party isn't for you, especially during pledge week. Things get pretty wild." As if to prove my point, someone hugging another mattress leapt from the second-floor balcony and landed no more than three feet from where we were standing. The fraternity pledge climbed off the mattress, grinning like a buffoon before staggering off. Between flying mattresses and the wrestling, which had escalated to an all-out mud-slinging war, the backyard was total chaos. The kind of chaos I would have enjoyed if I wasn't babysitting "Clark Kent," as Derek had called him. Normally, I would have been in the thick of things. I freaking loved pledge week. It was cheap entertainment to see what the pledges would do to get into a fraternity.

"What makes you think I can't handle wild?" he asked,

adjusting his glasses. I could tell by the way he shifted his weight he was uncomfortable. Yet another way we were so different.

"You're joking, right? I bet your computer brain feels like it's been invaded by a virus."

The corners of his mouth quirked upward. "Who am I to judge? If killing brain cells is the theme of these parties, so be it."

Despite myself, I grinned. "Damn straight."

His eyes lit up at my words. It should be a sin to waste such beautiful eyes on someone so different from the guys I usually went for. The thought had barely materialized in my head before I gave it a mental bitch slap. I needed to keep my shit together. "He's over there," I said, pointing to the far side of the backyard where Tristan had two pledges showing their goods to a group of sorority girls holding up scores to vote in some sort of contest. I turned and walked back to the house, ready to put some distance between Trent and me. I was pretty sure I heard him call my name, but I ignored it. He could sink or swim here, but there was no way I was sticking around to be his life raft.

"What did you do with your cub, momma bear?" Derek teased as I joined him and Cameo, who were on one of the sofas.

"Bite me." Sinking down on the couch next to them, I reached over and snagged the red Solo cup Cameo was clutching.

"Hey, that's mine," she complained as I sniffed the contents. Rum. That would do the trick. Ignoring her grumbles, I downed the contents in one gulp. The rum burned a path down to the pit of my stomach, numbing my teeth along the way. My eyes took on a slightly fuzzy view. Rum was definitely what I needed to forget about jerky ball-scratching ex-boyfriends and electric blue eyes on nerdy superhero look-alikes.

"Don't mind me. Go ahead and have my drink," Cameo said sarcastically.

"Thanks, sugar lips," I said, giving her a smacking kiss. The rum had given me a nice buzz.

"Gross. I don't know where those lips have been," she complained, swiping a hand across her mouth.

Grinning, I reached for her again, this time giving her a spectacularly sloppy kiss on her cheek while Derek laughed next to us.

"If you two are done making out, I'd like to do some more dancing," he said, bobbing his head to the music.

"I need another drink first," I said, pulling Cameo to her feet. She accepted my help, though she was still rubbing her cheek where my lips had been. "Sheesh, it's not like I have cooties."

"As far as you know. You owe me another drink."

"Ouch. Don't bother to ask me when you decide you want to experiment with being a lesbian," I said, pulling her to the kitchen to make us another drink.

The rest of the evening passed in a blur. I know we danced for several hours, and I'm pretty sure Cameo and I did an impromptu karaoke show when Justin Timberlake's newest song came on. One thing was certain: Chuck and Trent became a distant memory.

3.

I was jarred awake the next morning by an unmistakably male body pressed against me. Oh hell. How much did I drink last night? Opening my eyes a crack, my first instinct was to reach down to check whether I was still wearing panties before I spun around to see who was spooning me. I sighed with relief when it turned out to be Derek. His large frame was sprawled across my bed, trying to steal every inch of available space. Not quite ready to be awake, I shoved at him until he rolled over. This wasn't the first time Derek had crashed with me. I didn't mind, but you had to claim your space with him around—otherwise you'd end up on the floor. With more room for myself, I turned on my side and pulled the blanket up to my chin, drifting back to sleep in seconds.

The next time I woke, my bed was empty and I could hear

the rustling noise of pans and plates coming from the small kitchen in the apartment I shared with Cameo. Rolling over on my back, I took stock of my hangover. On a scale of *I need to throw up* to *I just need some coffee*, I'd say I was more on the needing-coffee side. I had a slight pounding headache, which I could handle with Advil, but my mouth tasted like something had crawled in there and died. It felt like I would need a sandblaster to remove all the gunk from my teeth. Grabbing a clean pair of sweats and a Maine State shirt from my dresser, I staggered to the bathroom to shower. The mirror over the sink showed no mercy. Not that I was somehow expecting to look any better than I felt. I popped three Advil into my mouth before giving my teeth the long brushing they needed. My face resembled something out of a zombie movie. Both of my eyes were rimmed in a thick layer of black eyeliner and mascara. I didn't remember being that liberal with the makeup, but the evidence was staring back at me. A dried patch of drool covered my left cheek. That was attractive. I looked like a hooker after a hard night at work. I reached around the shower curtain and turned on the water, leaving my freak show reflection behind. If a hot shower didn't make me feel more human, I guessed I'd have to resort to a paper bag over my head for the day.

Derek and Cameo were cooking breakfast when I finally stumbled into the kitchen twenty minutes later. Derek set down a platter of crisp bacon and eggs on our small dining room table that would wobble slightly if not for the piece of folded-up cardboard under one of the legs. Classy, that's the way we rolled. Cameo and I rescued the table from a Dumpster at the start of summer after the previous owner threw it out before heading home at the end of term.

Last year, our apartment had been pretty sparse when it came to furniture. We had nothing more than our beds and one futon couch, but when Cameo decided to take summer classes, we stuck around, keeping a sharp eye out for any furniture that would fill the gaps. We were shocked by what people would throw out, and in no time our apartment was filled with the treasures we had found. Most of it had seen better days, but we used strategically placed scarves to cover scratches and water marks. Nothing matched, but somehow it still looked good in a bohemian sort of way.

"She lives." Derek greeted me in a booming voice that earned him one of my patented glares. He laughed, opening the cabinet to pull out more plates.

"You're a bed hog," I complained, filling my favorite oversized mug to the brim with hot black coffee. It had a cartoon dog with the caption: *If you don't want me to be a bitch, give me caffeine.* My brother gave it to me for Christmas the previous year. He thought he was so clever, laughing his ass off when I opened it. He was a little shit, but I loved the mug. It could have read *Tressa is a whore* on the side and I would still use it because of the sheer size of the mug.

"You snore," Derek returned, handing us each a plate.

"Liar," I said, shoving him with my hip.

"You were pretty toasted last night," Cameo said, placing her coffee and an energy drink beside her plate.

"Caffeine and an energy drink? You planning on hiking Baxter Peak?"

"I wish it was something that easy. I need to crack down and finish my bio chem paper or I'm seriously screwed. What about you? Don't you have a paper due in your business management class?"

I shrugged. Schoolwork wasn't high on my priority list at the moment. To avoid answering her question, I shoveled eggs into my mouth. I chewed slowly, making sure my stomach, which had been relatively tame, wouldn't boycott. After several bites, I figured I was safe. Cameo and Derek chatted while I ate my breakfast and nursed my coffee. I wasn't a big morning person. Both of them knew me well enough to allow me to finish my coffee before involving me in any conversation. Derek teased me, claiming I was like a bear being poked with a stick in the morning.

"More like a ticking time bomb," Cameo joked.

"Drama much?" I countered. "Bite someone's head off once and suddenly you're labeled." Cameo started to say something more, but Derek covered her mouth with his hand.

I was finishing the last of my bacon when I finally felt I could join the conversation with any civility. It didn't hurt that the food was delicious, as usual. Derek was a wiz in the kitchen, where Cameo and I were both hopeless when it came to cooking. Cameo at least had an excuse for her lack of culinary skills. Her parents were doctors and rarely cooked while she was growing up. Catered meals and takeout had been as close as she ever got to a home-cooked meal. I, on the other hand, had absolutely no excuse considering my mom was practically Susie Homemaker. Three squares a day and extravagant Sunday dinners were the norm in my house. Mom had tried to teach me to cook, but it never stuck. Finally, after I burned her favorite set of pans, I was officially banned from the kitchen. I'd be lying if I said I wept at being exiled.

Derek was a regular Gordon Ramsay who could easily compete in one of those cooking challenges on TV. Cameo and I capitalized on his skills and worked out a deal with him: He cooked for us on occasion, and we let him crash at our apartment whenever he wanted. His roommates were complete douchecanoes this year, so he was at our apartment more often than not. Cameo and I had considered the idea of telling him to move in with us, but hadn't broached the subject with him yet.

Once my plate was empty, I stood up to do the dishes. Early on in our roommate relationship, we learned that if the apartment was going to remain clean, we would have to work out a chore schedule. This week, I had dishes and vacuuming. Dishes weren't bad. Vacuuming was tolerable, but I hated when I drew laundry. Laundry was the bane of my existence.

I filled the sink with hot soapy water as Derek and Cameo carried the rest of the dishes to the counter. "So, are you going to tell us the deal-i-o with your friend?" Derek asked, hoisting himself up on the counter while I washed.

"There is no deal-i-o," I answered, swatting his hand as he tried to snag some bubbles. I heard Cameo snort behind me. Without even looking at them, I knew they were exchanging a doubtful look. I focused my attention on the dish in my hand, continuing to scrub while I came up with a plausible excuse for my behavior the night before. When neither of them left the kitchen, I knew I wasn't going to be able to weasel out of answering. "Fine. It aggravated me that Panty Muncher had her claws in him. I felt responsible for him," I said lamely, drying my hands on a towel.

"Bullshit," Cameo coughed.

I flicked the towel at her. "I'm serious, bitch."

"Right," she laughed mockingly as she left the kitchen. "You need a reality check."

Derek stayed with me while I put the dishes away, remaining silent as I worked. This was one of his sneaky tactics I was all too familiar with. Eventually, the silence would wear on you and before you knew it, you were spilling your guts to him. But he could sit there all day as far as I was concerned. I would not buckle. There was nothing to say. Okay, for some odd reason Trent had snagged my attention. Who cares? It's not like it was the first time I showed any sort of interest in a guy. Why did this time need an explanation?

Derek sat watching me like he could read my thoughts. He wasn't going to wear me down. I was as strong as a brick wall.

I pulled the vacuum out of the small linen closet, glaring at him as he perched himself on the futon.

He returned my glare balefully.

Pushing the vacuum along, I tried to drag out the process, hoping he'd give up, but I could only vacuum the same spot so many times. Shooting him another glare, I shut off the vacuum.

"Fine! You freaking stubborn ass!" I began to spill my guts, just as he had planned. Damn him.

It poured out of me like sewage I couldn't wait to get rid of. I told him how my friends back home were convinced that Trent had a crush on me, but I felt he so wasn't my type, and how off-the-wall my sudden possessiveness had been.

"So you have the hots for Clark Kent. Big deal," he said when I ran out of steam.

"Have you not been listening at all? I have the opposite of the hots for him."

"'Most men would rather deny a hard truth,'" he stated. Derek loved quoting his favorite books, and he seemed to have one for every occasion.

"Hemingway?" I guessed.

"George R. R. Martin."

"Who?"

"Seriously? You don't know who one of the greatest authors of our generation is?" he asked, looking scandalized. "He only wrote the saga of literary genius that includes *A Game of Thrones*. Maybe less partying and more studying," he said, sticking out his tongue at me when I swung at him. It was no secret that studying wasn't exactly my forte. I had to really discipline myself in junior college to pull good enough grades to transfer to MSC. I still don't think I would have gotten in if not for a glowing letter of recommendation from Professor Nelson, a bigwig at the college and longtime resident of Woodfalls. He even offered to act as my advisor throughout school. Things started okay, but I had been avoiding him since fall classes started. I was supposed to sign up for a particular summer course he recommended, but I blew it off. Last year he was relentless as he pushed me to work harder. He seemed genuinely disappointed when my grades slipped. I shuddered at the idea of facing him at the moment, especially since I had bombed the first exam in business communications, and statistics wasn't going any better. For some reason, I couldn't seem to wrap my brain around it.

"Who cares about grades when there's always dancing to be done?" I held out my hand so Derek and I could fist-bump.

"Damn straight," he agreed, knocking his fist against mine and then spreading his fingers like his hand was exploding. "You guys want to hit that new underground club that opened up on the east side? I heard it's freaking hard-core. The acoustics are supposed to be out-of-this-world insane. Brant went last week, and he said the bass booms so hard the floor vibrates."

"Brant? I thought you two were done?" I asked, digging through a basket for a nail file. Cameo and I had an extensive collection of nail polish that made it hard to locate the files that always became buried at the bottom of the basket.

"We are," he answered defensively. "We're just friends." He sighed, grabbing a nail file for himself. He sat buffing a nail that was already pristine, obviously trying to evade my question. It served him right to get a taste of what probing felt like. Derek was idealistic. He believed in love and soul mates, and was determined to find his perfect match. The only problem was he kept falling back into the same toxic relationship with his ex. That's one thing Derek and I had in common. We gravitated toward the jerks. I had done it countless times with my ex Jackson. I would break up with him over and over again, but he always had an uncanny knack of dragging me back in. Brittni claimed it was because he played on my insecurities. I would always snort my disgust at her interpretation of our relationship, but deep down I knew she was right. Jackson always knew what to say to make me feel like I needed him. Eventually, the time came when I realized I needed to end it for good. My acceptance into MSC gave me the perfect excuse to make Jackson nothing more than a memory. I tried several times to bully Derek into cutting his losses with Brant, but I also knew from personal experience that no one can force you to end a bad relationship.

That decision is one you have to make on your own.

"Right," I finally answered, working to keep the skepticism out of my voice.

"I'm going to stay strong this time," he said resolutely.

I nodded my head in support. "I believe you."

"I will," he replied passionately. "I have to do it," he said before sagging like a balloon that had lost all its air.

"Time to man up, big boy," I said, dropping my supportive tone for a harder edge.

"Man up, yes." He repeated my words as he stood. "I better go home and try to grab a shower. That is, if no one has passed out in it." He headed for the door looking disgruntled.

"Why don't you crash here for a while?" I suggested, stowing the nail basket on the shelf under the heavy-duty coffee table. It was the sturdiest piece of furniture we had in the apartment. Too bad it was maybe the ugliest table you could ever lay eyes on. We tried to make it look more presentable by covering it with a lace runner Cameo had found at the Second Chances consignment shop. It helped some, but not much. We talked about painting it too, but neither of us felt like putting in the effort.

Derek turned to me with a hopeful puppy-dog look on his face. “I can’t just take over your apartment. That’s no different than what’s going on at my place. I won’t impose.”

“What about the fact that we’re asking you to stay? You’re not imposing, nimrod. It just means you’ll be cooking for us a whole lot more,” I said, grinning at him. “You can crash on the couch and stash your junk in my room. It won’t be Buckingham Palace, but it has to be better than what you have now.”

“Seriously, you guys wouldn’t mind?” he asked, striding across the room and swinging me up in his arms. “Shouldn’t we check with Cameo?”

“We’ve already discussed it,” I laughed. “No overnight guests, though. Our generosity doesn’t stretch that far.”

“Deal. Wait, does that rule apply to you too?”

“Hell no. We can have all the guys over we want.”

“Classy. You should make flyers and post that all over campus.”

“Whatever, douchehead. Even if I wasn’t kidding, it’s not like I have any prospects. Let’s just say we’ll cross that bridge when we get to it. Does that work?”

“I can deal with that.” A wide grin split his face and he let out a loud whoop.

"I'm guessing you told him?" Cameo stood in the doorway with a textbook cradled in her arms.

"What was your first hint?" I grinned as Derek scooped up Cameo into a bear hug, spinning her around. Her squeals filled the small apartment.

Derek stuck around another hour as we sorted through the logistics of our new roommate arrangement. Eventually, he had to go to work, and Cameo returned to studying. If I was smart, I would have worked on my own paper, but no one ever accused me of having any sense. Instead, I continued procrastinating, deciding to call Brittni and update her about my single status. Again.

Brittni picked up on the first ring. "I was hoping you'd call."

"You were?"

"Yes, my eyes are literally bleeding grading these papers." She sighed into the phone. "Remind me again why I thought teaching was a good idea."

"Um, you wanted to corrupt a new generation."

"That's right. I plan on taking over the world by turning them all into my minions," she said, laughing sinisterly. "Enough about my mouthy rug rats. How's your newest heartthrob holding up?"

I bit back a sigh. I should have counted on the conversation going in this direction so quickly. Now that Brittni was settled down, she was ready to hitch me to the first acceptable bachelor we could find. I couldn't understand her rush. We were all still so young.

"Tress, are you there?"

"Yeah, I'm here. I was just deciding whether to evade your question and switch to a less painful topic. Like a gynecologist with freezing hands."

"As if I'd let you change the subject," she reminded me.

"Fine, he turned out to be a total ass," I answered, sinking onto my bed. "I couldn't get past his constant nut scratching."

She snorted. "It couldn't have been that bad."

"Think of a hound dog with fleas and it was twenty times worse than that. It was seriously wrong. I guess it's back to the end of the loser line for me again."

Even with a thousand plus miles separating us, I could see Brittni's eyes rolling through the phone. I prepared myself for the lecture that was sure to come.

"Why do you always go out with assholes?"

"Oh, didn't you know? It's part of my personal ad on matchmewithadickhead.com. 'Only pricks need inquire' is one of my stipulations before I'll even consider them," I said dryly.

"Tress, you deserve so much better."

"Yeah, well, maybe you and Ashton got the last good guys around. Thanks for stealing my soul mate, bitch," I joked as she snorted with laughter.

"Your soul mate is out there, you just need to stop looking under rocks for your next date."

"Gee, thanks for the advice. I was wondering what I was doing wrong."

"Don't get your panties in a bunch," she said, trying to pacify me.

"Not wearing any."

"Eww, TMI, Tressa."

"Kidding. Laundry day was yesterday, so my lips are covered."

"God, you can be so vulgar sometimes." She laughed for a moment before turning serious. "You have to know you deserve better, right?"

"Right, better like Trent?" I instantly regretted bringing him up. With good reason. His name was all the ammunition Brittni needed.

"Yes. Exactly like Trent. He's completely different than the asswipes you normally go out with. It was obvious at Ashton's wedding he still has a thing for you."

I rolled my eyes even though she couldn't see the effort.

"Have you seen him since then?" she asked with her uncanny sixth sense.

I weighed my options on how I should answer her. I could fib and say I hadn't seen him, but knowing the way gossip spread through Woodfalls, even when you're not there, she would most likely find out. For all I knew, Trent had already told someone, who told someone else, who told Brittni and this whole conversation was one of her typical traps.

"Yeah, I saw him at a party last night," I admitted, holding the phone away from my ear as she screeched loudly. Okay, so maybe she hadn't heard about our encounter.

It took me five minutes to give her a glossed over version of the events from the night before. I left out the part about my freak show possessiveness over him and the fact that I had noticed his eyes.

"So he didn't ask you out?" She sounded disappointed.

"No. I think you're wrong about him. I've told you a million times: Trent and I are complete opposites. Besides, I'm thinking of swearing off guys completely. They're not worth all the baggage. Maybe I'll give girls a try."

She snorted. "You think we're any easier? Anyway, you like guys too much for that." Her tone turned serious. "You just need to give the right guy a chance."

"Maybe I'm different than you and Ashton. I'll be She-Ra, queen of myself. That's all I need."

She laughed. "Look, we're going to talk about this more, but I better go help Justin, who is attempting to hang shelves in his studio. I can hear him swearing already, so I'm pretty sure if I don't go in and help, this could turn into a disaster. I love you, sweets."

"Love you too, whore. Go help my soul mate," I teased, hanging up while she was still laughing.

4.

I was screwed.

My hand tightened around the note an aide handed me after my business communications class ended. I didn't have to look at it. I knew what it would say. After several unsuccessful attempts to contact me by phone, Professor Nelson obviously decided to take matters into his own hands.

Hence, why I was screwed.

I could no longer avoid him. My stomach felt like it was full of bricks as I detoured from my apartment, where I had been heading, to the science building, where Professor Nelson was expecting me. If only I would have done some schoolwork this previous weekend like I intended to, I wouldn't be in this situation.

I swear on Sunday I'd woken up with every intention of

studying the entire day, but Derek and Cameo dangled consignment store shopping and Starbucks in front of me. How could I pass that up? I told them I couldn't be gone all day, but one shop had turned into two shops and then two turned into three. My attempts to protest proved futile as Cameo and Derek dragged me along. Before I knew it, the day was gone, and I'm definitely not a "study all night" kind of person.

Now, in hindsight, I was mentally kicking myself in the head for my utter foolishness. The term was officially four weeks in, and I was failing three of my four classes. Even in the fourth class, I was barely maintaining a low-C average, and that was only because we had yet to take an exam. Rest assured when we did, my grade would match my other classes.

The science building was like a mausoleum when I pulled open the heavy door. During my walk of shame, I could hear muffled voices behind closed doors with lectures and classes going on. I looked at them longingly as I passed. I never thought I would wish to be in class, but right about now, I'd take anything over what I was about to face.

Professor Nelson's door was closed when I reached it. It wasn't too late to flee. That's if I was a runner, which I wasn't. My boobs would give me a concussion and a black eye.

Ripping off the Band-Aid before I could change my mind, I rapped my knuckles against the door before walking inside.

I breathed in deeply as I stepped into the office. The welcoming smell of rich leather, sweet spice, and pipe smoke assaulted my senses in a good way and reminded me of Woodfalls. For a brief second, I almost forgot about the trouble I was in.

I met the eyes of my mentor, who was sitting behind an imposing cherrywood desk that matched the floor-to-ceiling bookcases that bracketed the window. "Tressa," Professor Nelson greeted me. "Have a seat."

"Professor N," I mumbled, sitting on the edge of the leather club chair that sat on the other side of the desk. I crossed my ankles and folded my hands demurely in my lap. He was the lone person who extracted this reaction out of me. I'd known him my entire life. His first name was Warren, but even as a child I had always referred to him as "Professor." He was a close friend of my father. They were old fraternity brothers who kept in contact after graduation. When the professor's wife died in a skiing accident, Dad talked him into coming to Woodfalls to grieve. What was supposed to be a one-year hiatus from his job at Princeton turned out to be a career move. Professor Nelson had a well-respected reputation and needless to say, Maine State College had been thrilled to offer him a tenured position. For as long as I could remember, he'd been around, and my brother and I always considered him a surrogate uncle.

He was the one I'd always turned to for advice, the one who sat with me when I broke the news to my parents that I would be taking a year off before going to college. He was the sole reason I'd gotten into MSC, which was why I was currently squirming sitting across from him.

I winced at his silence, unable to return his stare. His normally warm molasses eyes behind his glasses weren't angry or filled with judgment. That I could have handled. As a matter of fact, I wanted him to yell at me. Call me a screwup. Tell me I deserved a kick in the ass. But his reaction was like a knife in the gut. Anything would have been better than his disappointment, which was so tangible I felt like I would choke on it if I inhaled.

"Are you done?" he asked, breaking the silence in the room.

His direct question made it obvious he didn't summon me here to beat around the bush.

I looked up, trying not to flinch. "No, sir."

"Are your courses too overwhelming?" He leaned back in his leather chair that creaked as it redistributed his weight.

I weighed his question. Either he was giving me an out or he was trying to trick me. I could claim my classes were too hard. I'm sure he would believe me. After all, it was common knowledge that I struggled academically. I had the perfect excuse. Statistics was totally making me its bitch, but deep down I knew that was my fault. All the partying I'd been doing since term started was the real reason I was feeling the pinch in all my classes. I knew if I applied myself, my grades would be different—maybe not stellar, but at least more respectable.

I shook my head, not taking the excuse he'd offered. "I'm just not focusing as much as I could be," I answered without looking away. "I just need to find my rhythm."

"Are you certain? You know, if you need help, it is up to you to ask for it. We have excellent tutors who would willingly step in if I asked. All you have to do is say the word." His chair creaked again as he reached for a sticky note on the corner of his desk. He picked up his pen and started scrawling on the small yellow piece of paper.

I balked at his words. No way did I want a tutor. The idea of having someone leaning over my shoulder while I muddled my way through assignments was not my idea of a good time. I was a solo kind of student. It might take me twice as long with a fair measure of aggravation, but in the end, I was always able to figure things out. "No, I got this," I interrupted him as he continued writing. I tried sneaking a peek at his note, but he finished up before I could get a good look. I suspected it had something to do with me.

He set down his pen, stroking the beard on his chin that was more white than brown. "A tutor could be vital in helping you get back on track. At the moment, you're facing academic probation. Getting expelled in your senior year would be a great shame."

"I won't get expelled, I promise. I almost have all the assignments done that I need to catch up," I lied.

He didn't answer, but instead stared at me with unwavering eyes.

"I'll catch up. I know I've let things get out of hand."

I could tell he had his doubts, but he finally nodded his head. "See that you do. Don't squander this opportunity,

Tressa. The hard work will pay off in the future. I can promise you that. Now, tell me, will you be returning to Woodfalls to cause your usual ruckus during the Halloween festivities?"

My eyes narrowed at the sudden redirection of our conversation. "Did Dad put you up to asking?"

A smile spread across his previously stony face. "He may have mentioned it when I saw him at Fran's a couple days ago."

I shook my head, not at all surprised.

"You know your folks like having you around. They miss you while you're away."

"BizCake, I was just home during summer break."

"BizCake?"

"Yeah, you know, like something that's so bizarre it takes the cake," I explained, grinning at him.

"Your vocabulary never ceases to amaze me."

I laughed. "Admit it. You learn something new every time I come to see you."

"Let's just say that you have more creativity than you give yourself credit for. All the more reason why I expect more than you are giving at the moment. Now, I hate to cut our meeting short, but I have an appointment in a few minutes."

Relieved to be getting off without more chastising, I jumped to my feet. "Gotcha," I said, heading for the door.

"Not so fast." His words stopped me in my tracks.

Nuts. So close.

"Yeah," I said, turning back to him.

"No more avoiding my calls. I'll send the posse after you next time."

"Yes, sir," I said, giving a mock salute and opening the door to leave before he threatened to throw my parents in the mix. In my haste to exit the office, I didn't see the person waiting to come inside, who I completely bowled over.

A set of warm hands encircled my biceps as we both tried to keep our footing. My momentum knocked us together as my chest bumped his.

"Shit, I'm sorry," I said. "Oh, sorry, Professor," I yelled over my shoulder, knowing he didn't care for cursing. I looked up at the poor soul I had bumped into to find a familiar pair of entrancing blue eyes looking down at me with complete shock.

"Not a problem," Trent answered. His intense stare held mine for a long moment and had me second-guessing all kinds of things, including my mixed feelings for him. After a moment, his eyes drifted to my lips, which were only inches away. Suddenly, it felt as if we were frozen in some kind of time warp. Nothing around us moved, and all I could think about was what it would feel like if he kissed me.

I drifted backward into the wall, which jarred me back into reality.

"What are you doing here?" My tone came out more accusatory than necessary.

Professor Nelson spoke up before Trent could reply. "Trent, my boy. Nice to see you. We were just finishing up here."

I wasn't surprised the professor knew Trent. After all, we were from the same itty-bitty town. What did surprise me was the comradeship they obviously shared. I wasn't trying to be selfish, but I always assumed Professor N was only my mentor, not anyone else's. I wasn't sure I wanted to share, and definitely not with Trent.

"Sorry about showing up unexpectedly, Professor. I finished the program earlier than expected. I thought we could go over it together before my presentation tomorrow," Trent said animatedly, stepping away from me like I wasn't there.

Within seconds they were completely engrossed in a conversation that lost me at the words *megabits* and *nanotechnology.*

I looked at Professor N in disbelief. I'd always considered him to be a bit stodgy and uptight, but as I listened to him talk to Trent, he was strangely the opposite. He was enthusiastic and engrossed in everything Trent had to say.

"Well, okay then. I guess I'll see you later," I finally said, not quite believing I had been forgotten.

My words at least broke through their geek-lingo-filled conversation. "Tressa, my dear, you know Trent, right?" Professor N asked, clapping Trent on the back.

"Um, does he live in Woodfalls?" I asked sarcastically. I was still a little miffed that I had obviously missed their secret relationship.

Trent's lips quirked at my sarcasm, but I ignored him as I stared blandly at Professor N.

"Don't get cheeky with me, my dear." His eyes narrowed as he reprimanded me. "Trent here is my protégé. He'll be vying for my job before I know it."

Oh brother. Go figure. This was just another prime example of why Brittni was wrong. Trent and I couldn't be any more opposite if we tried. I get called to the professor's office because he's afraid I have one foot in Loserville. Meanwhile, Trent is his golden geek boy.

"Not your job, sir," Trent said, pushing his glasses back up on his nose. For some reason, the gesture aggravated me. Why was he always pushing his glasses up? Why not just get his glasses tightened or get a new pair? I knew I was being ridiculous. Actually, I was being petty and mean, but it felt good at the moment.

"That's my boy. Aim higher. One day you'll be my boss."

Trent's laugh seemed a bit forced. "I wouldn't go that far, sir," he answered, looking uncomfortably at me. That was surprising since most of the guys I knew had egos so big they could barely get through a double doorway. Watching Trent now flushing made my stomach flutter slightly, and my aggravation from a few seconds ago evaporated.

"Don't be modest, my boy. You're destined to do great things," Professor N declared, turning back to me. "Young Trent here was the tutor I had in mind for you. He has agreed to help as a favor to me."

His words were like a bucket of ice-cold water dumped over my head as embarrassment flared through me.

Trent nodded his head. That was just great. They'd been discussing me. I was literally in hell. My feelings of goodwill toward Trent from a moment ago disappeared.

"No, thanks. I don't need your help." Acid dripped from my words. Turning on my heels, I stomped away from the office, slamming the door behind me.

I was halfway down the hall when I heard the office door open and footsteps running after me a second before a hand encircled my wrist. Unable to hold back my anger and embarrassment, I abruptly turned to let Trent have it, but I was unprepared for his close proximity and concerned expression. My eyes moved down to his fingers that gently held my wrist. Usually when a guy grabbed me, I felt trapped and overcome with the urge to fight him off, but here, now, I was feeling anything but entrapment. I felt oddly comfortable, like I was anchored to something important, something significant. My eyes moved to Trent's face.

He looked at me earnestly before finally speaking. "Please let me help you." A shiver ran through me. His voice was soft yet husky. Had it always sounded that way? A geek with a voice like his went against nature. That deep sexy tone belonged to some mysterious business tycoon trying to entice a sweet innocent virgin into his bed. Rational thoughts were finding it hard to hold court in my mind at the moment. It was time to lay off the steamy books that Ashton kept sending me. This was nerdy Trent, for God's sake. My complete opposite. Electric blue eyes and sexy voice be damned.

"Tressa, I can help you catch up." His words finally wormed their way through my mind, which was acting like a horny teenager.

I glared at him before jerking away stubbornly. "I don't need your help."

"It's nothing to be ashamed of. College can be hard for

some people." I bristled at his words. Hard for some people? He might as well have attached *morons like you* to the statement.

"Don't worry about us stupid folk. You can go play with your intellectual kind," I drawled before turning around and stalking away.

It wasn't until I was out of the building that I finally allowed my shoulders to slump.

Mother of all donkey suck. I wasn't sure I could remember a time when I felt as mortified as I was at the moment. The idea that Trent knew about my academic failures felt like a sucker punch to the gut. I couldn't believe Professor N had blabbed. Wasn't there some kind of student confidentiality or something he was supposed to uphold?

My anger carried me across campus to my apartment. I was still fuming as I stomped up the four flights of stairs. I shoved through the front door, slamming it closed behind me.

"Whoa, Hurricane Tressa," Derek joked, looking up from his laptop. I ignored him, throwing my book bag on the floor and then kicking it across the room in a complete fit of anger. "Whose ass needs to be kicked?"

"Professor N's," I answered through gritted teeth, hurling myself on the couch beside Derek.

"Oh, well, I'm out on that one."

"Gee, thanks." I glared at him.

"What happened?"

I shrugged, not wanting to tell him the real issue. It was

bad enough Professor N and Trent knew the current dismal condition my grades were in. I didn't need my friends to know I was a total loser. "Nothing," I mumbled, climbing off the couch.

"Hey, you can talk to me." He sounded sincere. For a moment, I was tempted, but the words stuck in my throat like a lump.

"It's nothing," I muttered, grabbing my book bag off the floor and heading for our room. I closed the door behind me and tossed the bag in the far corner. At the moment, I wasn't in the mood to deal with it. I collapsed on the bed as the last of my anger faded and was replaced with remorse and something akin to pain.

"Tressa," Derek called, knocking cautiously on the door.

"Come in," I answered in a monotone voice.

Derek turned the knob and entered the room slowly. If I wasn't in total mopeville I would have laughed. My friends knew me well enough to know that if something got me this steamed, it must be serious. "If you need me to kick your professor's ass, I'll do it," he said, looking pained. He slid an arm around my shoulders and squeezed.

I debated his words like I was actually giving them serious consideration. "No. He's a tough old bird. It would be embarrassing for you if he was the one who ended up doing the ass-kicking."

"Hey, I'm tough. I'm just not sure I could punch an old dude, let alone Professor N."

"It's the thought that counts, sparrow." I felt marginally better. Derek excelled in this area.

"What else can I do to make it all better?"

"Do you and Cameo feel like going out?" I asked hopefully. I kept my eyes averted from my book bag, ignoring my promise to buckle down.

"I'm game. I think Cam said she had to work until eleven, though. What time do you want to leave?"

I glanced at my phone to check the time, seeing that it was later than I thought. "Does six work for you?"

"That works. Now, put on a happy face. We're going out," he said, dropping an endearing kiss on my head.

What a relief. Going out was exactly what I needed. I would deal with my mess later.

5.

In typical Tressa fashion, dealing with my schoolwork mess meant basically ignoring it altogether. I had recently gotten a job at a coffeehouse near the campus that kept me busy and made it easy to temporarily forget about my academic nightmare. In my twisted justification, I convinced myself the extra money was more important than improving my grades. What MSC really needed was a procrastination class. That's a subject I would excel in.

Saturday night rolled around and my book bag was still taunting me from the corner of the room where I had left it. I knew it needed my attention, but the big Sigma Pi throw-down was tonight. It couldn't be missed. I made a vow to myself that tonight would be the last party I attended until I was caught up in my classes. It felt like the entire campus was buzzing over rumors about what the fraternity had in store for the pledges. If half of them were true, tonight would be the party of all parties.

"Tress, what do you think of this?" Cameo asked, joining me in the bathroom, where I was liberally applying my eye makeup.

"Whoa, this is smoking." I whistled, admiring the practically see-through sheer blouse she'd bought last weekend. Instead of a camisole underneath, she paired it with a plum-colored Victoria's Secret bra, skintight jeans in the same deep plum color, and six-inch heels to complete the look. "You look like a total sex kitten."

"Meow," she responded, tracing her lips with liner. "I'll probably freeze my ass off, but it'll be worth it."

"It's not like you have a whole lot to freeze off," I said, smacking her butt on my way out.

"Hey, you have to buy me a drink before you get to test the merchandise."

"You liked it," I teased, adjusting my clothes. Just a few minutes ago, I had been satisfied with the way I looked. Now, standing next to Cameo's petite frame, I felt self-conscious. At times like this, it was hard not to feel inadequate.

"Eventually I'd like to use the bathroom too," Derek complained, joining me in the hallway.

"Sorry, sparrow, you can't rush this," Cameo said, leaving the bathroom with a cloud of Viva La Juicy perfume in her wake.

Derek coughed, fanning his hands in front of his face to clear the fragrant fumes. "Viva should be spritzed, not bathed in."

"I'm not sure what I find more alarming. That you used

the word *spritzed* or that you know Viva by smell," Cameo called after him as he closed the bathroom door.

"I have four sisters." His voice was muffled through the door.

"I'm sure that's what it is," I said, winking at Cameo.

Ten minutes later we were chattering away as we walked down the second flight of stairs when a familiar voice called Derek's name.

Derek's eyes looked panicked even in the dimly lit stairwell. *Run*, he mouthed, grabbing our hands and dragging us down the stairs.

"Hey, these shoes aren't made for running," I hissed, trying not to fall down the stairs. My hooker heels were impractical for most vertical activities, but they looked uber hot.

"Just hurry," Derek squeaked in a high-pitched voice that should have embarrassed him.

"If you break my heels, I'm going to break your head."

Derek nodded, though he didn't slow down. We could still hear the thumping of footsteps on the stairs above us.

The door leading outside was within sight when we heard "yoo-hoo" right behind us. Derek groaned under his breath.

"Gird your loins," I teased, turning to face Destiny, the colorful cross-dresser who'd had his eye on Derek for months. Cameo and I found the situation hilarious, but Derek avoided him at all costs. Destiny was harmless, and definitely not shy about checking out the "merchandise," as he called it.

"Didn't y'all hear me calling you?" Destiny drawled, not the slightest bit out of breath. Unlike the three of us, who were sucking air like we had been chased by a pack of wolves.

"Sorry, Destiny, we're late for a party and didn't hear you." Cameo lied smoothly as Derek wedged himself behind us.

"Oh, I like to party," Destiny cooed, eyeing Derek meaningfully.

I nearly laughed when I heard Derek gulp behind me. "Sorry, it's only for MSC students," I answered, stepping in before Derek started hyperventilating.

"I understand, honey darlin'. Maybe we can have our own party sometime. You know I'm free anytime, and y'all are always welcome."

This time Derek blanched, looking like he could pass out.

"Sure, Destiny, but we better head out."

"Y'all have fun, and, Derek, don't you be a stranger," he said, throwing a sizzling look Derek's way.

Cameo and I barely made it outside before we dissolved in a fit of giggles.

"Not funny," Derek complained, looking green in the face.

"Maybe you should take him up on it. I bet Destiny could teach you things you never knew you were missing," I pointed out.

"Oh God, I just threw up a little," he said.

"Come on, don't be a prude. What's wrong with a little variety?" I continued, grinning at Cameo, who was laughing so hard she was holding her side.

Derek held up his hand. "Don't say another word."

"I'm just saying you never know," I teased.

"And I don't want to know, thank you."

We continued to mess with poor Derek as we drove to the party. The frat house was less than a mile away, but there was a definite nip in the air, finally providing relief from the unseasonably warm temperatures we had been experiencing this fall. The heat in Derek's truck barely had time to warm up before we got there. Stepping from the vehicle, Cameo stood shivering beside me while we waited for Derek, who was primping in the mirror. Finally satisfied with his appearance, he climbed from the truck and put an arm around Cameo to keep her warm.

Sigma Pi was already thumping when we arrived. I'd never seen so many people crammed into one house in my life. Derek darted away when his name was called by a couple of buddies, leaving Cameo and me to push our way through the crowd, looking for her current fling, who happened to be a fraternity brother.

"He's over there," I said, spotting him first. "Is that a pledge he's walking?" I added, laughing at the leash that was hooked to a collar around the pledge's neck. The poor dope was dressed in nothing but a Speedo with a dog tail attached at the ass. His nose was painted black, and he was wearing a set of dog ears.

"They all are," Cameo said, pointing to a couple of other guys walking their own pledges.

"That's classic. I want to walk a dog too."

"I'm sure Chad will share," she said, throwing herself into his arms. Her lips met his as he wrapped his arms around her. He easily lifted her slender five-foot frame off the ground.

After a moment, they broke apart. "Share what?" Chad asked, looking at me appraisingly. "I'm always willing to share," he added, winking outrageously. "There's plenty of me to go around."

"Oh no, if only we'd known. Cameo and I already got it on before we headed out tonight. We didn't realize you'd want to join in," I said, innocently brushing a finger across Cameo's bottom lip. Her eyes sparkled with mirth.

"Whatever, evil twins," Chad muttered, adjusting himself.

We both burst out laughing. Guys were so easy. If I had a drink for every time Cameo and I were propositioned for a threesome, I'd be an alcoholic by now.

"You know you love it," Cameo cooed at him.

"Please, I was just kidding," he answered.

"That's too bad. We weren't," Cameo said, stroking his chest.

Chad's eyes widened like he'd won the lottery. "Really?"

Cameo and I laughed again, making the pledge at his feet snicker.

"Evil, just plain evil," Chad complained, adjusting himself again.

"Nice dog," Cameo said, patting the pledge on the head.

"You like my bitch?" Chad asked, pulling on the leash so the pledge's head lifted. Cameo and I both snickered when his tongue lolled to the side. Pledge week was always better when the pledges went with the flow. For the most part, MSC was pretty tame when it came to hazing. We'd all heard the horror stories about fraternities using feces or urine in their pledge rituals. The most you were going to see here was some harmless streaking or crazy antics like jumping off the roof gripping a mattress. That really couldn't be counted as hazing since all the frat brothers had done it at one point or another. Hell, even I had tried it for the rush.

I scratched the pledge's head at my feet, patting him like a dog. "Where can I get a bitch of my own?"

My question went unanswered since Chad and Cameo were currently playing tonsil hockey.

I pulled out my phone and snapped a quick picture of the pledge on a leash so I could post it. "Good luck with that," I said to the freshman, who didn't look all that thrilled at being strapped to a make-out fest. Leaving them behind to suck each other's faces off, I decided now was as good a time as any to scope out the rest of the party. Snagging a beer from a nearby cooler, I made a circuit around the room, stopping to chat every few seconds.

"Hey, girl, I was wondering when you'd show," our friend Melissa greeted me.

"Hey, Mel. We just got here a few minutes ago. I love the dog theme," I said. "Steve's idea?"

She nodded. Steve was head of the Sigma Pi fraternity. He and Melissa had been dating since freshman year, and they pretty much dictated most of the social events at MSC. Melissa's sorority was notorious for pranking Sigma Pi, which made her my kind of girl.

"Yeah, the other brothers voted on ideas, and this was one of the winners. You should have heard some of the other suggestions—downright disgusting."

"Like what?" I was pretty confident there was nothing that would shock me.

"Dipshit John suggested all the pledges eat vanilla pudding. He said they'd wait until they were almost done and then tell them they all put their jizz in it."

"That's just wrong," I said, shaking my head.

"It's effing sick. I don't care if it is a joke. You know John, though. He can be such an asshole."

I nodded, having experienced it firsthand. I made the colossal mistake of agreeing to a date with John last spring. He was a total flirt who believed women should be flattered by his ogling and lame-ass comments. It only took one date to realize he was a shit.

"What else do Steve and the guys have up their sleeves?" I asked, dying to know what their grand finale would be this year. Last year their master plan fizzled out when security busted them for breaking into the library. The pledges were supposed to erect thrones for the fraternity brothers out of books. They were going to record it and post it on YouTube.

Melissa's eyes narrowed slightly, seeing through my ploy. "I'm not that easy. You have to wait just like everyone else."

"Come on, I'm not going to tell anyone."

She hesitated for a moment, so I went for the kill. "I'll give you total credit when I post the pictures on Instagram," I said, coaxing her. I could see she was close to caving. My Instagram account had become legendary around campus. I'd been posting pictures before Instagram was considered cool. Word of mouth spread and now I had more than ten thousand followers. People say I have a gift for snarky taglines and hashtags. Not to mention the pictures of pranks that most of the time were initiated by me, not to toot my own horn any further.

"Total credit?" she asked, lowering her voice to a whisper.

"Total credit. Steve won't even be a blip on the radar." I knew that's what she was going for. Mel and Steve were tight, but they were always trying to one-up each other. I guess that's what you got when you paired two alpha dogs together. Someone always had to win. I really couldn't care less about their competition. I just wanted to know what the frat house had planned.

She looked around one last time before answering. "Okay, but not a word to anyone. I'll have to seriously cut you off if it gets back to Steve. He made me swear not to tell anyone."

I looked at her blandly. Everyone knew I wasn't a snitch.

"They're going to make the pledges raft down one of the tamer runs on Penobscot River," she said in a hushed tone, waiting for me to be impressed.

I waited for her to continue. I knew there had to be more.

She sighed after a moment, knowing she'd have to dish all the goods. "Fine, but not a word. They're making them do it buck naked."

"Nice," I said, grinning broadly as we fist-bumped.

"Yeah, they want to do it as a race. They'll dump the guys and their rafts at the starting point, and the first five who make it back will become brothers. The others will be shit out of luck."

"That's effing brilliant. Are they doing it in the morning?"

"Hell no, that's the brilliant part. They're doing it tonight. Half the fun will be making them fumble through the dark."

"That'll suck for taking pictures."

"You can take a picture of the guys as they load into the rafts."

"That works. The chilly weather ought to make for some interesting pictures. I heard shrinkage is not just a myth," I said, grinning wickedly at her.

"Trust me, it's not. Steve talked me into skinny-dipping last spring at the lake near my parents' house. It was butt-ass cold and Steve's penis looked like a turtle head scared to peek out of its shell. I was scared it was permanently damaged and I was going to have to turn it in for a new model." She winked at me.

"Can't blame you there. A broken penis is a no-fun penis."

"Totes," she said, grinning.

"When are they going out?"

"Ten, I think. Whoops, I think Steve is looking for me," she said, glancing at her ringing cell phone. "Remember, not a word until they head out, okay?" She placed her hand on my shoulder to emphasize her point before leaving to join her man.

I was pondering Melissa's words when Cameo danced over to me, dragging Chad behind her, who was in turn dragging his human dog behind him.

She was practically bursting with excitement. "Guess what?" For a second I thought Chad had spilled to her about the rafting prank. This was college life. No secret was sacred.

"What?" I tried to look surprised, expecting to hear news of the prank I already knew about.

"Chad told me they installed a stripper pole in the rec

room. Do you want to give these boys a real show?" She looked knowingly at me, making me smirk.

Cameo and I decided last year it would be fun to take a pole dancing class. The class turned out to be a lot more intense than we thought. To put it mildly, we now had a healthy respect for the chicks that did it for a living. When it was all said and done, we had managed to squeak through enough lessons to give a decent showing.

Our small group headed downstairs, and I noticed others starting to follow as word began to spread of what Cameo and I had planned. The chatter crescendoed as we made our way into the rec room. The Ping-Pong table and air hockey table had been moved from their normal locations in the center of the room to make space for the shiny new pole. Currently, a drunk blonde with boobs that rivaled mine was straddling the pole. Whether it was her intoxication or just a lack of rhythm, she looked like she needed the pole more to hold herself up than to do any dancing. She was unceremoniously booed from the pole when she tried to make up for her lack of skills by humping it. Another girl stepped in to take her place. I recognized her from the speech class I took last fall. She was at least a halfway decent dancer, but she didn't have a clue what to do with the pole.

"This is painful to watch," Cameo murmured in my ear.

"Tell me about it. If she runs her tongue up the pole one more time, I may have to gouge my eyes out."

"When are you two going to put her out of her misery?" Chad interrupted.

"We're biding our time. If all the dancers perform like this, it'll make ours more meaningful," Cameo mumbled out of the corner of her mouth.

We endured two more showgirl wannabes when we finally decided enough was enough. The atmosphere changed abruptly when Cameo and I approached the pole. During the class we had taken, we pretty much perfected a dance that teased and enticed without giving anything away. The catcalls and groans got louder and louder as Cameo and I moved our hips in a rhythmic motion. Part of the routine had us unclasping the top few buttons of each other's blouses, exposing just enough cleavage to have all the guys yelling. In the big finale, I slid slowly down with my back against the pole and my face just inches from Cameo's bosom. She then spread her legs, as I ducked underneath and swayed up her backside as she turned her head back to me, looking like we were about to kiss, but stopping just before. By the time we were done, every male in the vicinity had taken off his shirt. They twirled them in the air as they screamed their approval.

We joined Chad, who was high-fiving the guys standing around him. He threw his arms around us like our dance had been an invitation. "Holy fuck, you sure you two wouldn't like to—you know?"

"That's as close as it's going to get, loverboy," I said, spotting Melissa, who was gesturing me over. "I'll catch you guys in a little while."

6.

"Okay, here's the deal," Melissa began. "The brothers are getting ready to round up the pledges. Steve knows you'll be driving with me. Everyone else will be at the bottom of the rapids so they can see the guys in all their naked glory when they finish."

"Or lack of glory," I snorted. We both laughed as we headed up the stairs. The rest of the partygoers caught wind of something coming up. Excitement rippled through the crowd when one of the fraternity brothers passed out flyers giving directions to the location where everyone should go.

After some mild confusion, Melissa was designated as a driver for the overflow of pledges. I probably should have found Cameo or Derek to let them know where I was going, but I was too excited. I claimed the front seat while three freshmen piled into the back. They had dumped their leashes, but were still wearing Speedos. The fraternity conceded and let them at least wear jackets for now, although none of the pledges knew it was only temporary. Melissa looked at me, giggling as I returned her grin. These poor saps had no idea what they were in for.

The drive to the drop-off point at Penobscot River passed with nervous bursts of chatter from the backseat as the guys mulled over what the final stunt was going to be. I felt a pinch of sympathy for them. This was one of the main reasons I never joined a sorority. It was fun watching what the pledges had to endure, but God knows I could never have tolerated some of the shit the wannabes are put through. I wanted to be the one doing the pranking, not the other way around.

The talking in the backseat hit a lull as we got closer to the river. Glancing back, I could see two of the pledges exchanging nervous looks. I couldn't blame them. In the pitch black of night, it was hard to imagine what they had coming. I caught the eyes of the third pledge. Unlike his comrades, he looked anything but nervous. His brown eyes sparkled with excitement and eagerness. He winked at me appraisingly and I shook my head. A fearless freshman. Very soon we would see if he still had his confidence.

Eventually, Melissa pulled off the road and drove down a path that was lined with mostly bare trees. In the darkness, everything looked spooky and had a sinister feel to it. Even the moon seemed to be teasing us by barely peeking out behind the clouds that were hanging low in the sky.

The dirt road was laced with ruts and protruding roots, making us bounce uncomfortably in our seats. We were relieved when the road finally ended abruptly near the water's edge. Melissa parked next to a line of other cars that were facing the water with their headlights on. Climbing from the vehicle, I spotted a row of rafts that were already blown up and ready to go on the shore's edge. Obviously, Sigma Pi was not taking any chances on this stunt going awry.

The pledges in our car piled out, following Melissa and me toward the rest of the group. The ground beneath our feet was damp, making our feet squish through the mud. I grimaced for my heels that would most likely be ruined. Mr. Brown-Eyed Flirt from the ride over chivalrously held on to my elbow, helping me walk.

"Thanks," I said, indulgently smiling at his hopeful face. He was cute, with warm brown eyes and dimples in each cheek, but definitely not my type. Despite my original assessment, I could tell he was likely an all-around good guy.

"I'm David," he said.

"Too young," I replied.

"What?" He looked confused.

"I don't date freshmen. Not even when I was a freshman."

"So, you're telling me you're a freshman hater?"

"Not a hater. Just not a dater."

"Ha, that's funny. You don't know what you're missing, though," he said, releasing my arm as we joined the others.

"I have a pretty good idea," I answered, grinning. His persistence was cute, I'd give him that. "You better join your friends before you blow your chance," I added before I could give in to his boyish charms.

"Maybe we can hang out after," he persisted, winking at me again before jogging off to join the others.

I shook my head. Can't blame him for trying, I guess.

The group was rowdy by the time I joined it. There was a lot of ribbing and pushing as they let off steam waiting for Steve's instructions. Several of the guys bounced around trying to stay warm. As if the night wanted to punish them further, a cold gust of wind blew through the trees. The half-dressed crew seemed to shiver as one. I felt their pain. It was downright cold near the water. I was thankful for once that this was a prank I wouldn't be taking part in. Melissa must have had the same sentiments since we both zipped up our jackets and stuffed our hands into our pockets at the same time.

"All right, asswipes. This last challenge is easy enough. When I blow the whistle, each of you will grab a raft and an oar and head downriver. The takeout is about two miles away. The first five to make it will earn their places in the fraternity. Simple as that. Before you crybabies start whining, this rapid is not even a class-three rating. They take kids on this run." His words seemed unnecessary judging by the roughhousing and taunts being thrown out.

It was obvious the pledges were raring to go. That is, until Steve lowered the final boom.

"One last thing. You'll be competing in your birthday suits."

Groans filled the air.

"You heard me. Drop your banana holders and shed those jackets."

My eyes found David, who winked at me again. He held my stare as he hooked his fingers around the waistband of his Speedo, lowering it slightly to reveal more of the small trail of hair that ran down his abdomen.

His eyes remained locked on my face as he grinned confidently. Cocky was more like it.

Not one to back down, I watched as he gently slid his Speedo to his ankles before kicking it off. He stood before us in all his naked glory without an ounce of embarrassment. Not that he had anything to be embarrassed about, I discovered, as I looked him over appraisingly before turning away nonchalantly. He was built and had a six-pack that I wouldn't mind exploring with my tongue, but I didn't date freshmen. That rule was written in stone.

The other pledges weren't nearly as daring as young David. They stared at Melissa and me like they were expecting us to turn around, but neither of us gave any indication of caring. They wouldn't be showing us anything we hadn't seen before.

After a few more grumbles, they finally conceded and stripped. I pulled out my phone, taking several pictures of the makeshift male revue, but had to crop them right above their junk. I didn't want to get my Instagram account shut down for posting nudie pictures.

I had just finished posting and giving Melissa the full credit for one of the pictures when Steve blew the whistle. I snapped one last picture of their white asses as each of the pledges scrambled to grab a raft and an oar. There was a lot of pushing and shoving, along with hooting and hollering from the onlookers. It was as hilarious as I thought it would be.

Even with several headlights lighting the area, it was hard to see in the dark, but we knew when the first raft hit the water by the sound of the splash. Within seconds, several other splashes followed by a string of cursing rang through the night as the pledges got their first feel of the ice-cold water. They'd be lucky if their nuts didn't freeze off. The fraternity brothers on shore seemed unconcerned about the temperatures. Judging by their laughter and congratulations to each other, they were satisfied with their well-executed prank.

Once the last raft hit the water, we all piled back into our vehicles so we could join everyone else at the finish line. The ride was short, and Melissa and I traded notes on who had the best body based on what we had seen. We were laughing about what the cold water would be doing to them when Melissa pulled into a lot that was nearly packed full with cars. It looked like most of the party had showed up.

"Catch you later," Melissa said, throwing me an air-kiss as she headed off to join Steve. Waving good-bye, I headed toward the bonfire that had been lit to search for Cameo and Derek. The flames from the fire cast shadows that only seemed to be enhanced by the tall pine trees that surrounded the clearing. I was just about to text Cameo when she snuck up behind me.

"Whore, where have you been?"

"Sheesh, don't be a creeper," I complained.

"Oh, please, as if tough-ass Tressa ever gets scared."

"Sure, look around. This party has classic slasher movie written all over it. I expected to find you stuck to a tree with a hatchet through your forehead or something equally macabre," I teased.

"Great, so you're telling me I'd be the first to die?"

"No. Big-Boob Trish would get it first. The chicks with the huge knockers always go first."

Cameo looked directly at my ample bosom without saying another word.

"I know. I'd be screwed, right?"

"True story." She smirked, taking a drink of some concoction from the red Solo cup in her hand. "Now, are you going to tell me where you were?"

"I was getting some epic pictures, my honey bear," I said, handing her my phone. I wobbled slightly as my left heel sank an inch into the soft soil near the water's edge. "Crap, I knew I should have worn those new boots I got a couple weeks ago. These heels are done, and that's the second time I've almost biffed it."

"Well, it's not like any of us were counting on hanging out at the river tonight," she said disdainfully, pulling on the hem of the MSC sweatshirt she was wearing.

"Chad's?" I asked, even though it was obvious by the way she was swimming in it. Chad was a lineman for Maine State's football team and had the bulk to prove it.

"Yeah, he was afraid I'd freeze without it." Cameo acted

like wearing the sweatshirt was somehow an inconvenience, but the dreamy look in her eyes said otherwise. Her tone was different from the usual way she talked about her flings. Usually, by the third or fourth date, she was already beginning to look for greener pastures, which was a shame since some of the guys were actually decent. Not like the asshats I dated.

"What's up with that? Am I crazy, or am I sensing something here?" I asked.

"I don't know yet. I still haven't decided," she answered, looking like she was waiting for me to criticize the situation. This was definitely interesting.

Derek joined us before I could dig any further. Cameo practically sighed with relief. Something was up. She may have thought she was off the hook, but I would pry it out of her later.

"Where were you?" Derek asked, twisting the cap off his beer.

"Taking pictures," Cameo answered for me as she handed my phone to him.

"Not bad," Derek said, flipping through the pictures. "Too bad they're babies. Some of these freshmen have it going on."

"I'm not too sure about that. Their junk looked pretty insignificant." I grinned at him.

"Hey, don't mock shrinkage. It's a real issue that plagues all guys." He coughed, looking uncomfortable.

I held up my finger. "Are we talking pinkie size?"

"Like I would tell you," Derek replied, swiping at my pinkie. I looked at him balefully. "Fine, it's worse," he admitted.

Worse, Cameo mouthed to me before we both started laughing.

"You girls have no sympathy for the plight of a man. How can you without a dick?"

"Oh, poor little teeny weenie. We're so sorry," I cooed.

Cameo doubled over, laughing.

"Maybe it's time for me to find some new friends," Derek said, making a move to leave.

"Come on, don't go. We love you," I drawled, looping my arm through his.

"No, you don't," he pouted.

"We do," Cameo assured him, finally able to talk.

We were trying to convince him that he was more important to us than our morning coffee, which was the highest compliment we could give him, when the first raft came into view. We all surged to the water's edge to cheer on the first new fraternity brother. Catcalls erupted from the crowd as everyone scored his shrinkage. He was given a Sigma Pi T-shirt and some sweats. He was grinning ear to ear as he pulled on the clothes. His new fraternity brothers clapped him on the back and handed him drinks. He'd be plastered within an hour.

The next raft arrived shortly after that, followed by two more. The previous scene was repeated as the new fraternity brothers were welcomed to the fold. With pledge week about to come to an end, the Sigmas began their house chant as they waited for the fifth and final brother to arrive. The rest of us joined in. The chanting hit a crescendo as four more rafts came into view.

From the shore we could see the competitors were playing

dirty, using their oars to splash water at one another and to push against the other rafts. We encouraged their tactics by calling out advice of our own.

In the end, it was one of the three pledges that rode with Melissa and me earlier who came out the victor. I cheered loudly for him when he looked my way. I had to admit, I felt a tinge of disappointment that it wasn't Mr. Brown-Eyed Flirt.

"New boyfriend?" Derek teased, catching our exchange.

"Please. He looks like he's twelve. Cameo may like playing with the young guns, but not me."

"Bite me, bitch. Chad's only a year younger than me."

"For half a year. The other half, he's two years younger," Derek added helpfully.

I snorted.

"He's mature for his age." I was surprised at the touch of insecurity that crept into her voice. She had it bad for him. Derek raised his eyebrows at me, obviously catching the same vibe.

He slung an arm around her shoulders, tucking her under the crook of his arm. "We get it, hummingbird, you like him." Cameo started to protest, but Derek shot her down. "It's okay to occasionally look at a guy as something other than a toy."

"Toys are better," she grumbled. "Or they used to be." She sounded bewildered.

"You have it bad, hummingbird," Derek said, placing a kiss on the top of her head as he winked at me.

She continued to argue as we stood around waiting for the last of the pledge hopefuls to arrive. Two more arrived after the last victor was crowned. They were forced to do the walk of shame to retrieve clothes from a stack the fraternity had piled by the road. They covered their junk the best they could as they made their way past so they could get dressed. More pictures were snapped as jokes and comments ran rampant.

Somewhere between the music being turned up and drinks being consumed, the vibe of the party subtly changed. Derek and I both sensed it at the same time. Our eyes moved to where a few guys had staggered through the shallow water to retrieve an empty deflated raft that had drifted ashore. Melissa and Steve huddled together with several of the fraternity brothers. Every few seconds they would cast worried looks upriver.

I watched as Steve discreetly found the other pledges that had been out on the water. From a distance, I could see him firing questions at them. Their concern level was rising. Several guys broke off from the group and walked along the shore, following the path the rafters had taken.

Steve turned off the music so he could tell the group what I had already figured out. A hard knot formed in the pit of my stomach. One of the guys wasn't back yet. Glancing around, I knew without a shadow of a doubt it was the persistent freshman who was missing. Gossip and speculation quickly began to ripple through the crowd. Out of the corner of my eye, I saw several people edging away from the fire toward the dirt lot where everyone had parked their cars. For a split second, I wanted to join them. I wanted no part of this. The carefree party atmosphere now had a feeling of unease. No one wanted to be associated with a possible accident.

Melissa came and found me as I stood at the crossroads of indecision. “Hey, Tressa, did you happen to take a picture of the guys who rode with us to the drop-off point?”

The knot in my stomach tightened to the point of becoming painful. “Sure. Why?”

“Because John can’t remember one of the pledge’s names. Steve is hoping the picture will jog someone’s memory.”

“It’s David,” I mumbled.

“What?”

“His name is David. He told me when we got to the drop-off point.” I didn’t want to believe something had happened to him. What was I saying? All of our panic was going to be for naught. David had probably run across problems and swum to shore. At the moment, he was probably a mile up the shore, freezing his ass off and wishing he had his clothes.

I willed that to be true, more than I had ever wanted anything. I had never been more wrong in my life.

7.

The authorities were called shortly after, and by the time they arrived, the party had completely dispersed. Cameo and Derek were both gone. They'd tried to persuade me to go with them, but I stubbornly refused. I had a strong urge to leave, but I couldn't shake the feeling that I was some kind of accessory in all this. Maybe it was because I drove with Melissa and took pictures, but deep down I knew it was because David and I had shared a moment. No matter how brief.

The authorities arrived in stages. First, it was one squad car. The cop was a total asshole. We were reprimanded and threatened with jail time for being at a state park after hours. Once he felt he had scared us, he proceeded to tell us that David probably smartened up and was back in his dorm room where we all should be.

The shit really hit the fan when his dorm room was checked and his roommate claimed he hadn't seen him since midday. At that point, more officers arrived, along with full rescue units. This time the line of questioning was different. The accusations were stronger. Words like *hazing* and *legal ramifications* were thrown into the mix. Steve and the other fraternity brothers remained stoically silent. Eventually, we were sent home, but were advised to not leave town and that we would be brought in for further questioning.

Melissa drove me home, and neither of us talked. We were both scared shitless.

Cameo and Derek were both waiting for me when I stumbled into the apartment. The events of the evening pulled at me. I wanted nothing more than to curl up in a ball and forget tonight had even happened.

Cameo and Derek didn't ask if we had found him. They didn't need to. It was written on my face. Walking past them, I headed to the shower to wash the stench of the party from me. I felt responsible for this. I wanted to believe David was okay, that in the morning all of this would be something we'd laugh about.

By morning we knew. It was on every news channel.

David Pierce's body had been found. Pierce—his last name was Pierce. Knowing that made it so much harder to hear. David Pierce was dead. Just ten hours ago he was an eager freshman ready to take on the whole world. Now he was dead.

Cameo and Derek went with me when I was called to the

police station for more questioning. My phone was seized as evidence. I wasn't surprised. I had documented the entire ridiculous stunt. That was my thing. I lived and breathed parties and watching these stupid antics. It was what defined me.

My dad showed up at the police station while I was being questioned. He was allowed to join me as my attorney, though he was really a tax lawyer. They assured him I wasn't being charged with anything. The Sigma Pi fraternity would be the one shouldering the blame for what happened. Hazing was a serious crime.

I was allowed to leave by midmorning. The four of us headed to breakfast, although my stomach felt like it was loaded with bricks.

The mood during the meal was somber. Dad and my friends thought I was worried about being charged.

"I'm not worried about that," I murmured.

"Then what is it?" Derek asked, dunking a piece of toast in the yellow egg yolk on his plate. "I'm not sure I've ever seen you this serious."

I shrugged my shoulders. I wasn't sure how to explain how I was feeling. Just because I liked to party and let loose didn't mean I had a heart of stone.

"It's going to be okay, pumpkin pie," Dad said, patting my hand. Cameo and Derek exchanged a look over his term of endearment, but didn't comment. Now wasn't the time for jokes.

I nodded even though nothing felt okay. The hazing stunt wasn't my fault, but did that automatically squash the guilt? To think otherwise was almost laughable. Hazing was done for entertainment. I'd always thrived on the ridiculous stunts. If my friends and I didn't encourage them so much, would the fraternities feel the endless need to one-up one another?

The questions rolled through my head like a highway pileup. Unable to eat, I pushed my food around my plate. I almost wished Dad would yell at me. Anything to pull me out of my slump. But he didn't. It wasn't his way.

The days following David's death were fraught with one consequence after another. I heard his parents were understandably livid and devastated. They demanded the school make an example of Sigma Pi. Steve and the other senior members were suspended while they were under investigation, but it seemed inevitable that they would be kicked out of school. Sigma Pi's charter was revoked and the fraternity was dismantled and shut down. The other fraternities on campus also paid a price for Sigma Pi's mistakes. Campus security scrutinized and checked over each house with a fine-tooth comb. It was as if all of fraternity row was on probation. I found it a bit hypocritical that many of the school's administration, who were likely fraternity brothers and sorority sisters themselves, acted so shocked that hazing was happening on campus. Like it was something our generation invented.

David's family decided to hold his memorial service the following Saturday so students would be able to pay their respects. The date loomed ahead of me, providing an eerie feeling of finality. In retrospect, I guess maybe David's death felt surreal since my life had been relatively untouched by death. Both sets of my grandparents were still alive, along with my uncle on

Dad's side and two aunts on Mom's side. My great-grandmother died when I was two years old, but that was the only death we'd had in our family. David's death was like a punch in the gut. It hurt like a bitch and nothing seemed to ease the pain.

I chose to handle my emotional upheaval by hiding out the rest of the weekend following David's death. Cameo and Derek didn't even try to hide their confusion over my complete one-eighty in personality. I couldn't really explain it to them since even I was confused. My entire existence up to this point felt wasted. The thought of partying or all the other shit I used to get off on made me want to hurl.

On Tuesday I was called to a meeting with the president of the university and found out I had not escaped the incident completely unscathed. Ironically, this almost made me happy. I felt this was a cosmic slap I deserved.

I knew before I arrived what the meeting would be about. My time at Maine State College had come to an end. Even if I wasn't directly involved in the scandal, I was failing all my classes. I received my summons on Monday evening, but didn't mention it to Cameo or Derek. They would know all the sordid details soon enough.

I decided to walk to the president's office from my apartment building the next morning, even though it was on the far side of the campus. I wanted to stall. Walking gave me a chance to clear my head. The air was crisp and the clouds were heavy with the promise of our first real snowfall of the year. In the last few days while I'd been holed up in my apartment, fall had staked its full claim on Maine. All the trees were barren and stripped of their leaves. They seemed so lonely without their normal foliage to cover their limbs. I felt an odd sense of kinship with them, like my own leaves had been stripped away, leaving me bare and neglected.

I reached Alumni Hall sooner than I expected. Pushing open the door, I was greeted with an influx of fall smells. I inhaled deeply, feeling oddly comforted by the scent of pumpkin spice.

"Can I help you, my dear?" A short, plump woman with a raspy voice and salt-and-pepper hair sat behind the reception desk. She was the spitting image of my grandma, putting me instantly at ease.

"I have a nine A.M. meeting." My voice didn't waver, which was surprising. I had worked so hard to get into MSC, and now it was all coming to an end.

"Name?" She waited with her hands hovering over her keyboard.

"Tressa Oliver."

"Let me tell President Johnson you're here," she said kindly as she picked up her phone. "Your nine A.M. is here. Yes, sir." She hung up the phone and smiled. "You can go right in, dear," she said, waving me toward the office.

Thanking her, I approached the office and opened the door, ready to face the consequences of my actions.

My resolve quickly changed when I stepped into the office and saw a pack of wolves waiting for me. Suddenly, the only instinct I felt was to flee.

President Johnson sat behind a massive mahogany desk that easily rivaled the size of a twin bed. He looked as hard as a statue, but it wasn't him who made me want to run. Nor was it Professor N, who was sitting in one of the three wing chairs to the side of the desk. Much to my dismay, the individual who made me feel like I wanted to be anywhere but here sat in the chair next to Professor N.

Trent's electric blue eyes met mine, holding them as I walked cautiously to the only available chair in the room. Would there be no end to my shame in front of him? Averting my eyes from Trent, I faced President Johnson and waited for the verdict.

"Ms. Oliver," he greeted me as I sat down.

"President Johnson." I nodded. "Professor N—Trent." I swallowed as his name stuck in my throat.

"I'm certain it is no surprise why we're all here today," President Johnson said gravely, sitting back in his chair, which swayed slightly with his weight. I had never actually seen him in person, and he was a larger man than I had pictured. Judging by what I could see, he was easily more than six feet tall and seemed at least half that size in width. His broad shoulders stretched the tweed material of the suit jacket that he wore over a starched light blue shirt. A sharp-looking red polka-dot bow tie added a whimsical touch to his professional dress.

I forced my attention away from his bow tie, which felt like it was mocking me at the moment, and worked on focusing on his questions. I knew why I was here, and why he was here. Hell, I even knew why Professor N was here. What I didn't know was why Trent was here. I glared at him, but he was oblivious since his eyes were fixed on the president.

"Eh hmm." President Johnson cleared his throat, summoning me back to his question.

"Huh? Uh, yes, sir," I finally answered.

"Your current grades are not up to the standards we expect from our students here at Maine State College."

I nodded my head but didn't answer.

"Do you have any information that might shed some light on your current academic status?"

I looked over at Professor N for a brief moment before answering. "I guess I fell behind," I answered. The lameness of my answer hung in the air. I deserved a smack upside the back of my head.

"You guess?" He sat back in his chair, exchanging a dissatisfied look with Professor N that spoke volumes.

Great. Not only was I a loser, but I had damaged Professor N's reputation. He had vouched for me and I had let him down. Indecision filled me. When I had been summoned to the office, I knew my stint at MSC was most likely over, but I wondered if I could say anything at all that might change their minds. I'm sure I had no credibility and they would probably laugh in my face. The question was whether staying in school was worth swallowing my pride and allowing Trent to see me at my weakest. I gnawed on my lip for a brief moment. I sensed the ball was in my court if I wanted it. Damn. Pride was a prickly son of a bitch.

My gaze moved to Professor N's one last time before skating over to Trent, who was still not looking at me.

"I allowed myself to fall behind," I blurted out. "Some of

the classes I'm taking are harder than I thought. I'm completely lost," I admitted, feeling slightly sick at my candidness. "I was too busy doing other things," I continued, squeezing the arms of my chair in a death grip. I focused my eyes on the rich wood flooring at my feet. Nothing like puking your pride and shame out in front of three intellectuals who intimidated you.

President Johnson sat forward again, addressing me directly. "You chose not to use the countless resources at your disposal to alleviate this situation?"

I raised my head up to look at him. I could shrug my shoulders in defeat, or I could continue to spill my guts in front of all of them. It all boiled down to how badly I wanted to stay. "I was too embarrassed to ask," I said, proud that my voice didn't shake.

"I see," he replied, rocking back in his chair and looking at Professor N again. "You know, ordinarily in a situation like this, considering your extracurricular activities, we would terminate your enrollment. Here at Maine State College, we stand behind the belief that we should challenge and rise above the activities you have been fraternizing in."

My gut clenched like I had been sucker punched. "I understand," I said, making a move to stand up.

"I'm not finished," he said gravely, stopping me midrise. Sinking back down, I waited for him to continue ripping into me before I was officially released. I guess I was getting what I deserved. My eyes moved again to Trent. I was surprised to see that he was now watching me. The intensity of his stare pulled an unexpected reaction from me. The embarrassment I had been struggling with completely evaporated and was replaced with something that felt like sadness. His stare was intense, but it was hard to fathom what he must be thinking. Not that I should care, but for whatever reason, I wanted to know.

President Johnson cleared his throat again, pulling me free from Trent's gaze.

"Ms. Oliver, I am trying to make a decision here that will determine whether or not you have a future at this university. Do you think you can provide me the courtesy of at least paying attention?"

"I'm sorry. I'm just embarrassed."

"The time for excuses is over. We've decided to put you on academic probation and allow you until the end of the semester to get your grades back in order. Trent has graciously agreed to help you with your studies. You will accept his help if you hope to remain a student here."

I wanted to argue. Who did they think they were to tell me what to do? I was an adult. The urge to throw off the restraints they were trying to put on me was strong. I hated feeling trapped. Work with Trent or leave? Neither were appealing options. I glared at Trent. He probably had something to do with this. Blaming him made me feel a bit better. At least I had somewhere to direct my rage.

Silence filled the room as everyone waited for my response. Now that the gavel had been dropped, the decision was mine. I could get up and walk out if I wanted. I may not like the choices I'd been given, but they were mine to pick from.

In the end, I made the only decision I could. I would not

leave MSC if there was even the slightest chance of staying. I simply nodded my head and sat quietly while a tutoring schedule and the parameters of my academic probation were outlined. School functions were out. My academic probation would be revoked and I would be asked to leave school if I was involved in any further questionable activities. A week ago, I would have balked at his words. Giving up school functions may not seem like a big deal, but that included football games as well. That was a low blow. For those of us born and raised in Woodfalls, where the most exciting thing happening was watching paint dry, football was our life. Cheering on the Maine State College Black Bears was almost as important to me as attending parties. I was being forced to quit everything cold turkey and throw myself into my classes.

The meeting eventually came to a close. I felt relieved and like I'd just had my ass kicked at the same time. God knows I had plenty of free time to stew over the weeks of endless tutoring in my future. I was halted by President Johnson's parting words to Trent as I was leaving.

"It is commendable that a student of your caliber is unselfishly volunteering your limited free time to help a fellow student," he said, reaching out to shake Trent's hand.

His words stopped me in my tracks. I was a selfish bitch. I never considered what tutoring me would mean for Trent. My only concerns had been about myself and my unwillingness to give him a chance. I was a total asshole. Without waiting to hear Trent's reply, I left the office.

Somewhere near the student union building during my

walk back to my apartment, my self-loathing changed to suspicion. President Johnson had brought a relevant question to the table. I'd done nothing but treat Trent with disdain. Why would he willingly give up his time for me? Was this nothing but a mad ploy to get in my pants? The more I thought about it, the more I was convinced I was on the right track. Why else would he give up his precious lab time or all that other shit?

That bastard was trying to boink me.

Feeling better and less indebted to his "sacrifice," I picked up my pace. My first tutoring session was this afternoon, and there was no way in hell I was going to be late.

8.

A couple hours before our tutoring session, I received a text from Trent because he found out the library was closed for the day with some sort of plumbing issue. He suggested we meet at his apartment off campus instead.

"Well, isn't that convenient?" I said out loud, rolling my eyes. That superhero-worshiping asshole would go to great lengths to get in my pants. If that's the way he wanted to play, that's fine. Game on. Just because my grades sucked didn't mean I was a moron. I called the library myself.

"Oh, so the library is closed until tomorrow?" I asked, confirming what the helpful lady who answered the phone had just stated. "Plumbing issue, you say? That's what I heard. Okay, thanks for the info—bye."

Fine. Send me your address, I texted to Trent. According to

the GPS on my cell phone, his apartment was on the other side of campus. I probably could have walked there, but it had been almost a month since I'd taken out my old reliable Jeep, so I decided to drive. Dad reminded me every time I talked to him to start the Jeep at least once every few days to save the battery, but anytime it came to mind, I always told myself I would do it the next day. And yes, that would turn into the next day and then the next. My pattern was clear.

Cameo came out of her room as I was gathering my things to leave. It had started to snow outside and I wanted to head out in case it got bad.

"Hey, you want to go to Stavro's for dinner? I'm in the mood for a little pasta and some house wine."

I shook my head regretfully. "Can't. I have tutoring." The idea of good Italian food and rich wine sounded more appealing than banging my head against a math book, but my ass was in a sling.

"Tutoring? You? Where is my friend and what have you done with her?"

"Very funny." I grabbed my bag, which felt like it weighed a hundred pounds with all the textbooks inside. "Believe me, I would much rather go to dinner with you."

"So blow it off."

The idea was laughable. At this point, if the college found out I was even thinking about blowing off tutoring, they would kick my ass to the curb so fast my head would spin. "Sorry, Cam. I can't." I knew she wanted more of an explanation, but I was too embarrassed to tell her about the trouble

I was in with my grades. It sucked being the dumb one in our group.

"Can't? Since when do you have a problem blowing things off? Besides, I don't want to go alone. We haven't hung out in a few days and I really need to relax."

What Cameo meant by *relax* was she was looking to get drunk.

"Please, I'll buy the first round of drinks," she pleaded.

For a second I actually considered calling Trent to reschedule the first tutoring session. It wasn't the same thing as canceling altogether. Of course, I was sure Professor N would feel differently. The image of his disappointed face filled my head. There was no way I could cancel.

"I really can't. Professor N is on my ass. Maybe some other time."

Cam looked completely taken aback. "Some other time? What does that even mean?"

"It means not now," I bit out in aggravation. "I'm on freaking academic probation, Cam. If I don't get my shit together, I'm out of here." I pulled on my jacket in frustration and threw a scarf around my neck.

"Probation? Since when?"

"Since now. So, no. I don't have time to go get drunk at Stavro's." Slinging my bag over my shoulder, I grabbed my keys and walked out, slamming the door behind me. I didn't mean to get so mad at Cam, but she wouldn't stop pressing. Hopefully, after a couple of hours we would both get over it and could talk again when I got home.

Ordinarily, I put more effort into my appearance before going out, but impressing Trent was the furthest thing from my mind. My plan was to buckle down during the tutoring sessions, figuring the sooner I improved my grades, the sooner things could go back to normal.

The snow was already coming down more than I'd thought and was beginning to stick. I grimaced when I approached my Jeep and saw the spiderwebs between the tires. Dad would have my head if he knew. The good news was that despite my negligence, Old Reliable started on the first try. I cranked the heat and waited for a few minutes to give it time to warm up before I pulled out. I still had fifteen minutes until T-Doom time, which is what I had deemed my tutoring schedule, so I decided to hit the coffee bar where I worked for some liquid sanity.

"What's up, Tressa? You working today?" Ben, one of the other part-timers, asked as I pushed the door open, inhaling deeply. If they could bottle the smell of this place, I'd buy it by the gallon. Working at Javalotta was like coming home to a second family. There was an easy comradeship that stemmed from the owners, Liz and Larry, who ran the coffeehouse like a well-oiled machine. Despite their strictness when it came to the rules, they maintained a lighthearted relationship with their employees.

"No, I have a studying session that requires a double shot," I answered, moving behind the counter to fix my drink. "Looks pretty dead today," I observed, adding whipped cream to top off my concoction.

"Yeah, it's kinda been this way since the accident . . ." His voice trailed off.

His words caused me to nearly drop my coffee. I had momentarily forgotten about David's death, pushing it to the back of my mind. It was like a game to see how long I could go without thinking about it. Ben had broken the longest stretch yet. I'd almost made it sixteen minutes. Time to start over again.

"Yeah, I guess I hadn't noticed," I mumbled, steadying my cup as I stared blankly at the walls. Ben gave me an odd look that I didn't acknowledge. For the past three days, I'd been fielding similar stares from Cameo and Derek. It was a *what alien species took over Tressa's body* kind of look. I hustled around the counter, suddenly anxious to leave.

"Catch you later," Ben called as I walked out without saying bye.

Climbing into the Jeep, I didn't know whether I should be pissed or embarrassed that everyone seemed surprised over my reaction to David's death. Were their perceptions of me really that I was just a party girl with no real feelings? Lost in my thoughts, I made it to Trent's apartment quicker than I'd anticipated. I sat in the parking lot, stalling for as long as I could before walking to his door. I took a big swig of my coffee before knocking. I didn't know what was wrong with me. This was just Trent, for crap's sake. My damn emotions were like a roller coaster lately. Anything I thought I'd felt for him earlier in President Johnson's office was nothing more than the result of the upheaval I'd been going through the past week.

I raised my hand to knock on the door before I could chicken out.

Trent answered almost immediately, like he had been standing by his door waiting for my knock.

"Tressa?" He greeted me awkwardly, looking surprised when I took a cautious halfstep backward. He pushed his glasses back up the bridge of his nose. I waited for a moment, expecting him to invite me inside, but he stood there like he was waiting for me to say something.

"Tutoring," I said, holding up my book bag to jog his memory. Sheesh, I thought he was supposed to be supersmart.

"Right. Sorry, I was just finishing up some notes for Professor Nelson." He held the door open so I could enter his apartment.

"O-kay," I replied, still not quite believing he'd forgotten I was coming over. What about the text he'd sent me just a few hours ago? Stepping past him, I stood in the middle of his living room, taking in my surroundings. My original assumptions about him were dead-on. I'd stepped into a pimple-faced teen-aged comic book lover's wet dream. Superhero memorabilia littered every available surface in the apartment. The shelves that bracketed a big-screen TV were lined with statues and action figures, much like what my brother was into. I could tell by the way they were reverently displayed that Trent cared more about his collection than my brother did about his. I moved closer and reached a finger toward a gleaming Superman statue.

"Don't touch," Trent said, stepping between me and the shelf.

"Wow, chill, Wonder Boy. I was just going to point out

that my brother has that same Superman. I think his is missing an arm, though." Trent flinched. He was definitely strange.

Backing away from his precious shelf, I took in the rest of the living room. Outside of the superhero universe, the apartment looked pristine. Unlike most apartments around campus I'd been in—including mine, which was made up of nothing but castoffs—Trent's furniture actually matched. A large leather sofa sat against the wall that shared space with the front door. The matching leather recliner sat near the patio door and was turned to face the television. Matching throw pillows adorned both the sofa and recliner like an interior designer had placed them there. Hell, even the coffee table and end tables matched the elaborate entertainment center.

His apartment looked like an adult had decorated it rather than a bunch of college kids trying to fill a space.

"Do you want to sit down?" He looked uncomfortable with my surveying of his territory, like he'd never had a guest before. I guess my actions could have been construed as intrusive, but he was the one who had invited me.

"Uh, sure." I walked over to the sofa and sat down next to a stack of papers, which was the only thing out of place in the room.

"Sorry, I was in the middle of entering data," he said, stacking the papers into a neat pile before placing them on top of a laptop that was sitting on the coffee table.

"That's okay. It feels normal."

He raised his eyebrows in response before sitting on the couch cushion he had just cleaned off. "A mess feels normal?"

Without any conscious thought, I shifted over, putting more space between us. If he noticed my movement, he didn't comment on it.

"I've been going over your grades in your classes, and I've come to the conclusion that statistics is the class you seem to be struggling with the most." He shuffled the stack of papers, searching for one in particular.

"You pulled my grades?" My voice sounded shrill to my own ears. Tutoring or not, who the hell did he think he was?

"Huh? Oh, no. Professor Nelson gave them to me this morning," he answered, looking confused over my tone. My eyes met his for a moment. The difference was glaring. His look was questioning, while I practically had lasers wanting to melt off his face. It took everything inside me not to snatch the papers from his hands. After a second, when the more rational side of my brain took charge, I realized it wasn't his fault my grades had been handed to him. Clamping my mouth closed, I silently counted to three to calm myself. Most people thought ten was the golden number, but if I forced myself to count to ten, I'd lose my patience all over again.

After I was able to form a sentence without biting off his head, I answered him. "Math has been a pain in my ass for years. I'll be the only senior in history that won't be able to graduate because I can't pass some math class."

"Not true. Statistically, no pun intended, hundreds of students drop out every year. Most are for economic reasons or a life-altering circumstance, but I'm sure you're not the only one in history not to graduate because of failure to master a class," he said in a dry tone.

I stared at him incredulously. Was he fucking with me? The way he sat, waiting for another response from me, I couldn't tell.

"It's better to analyze it like you would a puzzle," he continued when I didn't respond.

Puzzle? What the hell did graduating have to do with puzzles? I swear, he was the freaking puzzle.

"Statistics," he clarified. "It helps people sometimes if they look at the problems like a puzzle that needs to be figured out instead of a complicated math problem," he said, pushing his glasses up on the bridge of his nose.

"Why don't you get glasses that don't do that?" I asked, momentarily distracted.

He looked startled by my question, like I was the one talking in riddles. "What?"

"Your glasses. You're always pushing them up. Why don't you get ones more appropriate for your face?"

"I like these. They're retro."

I snorted. "Just because they're ten years old doesn't mean they're retro. They're too big for your face. With your bone structure, you should have smaller plastic frames. Like the stylish ones all the guys are wearing. You look like Clark Kent from the old movies my dad likes. Is that what you're going for?"

"You got me. This is just a disguise for my alter ego. Now that you're onto my secret, I'll have to lock you away in a gilded cage." He pulled a Tootsie Pop from a Spider-Man cookie jar that was perched on the end table.

His words made me laugh. Who knew Nerd Boy would have a sense of humor. It was dry, but it was still there. His eyes sparkled behind the overly big glasses as he responded to my laugh. He pulled the wrapper off the lollipop and stuck the orange sucker into his mouth. His eyes never left mine. My laughter instantly dried up. No guy had ever looked at me like he always managed to. His intensity sobered me.

He held out the jar filled with suckers. "Want one?" I wasn't a big hard-candy fan, but I reached for one.

"Thanks." I pulled the wrapper off the Tootsie Pop and cleared my throat. "Okay, so are you going to teach me how this mumbo jumbo in here is a puzzle?" I asked, pulling my book out of my bag.

My words had their desired effect. Trent abruptly switched his focus from me to the textbook in my hands like someone had hit a button. Within minutes, he was explaining problems that for the first time ever started to make sense. We worked for more than an hour until I felt I had a good enough grasp to take the first practice test online when I got home.

During the second hour of tutoring, Trent set up a study schedule for me on my laptop to help me catch up on my other classes. He gave pointers that would help me cut my missing-assignments list in half. The schedule was grueling, and a week ago I would have nixed the idea of cutting into my social life, but things were different now.

I was shoving my books and laptop in my bag when Trent switched the conversation from my dismal academics to food. "It's past dinnertime. How about a pizza?"

"Dinnertime? What are you, forty? We're in college. We don't follow any dinner bell. We eat when we're hungry, day or night. Haven't you ever been on a two A.M. taco run?"

"An irregular diet is bad for your body," he answered before blushing. "Not that there's anything wrong with your body." He looked away quickly when I caught his eyes drifting down my midriff.

"You need to get out more often," I mocked him, standing up with my bag. I kept my voice neutral so he wouldn't become more embarrassed. "I need to run anyway."

"You run? Maybe we can go together one time."

My jaw dropped at his words before a laugh bubbled up through me. The way he took everything so literally was a bit adorable. Quirky, but adorable. We were as different as night and day. It was easier that he was like this. It would help remind my hormones that I should be keeping him at arm's length.

"I meant I have things to do. The only time I run is when someone is chasing me," I joked, pawing through my bag for my keys.

"I know. I was teasing you," he said in a deep, husky voice.

My eyes jerked up and I felt my pulse quicken. You'd think I'd never heard a sexy voice before. In my defense, that smooth, deep voice coming from his mouth was a bit of an oxymoron. The fact that he continued to surprise me was throwing me off guard. I was fine when I could put him in a box and tell myself he wasn't for me, but keeping him there was proving to be harder than I expected.

I had to get away before I did something stupid that we would probably both regret.

"Just stick to what you're good at," I said. I threw out the snarky comment, pretending I didn't notice the way his face fell as I walked past him. "See you tomorrow."

"Sure," he answered as I closed the door.

I berated myself during the short drive home. Why was I letting him get to me? If I was going to get through this mess, I needed to pull my head out of my ass.

9.

For the next few days, I was able to stick to my guns and focus on the actual tutoring. It was only occasionally that I noticed small things like how his forearms were more muscular than I'd realized, or the way he liked to hum game show theme songs while he waited for me to answer a question. Holding our tutoring sessions at the library provided a more formal setting, which seemed to help. Although Trent's humming garnered continuous looks from anyone sitting around us. Between that and his Tootsie Pop obsession, he was driving the library staff nuts. He'd been warned more than once that there was no eating or drinking in the library. Each time he was reprimanded, he would inform them that, technically, he was sucking on his lollipop, not eating or drinking it. Different staff workers would approach him each time, but their reaction was always the same. They would stand for a moment, trying to figure out if he was serious or just screwing with them. Eventually, they would walk away. I would laugh, but I empathized with them. Half the time I didn't know if his dryness was real, or if he just liked effing with people's heads.

On Friday I arrived at the library before Trent, which was nothing new. I'd quickly realized that he was never on time. His brain, which was so brilliant in some respects, seemed oblivious to time schedules. It was ironic considering he was helping me become more organized.

I was working on an assignment for my business management class when he finally showed up.

"Late again," I mocked. "You need an alarm clock superglued to your forehead."

"My eyes don't roll up that high," he answered, sinking down in the chair next to me.

My eyes zeroed in on his mouth. I'd noticed the other day that his lips quirked slightly when he was teasing. It was the only tic I had picked up on to tell if he was screwing with me. "You need some new material. You know how some people go to fat spas or relationship camps? You need a sense of humor makeover," I said.

"My humor is just too sophisticated for regular people."

"Regular people? You mean human beings, right, Spock?"

"Do you even know who Spock is?" He sat forward in his chair like the end of the world hinged on my answer.

"Sure, he's Luke's father," I said, looking down at my book

so he wouldn't see my smirk. I'd learned on Wednesday that Trent's biggest pet peeve was when characters from his favorite shows or movies were mixed up.

"First of all, Spock is from *Star Trek*, while Luke's father—whose name is Anakin Skywalker, or Darth Vader to the layperson—is from *Star Wars*."

I egged him on further by looking down at my book, disinterested.

"Furthermore, the two are not even in the same universe or time period, for that matter. One happened a long time ago in a galaxy far, far away, while the other takes place in the future. It couldn't be any simpler," he sputtered.

It was almost too easy, like taking candy from a baby. I let him suffer for a few seconds before looking up and grinning at him. "Don't get your undies in a bunch, Captain Kirk."

"Do you always use nicknames as a shield?" he asked, moving my statistics book closer to him.

My grin faded. Damn him. He always seemed to be able to do this to me. With a few words he could knock me down several notches. I clamped my mouth closed, even though I was dying to retort, but that would only waste more time.

"I took the last practice test in unit one of statistics. I asked Ms. Joyner about the makeup exam. She said I could go in on Monday and take it. Even if I ace it, the highest grade I can get is an eighty-five." Changing the subject was how I got around his random probing questions that always seemed to make me uncomfortable.

He took the bait. "What did you score on your practice test?"

"Ninety-eight. I missed a damn ratio problem."

"Ratios," he announced, flipping open the book to the appropriate section. "We'll go over them again." His tone was animated as he searched for the page. For once, I was happy to dive into a textbook.

The next hour passed with Trent covering ratios yet again. He was patient in his explanation and deemed me ready for the test when I correctly answered ten complicated problems that he had randomly pulled out of his head. It must be nice to be a total brain.

After we finished with ratios, Trent proofread my paper for business communications while I worked on a mock employee schedule for a group assignment in my business management class. We had to create a fictional online company, which was surprisingly fun. The group voted and decided on an online shoe company. The project was worth 80 percent of our overall semester grade, so it was important my group did well. I was struggling with how many employees would be required to ship out shoes each day when Trent finished proofing my paper.

"Was it awful?" I asked, clicking the track changes button on my computer to read his notes. Just two days ago, I had broken out in a cold sweat over the idea of him reading my stuff, but I had come to realize that although he was very analytical, he was also an excellent tutor. Without sounding critical, he had a way of clearly explaining things so they made sense.

"No, you covered many of the points that were in the rubric. I noted a couple more points you might want to add." I nodded my head absently at his words since I was already reading his notes. I was a little embarrassed over the grammar mistakes he found. I always seemed to mess up *there*, *their*, and *they're*, which was pretty aggravating since I knew the difference. I shut down my laptop once I finished reading through his notes.

Stowing all my stuff in my bag, I stood up and was quite pleased with myself for getting through another session. It was all about mind over matter. Trent stood up with me.

"I guess I'll see you on Monday," I said at the same time he started to ask me a question, so our words jumbled together. "I'm sorry, what?"

He pushed his glasses up, which meant he was either nervous or thinking hard about something. "I asked if maybe you wanted to catch a movie," he said, clearing his throat.

"No," I barked out like a drill sergeant. I didn't mean for it to come out that way, but his question took me by surprise. I tried to smile so the rejection wouldn't seem so harsh.

Surprisingly, he didn't seem to be bothered by the shortness of my answer as he leaned back against the table we had been sitting at. "Why not?"

Did I really need to break it down for him? Judging by the way he stood waiting for an explanation, that's exactly what I needed to do. I sighed loudly, placing my heavy bag on the table.

"Because we're the least compatible couple on the planet. We have absolutely nothing in common."

"That's not true. We're both from the same town."

"So? Millions of people live in New York City, but that doesn't mean they're all compatible."

"Fine. We went to the same high school."

"You're making my case for me. We went to the same high school and yet our circles never overlapped. What does that tell you?"

"That I was biding my time," he said, taking off his glasses so he could clean them with his shirt.

My mouth dried, making my next retort die in my throat before it could even emerge. Seeing him without his oversized geek glasses was an instantaneous knee-jerk kind of moment. His blue eyes were even more pronounced without the glare from the lenses. Plus, I was seeing an unobstructed view of his entire face. To say the overall effect was panty dropping would be putting it mildly. Heat moved through my body, latching on to every single nerve ending.

I tried to focus on his last words, but my brain was on vacation on *smexy island*. I was having a hard time remembering what we were even talking about. I knew I was rejecting him. I just couldn't remember why.

The buzzing of my cell phone provided the interruption I needed to pull my eyes away from his. "I have to get this," I said, grabbing my bag and fleeing the library. Thank God for lifelines when you're about to drown is all I have to say.

I hit the ANSWER button as I pushed the library doors open.

"Hello."

"Where are you?" Cameo demanded.

"At the library. Why?" Things had been a little tense around our apartment the last few days. Cameo and Derek were still trying to adjust to the new me and the fact that I spent more time lately studying than partying. At least Derek seemed to understand my situation and was handling it better than Cameo. She continued to act like it was something I could fix with a weekend of cramming. As for not going out every other night to drink, she dismissed my new lack of interest as me being too dramatic over David's death. What she didn't understand was that I just didn't see the point of wasting my time here at school. Sure, it took David's death to make me realize that, but Cameo wasn't going to change my mind because she called me overly dramatic. Anytime she brought up his name, I would cut her off. It was a taboo subject for me.

"Derek heard there's an underground party at Phi Beta. We're going to check it out, so you need to hurry home."

A week ago those words would have filled me with an almost euphoric feeling. Regular parties were superb on their own, but an underground party was downright killer.

"Are you sure? I thought every frat house was on lockdown. They could get in serious trouble if word gets around."

I could hear Cameo's sigh. I didn't need to see her to know that she was probably making a face at her cell phone. "What do you think *underground* means? The school's not going to find out. Are you going with us or not?" She was clearly irritated, but that didn't mean she had to act like a complete bitch.

Now I was aggravated and never one to respond well to bitchiness. "I'm on academic and extracurricular probation, in case you forgot?" I snapped.

"How could we forget since you like to remind us constantly," she snipped back. "Are you never going to go to another party, ever?"

I wanted to lash out more, but I bit my tongue. My silence was all the answer she needed. "Fine, suit yourself," she said, disconnecting the call. Her parting words lacked the bite that she had started with. She sounded more hurt than anything else. Feeling guilty for snapping at her, I put my phone back in my pocket and leaned against the rough brick exterior of the library. I closed my eyes, trying to calm the twisty emotional monster mucking up my brain. What was happening to me? I felt like I was going through some kind of identity crisis.

"Everything okay?"

"Damn it. Don't sneak up on me like that!"

Trent looked as surprised as I felt. He's lucky he didn't get a punch in the throat or a kick in the balls for sneaking up on me like a freaking ninja. "Sorry. I assumed you knew I was there since I was right behind you when you came out here," he pointed out. "I can't help it you're so self-absorbed you missed that part."

"Self-absorbed? Are you kidding me?"

"What's wrong?" His eyes cut through me, seeing past my defensiveness.

I glared at him for a moment. I didn't need any psychoanalysis bullshit. "My roommate is pissed at me, all right?"

"Why?"

"Why do you care? You're not the Tressa Whisperer. You're

already involved enough in my life as it is." I turned to walk away.

Trent's hand reached out, encircling my bicep. It was probably my imagination, but the warmth of his touch traveled through the two layers of clothing I was wearing. Luckily for him, my normal instinct to knee a guy in the balls for handling me that way never surfaced. I chalked it up to the fact that Trent was different because I felt nothing for him.

"Don't be like that. Tell me why your roommate is pissed. By the way you talk, you two are close. Maybe it's a simple fix."

"What makes you think everything can be fixed?" I already knew the answer to my own question. His analytical mind always looked at everything like an equation that could be solved.

"Because it can. You just have to take the emotion out of the situation to find the root of the problem. Conflict is caused by emotion. As human beings, we allow and even thrive on the emotions that ultimately lead to our destruction. Look at the root of every war and you will find a dictator who allowed his emotions to control his thinking until it curdled into something else."

"People are not math equations, Trent. Your concern is touching, but for such a smart guy, you don't know shit. For your information, emotions don't always cause conflict. They also cause good things, like love. For every emotion that leads to our destruction, there is another that makes us stronger."

"Interesting hypothesis. I think—"

"Wait a second. Let me cut you off right there," I interrupted. "What I said wasn't a damn hypothesis, it's a fact, you goober. Look, people don't choose to have emotions, they're part of us. Like it or not, you can't just turn them off. Without emotions, we'd all be robots. My roommate is miffed because of the decisions I've made to change my lifestyle. You think she gives a rat's ass about the logical reason for my decision? Hell no. She's pissed. Hence, human emotion."

He raised his eyebrows at my choice of words. "I see. So the student becomes the teacher."

I doubled over laughing. "God, you can be such a nerd, but I'm glad you understand. Welcome to Earth."

"I still say she should understand you're on probation," he said, folding his arms across his chest.

"Yeah, well, that's easier said than done. I'm just not sure I care anymore, but who knows? Maybe where there's a will, there's a way."

"And you no longer have the will?" he asked, shoving his hands into his pockets.

"Nope," I admitted, turning to walk to my car. This chat was stimulating, but wasn't helping my current situation. It really wasn't Trent's fault. Not even my friends understood where I was coming from.

He kept pace with me by jogging along my side. "Why not?"

"No offense, but I don't want to talk about it anymore." I'd yet to confide in anyone about the way I felt about David's accident. I tried with Cameo, but all she wanted to do was tell me I was being stupid, so I buried it in my gut and spent the last week being twisted into a tight knot of guilt. Logically, I knew I wasn't directly responsible, but I had been there. I couldn't help dwelling on what would have happened if I'd never talked to him, or maybe if I could have talked to him longer. Was our conversation the point on the pendulum of life that triggered his death? Would it have mattered if he went into the water sooner or later? This was the morbid shit that was keeping me up at night. The coroner's report had come out and concluded that David had smacked his head on an outcropping of rocks when he tumbled overboard. They believe he lost consciousness and drowned. Would that have happened if he had been in the water a few seconds earlier?

I confided none of this to Trent. It wasn't in my nature. I didn't talk about insecurities and, until now, never considered the cosmic ramifications of anything. I was the dial-a-laugh girl, the gutter-minded rock star.

Trent walked beside me all the way to my car without saying anything more. I avoided his eyes. They were becoming my kryptonite. Obviously, the Superman theme was sticking. God help me if I started thinking of myself as Lois Lane. I'd have to find the tallest building around and jump off.

Neither of us spoke as I climbed into my Jeep. Trent stood on the sidewalk watching me while I backed out. His attentiveness was disconcerting. Why couldn't he just be a douche like every other guy I attracted?

10.

I spent Friday evening holed up in my apartment by myself. After leaving Trent, I'd driven around aimlessly for over an hour, hoping to avoid Cameo and Derek. My ploy worked. By the time I entered our apartment with a bag of junk food, our apartment was empty. Just the way I wanted it.

The evening was a far cry from my normal Friday activities. I ate crap I knew I would regret and watched mindless TV. Toddlers competing for tiaras was new to me, but that didn't stop me from watching six episodes in a row.

I hated that Cameo and I couldn't seem to get past this hump. It was as much my fault as hers. My life was changing and I wished she would accept that, but maybe it was too much too fast. Maybe she needed more time to adjust to my shift in priorities. I debated staying up until she got home so we could hash it out, but in the end I headed to bed earlier than I had on a Friday night in years. I wasn't sure what I could say to fix the situation. There was a chance I would just make it worse. Normally, we were joined at the hip and did everything together. This week had proven that things had changed for us. Maybe they would never be the same again.

Unfortunately, lying in my dark, quiet bedroom only encouraged me to think about David's death. The guilt festered in my stomach like some alien had inhabited my body. I was still tossing and turning two hours later when I heard the front door open and close. I feigned sleep when my bedroom door squeaked open a few seconds later. Derek's footsteps echoed on the wooden floorboards as he approached my bed. Though my eyes were closed, I could feel the weight of his stare as he stood beside my bed. I don't know if he bought my ploy or just didn't want to make the situation any more awkward by calling me out, but after a moment, he retreated from the room. I could hear Cameo's and his muffled voices through the thin walls. I couldn't make out what they were saying, but I knew it was about me.

I contemplated how much I'd changed in a week. The old Tressa would have stomped out to the front room and confronted them. Now I stayed in my room, not certain I could muster enough fuel for a fight.

Maybe I was broken. I felt broken. I'd never experienced this crushing sense of hopelessness. I wasn't used to feeling like I was letting down so many people at once. The list felt endless.

Eventually, I drifted off to sleep, uncertain of what I was

morphing into. In the end, my last thoughts were about David's memorial service the following day.

I learned several things the next day that I would have rather lived my entire life without ever knowing. Funerals are nothing like they seem on TV or in movies. On a screen, you get a one-dimensional sense of the despair, but in real life, it's painful and ugly. Even if David and I didn't have our moment, if I'd never talked to him, I'm not sure I could have attended his service and remained dry-eyed. His parents' grief was real and seared through you like a hot poker being shoved in your eye.

Sitting on one of the hard pews, sandwiched between Derek, Cameo, and her maybe, maybe not boyfriend, Chad, provided my crazy muddled mind with sudden clarity. Giving up my old lifestyle was the right thing to do. Partying, hazing, pranks, and everything else I had ever been involved in were part of a life I no longer wanted.

The somber memorial service started with the minister giving a long-winded eulogy. For the benefit of the younger crowd, he thundered on about responsibilities and the consequences of bad choices.

After he finally ran out of steam, David's best friend from high school got up to say a few words. A picture of David filled my mind as his friend talked about their friendship. The way he described David reminded me of the flirtatious, cocky guy I had gotten to know moments before he jumped into the raft. Unlike David's parents, his best friend, Troy, didn't point fingers or accuse anyone of any wrongdoing. Judging by the stories he told, David had always been a daredevil.

I was relieved when neither of David's parents got up to talk. Seeing them lean on each other, trying to draw strength from the other was hard enough. I couldn't imagine how suffocating the grief of losing a child must be.

The four of us opted out of attending the luncheon that MSC was hosting following the service. Trying to eat a big meal after having your guts spoon-fed to you just felt wrong on so many levels. Instead, we headed to Javalotta.

The others grabbed a table while I went to the break room to check my schedule for the following week. Thankfully, Larry and Liz were completely understanding about my probation and tutoring. They agreed to cut my hours during the week, and I volunteered to work whenever they needed on the weekends. Liz was even nice enough to schedule me off for the memorial service. I had to work open to close tomorrow, but it was cool. The store was only open eleven to six on Sunday. My schedule for the following week looked similar with the exception of working until nine next Saturday.

Between tutoring and working all weekend, I would be too busy for anything else, which was my intention all along.

Leaving the break room, I headed back to my friends, who were in the process of giving one of my coworkers, Heather, their drink orders.

"Hey, ho, you want your usual?" Heather asked, nudging me with her hip before I slid into the booth beside Derek.

"Don't be jealous, blow queen," I said, making a gesture with my mouth like I was sucking on something.

Everyone laughed and after a moment I joined in, even though it felt forced and a little phony. Still, for the first time in a week, I felt almost normal. Cameo looked satisfied, which didn't escape my attention. I rolled my eyes, but didn't comment.

I turned my attention to Chad, who I hadn't seen since last weekend. "How's it going?" My question was fraught with double meaning.

He shrugged before answering. "It pretty much sucks. The entire fraternity was dismantled, so most of us were left scrambling for available housing. MSC isn't being very sympathetic. They're the biggest bunch of douche-hypocrites ever. Even my dad is being a total prick. I remember when we were in high school, he used to brag to my brothers and me about all the shit he did in college. Suddenly, he's a fucking saint and I'm the bad guy," Chad complained, running his hand through his hair in aggravation.

"You're not being expelled, right?" Derek asked as Heather returned with our drinks and the platter of pastries we ordered.

Chad shook his head. "Nah, just probation. None of us underclassmen got anything worse. It's the seniors that got fucked. I know Dawson and Kevin both lost their scholarships. They both left yesterday." The school basically blamed the upperclassmen for everything.

Cameo, Derek, and I collectively gasped at the same time. This shit was real.

"I didn't know that," Cameo said, picking the pecans off one of the croissants. "You only told me about Steve."

"What about Steve?" I asked, losing my appetite midbite.

Cameo answered for Chad. "He was asked to leave on Thursday."

"That doesn't seem fair. Why just Steve?"

"He came forward and admitted the prank was his idea. The other brothers were mad. Their plan was to stay quiet and ride out the wave together. Steve went all kamikaze and took the fall for everyone." Chad shook his head as he took a big bite from a strawberry-filled pastry.

"Holy shit, that's crazy. I bet Melissa is pretty torn up," I said.

"No shit. Supposedly, she threatened to break up with him if he went through with his plan," Chad explained.

"Can't say I blame her," Cameo stated.

"What?" Derek sputtered, glaring across the table. "You can't be serious. What about the whole stand-by-your-man thing?"

"Like we live in nineteen sixty? Steve should have kept his mouth closed and eventually everything would have blown over." Cameo's answer surprised me. It was as if David's death wasn't important.

"Someone died and you really thought it would just blow over? Come on, Cam, get real," Derek argued.

Disgusted by Cameo's attitude, I focused on my pastry that I had slowly but methodically mutilated. Would my attitude be the same as Cameo's if I hadn't gone with Melissa and met David that night? I wish I could believe otherwise, but truthfully, I didn't know.

The topic of conversation switched after that before things got too heated, but everyone was pretty much done, so we left. When we got home, Cameo didn't bother to ask if I wanted to go out with her, so I guessed that meant the truce was over. Derek opted to stay home with me. Cameo didn't hang around long, and once she left, most of the tension that had cloaked our apartment during the last week evaporated.

I sank down into the sofa where Derek joined me with a couple of Cokes he had grabbed from the fridge. "I really don't get Cameo right now," he said, sitting next to me.

I wasn't sure how to handle his remark. Obviously, he was talking about their semi-heated exchange earlier, but I couldn't be sure anything I said wouldn't get back to her ears. "I think everyone is still just trying to figure out how to deal with what happened."

"I get that, but thinking everyone should keep their mouths shut so someone's death will just blow over? That's kind of fucked-up. It's like she doesn't even believe anyone is responsible."

"Yeah, but who is responsible? Steve and the others at the fraternity are taking the fall, but isn't everyone that participated responsible? What about the ones like us who watched it happen? Hell, we all encourage hazing." I sounded more mature than I think I had ever sounded in my life. The guilt I had been suffering with was burning on the tip of my tongue.

"I guess. The hazing parties do get pretty out of control,

obviously. Maybe that's Cam's problem. Maybe she feels guilty. It doesn't seem like it, but who knows."

"I don't know. That's the problem. She won't take me seriously when I try to tell her my feelings. After David's death, the idea of partying every night just seems pointless to me. And all she wants to do is tell me I'm being dramatic."

I'm sure I sounded crazy to Derek, but I was trying to make him understand the way I'd hoped Cameo would. Maybe he would run and tell her as soon as my back was turned, but I didn't care anymore. Eventually, Cameo would learn to adjust to the new me, or she could take a flying leap for all I cared. Or so I told myself.

Derek could tell I was over it and let the subject drop. He suggested a game of poker. I readily agreed. Anything to pass the time. Maybe then I wouldn't dwell on the fact that I was spending another weekend night at home. Derek made a few calls, rounding up a couple more players.

The night turned out to be more fun than I would have ever thought. Adam and Tim, who joined us, had been dating for years. The way they talked to each other reminded me of my parents. Adam was over-the-top dramatic and terrible at poker. You could tell how good his hand was by the degree of *gasp* he let out each time the cards were dealt. Tim kept reminding him poker was a game of mystery and the goal was to try and fool the other players, but Adam couldn't care less about deceiving anyone. Derek thought he had game, but I'd played cards with him enough times to know his tells. If he sat forward in his chair, his hand was good. If he leaned back like he didn't have a care in the world, he had a crappy hand. It was Tim who was harder to read. I lost thirty bucks to him before I finally figured out his particular weakness. Once I realized he would pat Adam's knee when he was bluffing, I not only won back my money, but most of his also. It was ironic that I sucked so badly at math but I was a poker stud.

"Damn, girl, you're on fire," Adam said as I added another pile of chips to my growing stacks.

"Yeah, thanks so much for the heads-up, Derek," Tim muttered, frowning at his cards.

Derek laughed. "Don't feel bad. Tressa always takes everyone to the cleaners."

"We can always play strip poker if you're tired of losing money," I joked.

"Honey, I haven't been to the gym in weeks, and the way you play, it sure as hell isn't going to be you sitting here topless," Adam laughed.

I blew him a kiss. Derek watched me like a protective mother bird. He looked satisfied by the fun I was having.

We ran out to get pizza and beer, which was my treat since I'd taken everyone's money. When we got back with our goodies, we sat around talking and joking. Adam and Tim were a lot of fun. It had been ages since I'd sat around shooting the shit with friends when we weren't at some party. The last time I remember it happening was when Ashton and Brittni were in Woodfalls this past summer.

Cameo returned home while we were hanging out. She staggered in looking more than a little tipsy. I felt guilty. We'd made a pact, and I'd left her high and dry by not going to the party. Chad walked in behind her, so at least she hadn't walked home alone.

Cameo tugged on his hand, leading him toward her room. He shot us a shit-eating grin before trailing behind her.

"On that note, I think it's time we call it a night," Adam said, climbing off the couch. He gave me an exuberant hug before doing the same with Derek. Tim's hug was more restrained, like he was afraid I'd get the wrong idea if he pulled me in too close. We made plans to hang out again after they chided Derek for hiding me away so long.

"Don't let her fool you. This is an all-new Tressa. Normally, she'd be hanging from the ceiling or trying to sled off the top of the roof," Derek defended himself.

They looked at me skeptically, convinced that Derek was messing with them.

"He's lying. I'm always mellow yellow," I answered, looking at them demurely. I started laughing almost immediately. "Okay, so he's right. I'm not exactly a princess, but I'm trying to buckle down a little."

11.

Meet at my apartment.

I swore under my breath when I looked at my phone. Trent had the texting skills of a baboon. No *Hey, let's meet at my apartment* or *Hey, I'm thinking we should do tutoring at my apartment tonight*. Instead, he comes across like a caveman. It would serve him right if I didn't show up, claiming I never got his text.

In the end, his suggestion made sense, which was why I didn't argue. The library had been unusually busy all week. I blamed the cold weather. There was still a week left in October, but it was already dipping close to single digits at night.

I arrived fifteen minutes early and didn't feel like waiting in my drafty Jeep. I made a point of checking to make sure

Trent's Nissan was in the parking lot before opening my door. It was one thing to walk in the frigid-ass temperatures. It was a whole other thing to stand outside freezing my nips off waiting on Trent. Spotting his car, I reached into my backseat and grabbed my bag before heading for his apartment.

I knocked on his door, thankful I'd had the foresight to grab my gloves before heading out. I was preparing to knock again after he didn't answer when the door suddenly swung open.

My mild shock turned into downright slap-my-ass-and-call-me-Dixie surprise when I saw how he was dressed, or rather, *undressed* would be the more accurate description. He answered the door in nothing more than a towel, rendering me speechless.

My mouth dropped open as I took in the very male sight before me. My suspicions about what lay beneath the endless array of geeky shirts he was so fond of wearing had now been verified. Although, even in my wildest of dreams, I'm pretty sure I didn't imagine this. Not that I had wild dreams about him. At least, not all the time.

With the towel knotted around his waist, I had an up-close-and-personal view of his very defined, and—I loathed to admit—very lickable abs. I wasn't even sure *six-pack* was the right word. Running my eyes down his naked torso, I was pretty sure I counted an eight-pack. Eight delicious abs that glistened with droplets of water from the shower he had just stepped out of. My mouth began to water at the sight of him, and I'm pretty sure I even swayed a little. I wanted to reach out to feel if his muscles were as firm as they looked. *God, the things I could do to that chest*, I thought.

"Hey, you're early," he greeted me, using an extra towel to dry his hair. His words were like a torrent of cold water splashed on my face. I took an unsteady step backward. If he only knew how close I had come to reaching out and touching him. How could nerdy T-shirts and glasses hide that much hotness? That was the question. Hell, even his hair looked hot now that it was tousled from the towel dry he'd given it.

I croaked out an answer that was a garbled mess. He looked at me like I'd just fallen off the drunken train. Trying again, I cleared my throat, hoping for something that sounded more coherent. "Too Jeep cold," I mumbled, realizing as I said it that I had effed it up again.

His look turned to puzzlement as he tried to make sense of my words. "Oh, sorry," he finally said, stepping back so I could enter his warm apartment. "It's cold outside," he added, closing the door quickly behind me. I didn't bother to correct him. Better for him to think it was the cold that had my tongue refusing to cooperate. Trent didn't need any more encouragement.

I skirted around him. Distance was my only ally at the moment.

"How'd your test go yesterday?" he asked, oblivious to the fact that I was secretly wishing for his towel to drop.

For the love of my horny sanity, could you please put on some clothes before I tear my panties off and jump on you? The words bounced around in my head like a rogue Ping-Pong ball. I was practically chanting them.

"Sorry. I'll go get dressed," he said, giving me a strange look.

No way, did I utter that out loud? Please for the love of

horny bitches everywhere, tell me that was all in my head. Son of a bitch, I couldn't remember. I was stuck in some hypnotizing dick trance.

I needed to flee the scene while he was in his room getting dressed. That would be the only rational thing to do. Maybe I could tell him I was drunk. By the looks he'd been giving me, he probably assumed that already. I could go home and pretend this never happened. The mental image of his very bare chest floated through my dirty mind. My nether regions throbbed. That alone should have had me fleeing the apartment like it was on fire. Only it was me who was on fire. *Damn it, Tressa. Get your mind out of the gutter.*

"Tressa, you okay?" Trent asked.

I whirled around at the sound of my name. He was dressed, which was disappointing. No, wait. I was relieved. Definitely relieved. Holy monkey balls, my brain was officially broken.

Now would be the opportune time to use the drunken excuse, or even that I was abducted by aliens. He was a man of science. He would definitely buy the alien story. "I'm fine, just trying to warm up," I said, taking a deep breath. I was still feeling pretty hot and bothered, but that was for me to know.

"Oh. Let me turn the heat up," he offered.

Little did he know he'd already done that.

"I was working out earlier, so I kicked the heat down. I hate being hot while I'm lifting weights."

Too late for that. Seriously, I needed to be euthanized. My brain was a total traitor.

"Right," I muttered as I sat down. "I hate being hot too." God, I still sounded like a blabbering idiot.

"So, you never told me how the test went," Trent said, sitting on the couch beside me.

Normal. Be normal, I told myself. "I got an eighty-three," I answered, grinning. I may have been currently thinking of ways to punish myself, but I was pleased I was able to retain enough statistics to help me pass my second makeup test of the week. I wasn't killing it in the grades department, but thanks to Trent, at least I understood what I was doing.

"Not bad. What were your issues?"

"The usual. My brain refuses to accept any semblance of understanding when it comes to ratios. I'm pretty sure when God was creating that part of my brain, he was distracted. I'm guessing by a scantily dressed angel or something."

"I'm pretty sure it's sacrilegious to talk about God checking out angels."

I shrugged. "I'm not saying it's a bad thing. I bet there are some pretty hot chicks up there wearing negligees."

"Ew, now that's a mental picture of my grandmother I don't need," he said, shuddering.

I patted his hand. "Every angel deserves a playdate," I teased.

He looked down at my hand. I realized my mistake the moment my skin touched his. The heat I'd felt moments earlier instantly crackled to life. I made a move to pull my hand back, but he stopped me before I could retreat.

"Trent," I warned, tugging on my hand without much conviction.

"Go out with me."

"No," I answered, tugging on my wrist again.

"Why?"

"I need to get my dog ready for her space mission," I answered, grinning. This was not the first time we'd been through this in the last week. Not a tutoring session went by without Trent asking me out. I was getting pretty good at turning him down. Each excuse I threw out was more outrageous than the one the day before.

"Your dog in space. Clever," he said, smiling.

"What can I tell you? She's a diva space dog. She needs her entourage to go with her."

"They have strict protocols. You won't be able to get in."

"I already got my clearance," I deadpanned, looking down at my hand that was still clasped in his.

"You can go out with me once she's gone. You'll need something to keep your mind off your dog being in space."

"I'll be too sad to date. I will be mourning her absence by sitting in her doggie bed munching on her treats."

He looked at me pensively before giving up. "Fine, how's your group assignment going?" he asked, dropping my hand as he shifted into all-business mode. I was used to his quick personality switches, but this time a feeling crept in that felt an awful lot like disappointment. For a moment, I wished I had accepted his invitation. During the last few days, I had discovered that with the exception of Derek, Trent was the easiest person to talk to that I knew. You had to get around his mega-geek lingo sometimes, but something about his voice made everything a little bit more interesting. Despite my denial, I was curious about what a date with him would entail. Now that I had gotten an eyeful of what lay beneath his clothes, that curiosity had morphed into something more like desire.

Pulling my thoughts back on track, I answered his question, which turned into a long-winded rant. The group project was hell. That was the only way to describe it. Everyone naturally had their own ideas of how our fictional company should be run, but getting everyone to agree had turned into an act of futility. The project was due right before Halloween, which was one week away, but I couldn't see us finishing in time if we couldn't agree on anything.

"Let me check what you have so far," Trent said, waiting for me to navigate to the online section of the class so he could view our project up to this point. He moved the project to a new document so he could add notes. Peering over his shoulder, I saw that he was able to solve the equations in our business plan so they now made sense. "You have to account for supplies from this company and the overseas company you plan to use for this brand," he explained, pointing to the notes he had added by our columns. "That's why your numbers weren't matching up."

"Hey, not my numbers. Acne Greg has that job."

"Acne Greg? You sure like your labels."

"What?" I asked, feigning innocence.

"Acne Greg, Panty Muncher," he listed. "Oh, and my favorite are my nicknames, of course. Nerd Boy, Geek Squad, Clark Trent. That's the best one, by the way."

I laughed as he listed all my pet names for him. It was something I'd always done. My friend Brittni and I had nicknames for everyone back in Woodfalls. Some were terms of endearment, while others were more of a label. Like the girl Brittni interned with that got busted for smacking a kid's hand. She was forever known as McSlappy to Brittni and me, even after she got fired.

"Nicknames are awesome," I replied when I had my laughter under control.

"What about the nicknames people have made for you?"

"Are you kidding? I dated Jackson for four long years. Do you think there's anything anyone could call me that would be any worse than what he would call me?" I asked, still laughing. My hang-ups over Jackson were quickly slipping away to no-man's-land. I wouldn't allow sour memories of him to drag me down any further.

"I always hated that dick. Someone should kick his ass," Trent mumbled, shutting down my laptop. "Maybe I should."

"I don't know, Jackson's a big guy." I didn't want to hurt his feelings, but even with the lean muscles that I now knew lay beneath Trent's shirt, it was hard for me to imagine how he would handle himself in a fight.

"I know how to fight," Trent said quietly, like he was picking the thoughts from my head.

"He's not even worth the effort," I said, stowing my stuff in my book bag. "Thanks for the help with the group project. Hopefully the boneheads and I will figure it out. I need at least a B on the project."

"Looking at the grading rubric, you should be okay. The group portion only counts for fifteen percent of your grade. Your own section counts for the other eighty-five percent."

I stuck out my tongue at him. He liked to deliberately quote percentages because I had told him how they tripped me up like ratios. "You're hilarious. I've got to go," I said, heading for the door.

"Big plans tonight?" He stood and stepped close to me, resting a hand against the door so I couldn't open it. It was a classic guy move and was completely out of character for Trent.

"I'm not going out partying, if that's what you mean." I hated the defensive tone in my voice. Tutor or not, I didn't owe him any explanations.

"That's not why I'm asking." His voice came out strangled as a flush crawled up his neck.

"Then what's your deal?"

He choked out an answer I didn't quite catch.

"One more time, Geek Squad," I teased.

"Do you have a date?" He was finally able to spit out his answer, but not before his ears turned a bright shade of red.

"Yes," I said, seizing the opportunity to put the necessary distance between us.

"Oh—cool. Well, have fun." The electric blue of his eyes that was so captivating seemed to lose its brilliant luster.

I sighed. I was being suckered by a pair of eyes. “I have a poker game at my house tonight with some friends.”

His face lit up like a kid on Christmas morning. “Poker? I’ve been known to play a few hands,” he said, looking hopeful.

Before I could even stop myself, I asked if he wanted to join us. It was the damn eyes. Like I said before, they were my kryptonite. Trent accepted before I could even attempt to retract the invitation.

Oh hell. What did I do?

12.

If I hadn't needed my feet to drive, I would have kicked my own ass all the way home. Two weeks of keeping Trent at arm's length completely down the tubes.

I needed to vent. Picking up my cell phone, I opened my contacts and tapped the name at the top of the list. "I hate you, bitch," I said as soon as she answered.

"What did I do this time?" Brittni asked, laughing.

"You brainwashed me."

"Well, honey, you had to know that was my ploy all along. But, just so I know, how did I brainwash you?" I could picture her sitting on the couch rolling her eyes at my dramatics.

"With Clark freaking Trent."

"Who?"

"Trent James. Don't act like you don't know who I'm talking about."

"Sorry, my sweet foul-mouthed friend. The name wasn't ringing any bells."

"Seriously? Clark Trent is brilliant. You know, like Clark Kent?" I said. Then I realized it. He was turning me into a nerd. My life as I knew it was ending.

"Okay, I get it now. Tutoring starting to wear you down?"

"No," I snapped. "I mean—maybe, I guess."

"Well then, what has your thong all in a bunch?"

"I invited Trent to my apartment tonight."

"Oh my. Is it me or are things heating up?" she purred.

"Stop. We won't be alone."

"Oooh, trying a little kinky college experimentation, look at you."

"Can you stop being a perv for a few minutes?"

"What's that phrase about people in glass houses?"

"Brittni, this is serious. In an hour, Trent will be hanging out with my friends and me while we play poker. With anybody else this wouldn't be a big deal, but we both know Trent's not going to see it that way."

"So, why is that such a bad thing?" She laughed when I growled over the phone. "Okay, seriously. Tressa, I love you like a sister, but your dating snobbery is getting a little old. You've gone out with every dickhead who's ever asked you out. Meanwhile, when a nice guy comes around, you don't even want to give him a chance. It's time to pull on your big-girl pants and go out with someone who doesn't treat you like a doormat."

"I'm not a doormat."

"Exactly my point. I dare you to go out with him," she said, raising the stakes.

"Brittni," I warned.

"Double-dog dare you."

I swore under my breath. Growing up, Brittni and I had a made-up rule that neither of us could back down from a dare initiated by the other. I made Brittni do some pretty outrageous dares over the years, and she took great pride in payback whenever she got the chance. The sad thing is that the rule was originally my idea when we were like six or seven years old, and now it was going to bite me in the ass.

"And no veto either," she added hastily before I could use that loophole.

"Bitch, I hate you," I grumbled, clicking off my phone without saying good-bye.

My phone chirped, alerting me to a new text message as I was pulling into my regular space behind my apartment complex. I smiled when I read the message from Brittni.

I love you, whore.

What could I say? I loved her too.

Love you back, sugar lips. Revenge is beautiful, though.

I'm quaking in my rain boots.

You just wait. It'll happen when you're least expecting it.

Bring it on.

Kiss your handsome hubby for me.

You wish.

True story. Text you later.

You better. I want to know all about your card game. Wink wink.

I tossed my phone in my bag and climbed cautiously from my Jeep. It was starting to sleet, so the pavement was becoming slick. Landing on my ass was never fun. I'd learned that lesson the hard way more than once.

I had less than an hour before everyone arrived, so I spent the time tidying up the apartment. Cameo helped me move our dining room table to the living room since there would be more people playing this time.

She and I had reached a tentative truce again on Monday when I helped her drag the bookcase she found by the Dumpster up the three flights of stairs. During the last few days we had maintained the peace by steering clear of the touchy subjects, most notably my new nightlife activities, or lack thereof. Where to put the new shelf, picking up more laundry soap, the teacher who gave her a D on a paper because she was five words shy on a five-thousand-word assignment—these were the safe topics we stuck to lately.

I thanked her for the help, but as we smoothed the wrinkles out of the tablecloth, I made the mistake of asking if she wanted to join us in the game. She shot me a look of disdain before stalking off to her room to finish getting ready for an evening out.

"I guess that's a no," I said to the empty room. I told myself it didn't matter, but truthfully, it hurt. It was becoming clear that Cameo and I may never have the same kind of friendship again. It amazed me how quickly things had changed in a few short weeks. Part of me was angry at her for being a bitch, but I was also pretty sad that she had dropped me so easily.

An hour later, Cameo left without so much as a good-bye. Luckily, the guys were beginning to arrive, allowing me to push my woes with her to the back burner. Adam and Tim showed up with dripping jackets from the sleet outside. Adam pulled me into his arms for a bone-crushing hug before spinning me around.

"You're getting me all wet," I said.

"Well, that's the first time a girl's ever said that to me," he said, grinning.

I barked out a laugh.

"Don't let him fool you. He had all the girls in high school panting after him before he came out of the closet," Tim said, giving me a spaghetti-arm hug. "Where's Derek?"

"He should be home in a few. I think he had to work till

seven. I told him to pick up pizzas and booze on his way home," I said, taking their jackets as someone knocked on our door. *Crap, crap, crap.* I had hoped Trent would change his mind.

"Who's that?" Tim asked, opening one of the bags of chips they had brought with them.

"A friend of mine. He's here so maybe you guys can win some of his money and not mine. Not that there was a chance of that anyway," I teased, trying to sound nonchalant as I opened the door. For the second time in one day I got to see water dripping from Trent's hair. He was at least dressed in more than a towel this time, but for some reason, I still felt my insides beginning to heat up as I looked at him. There was something different about him, but I couldn't pinpoint what it was as he unzipped his jacket. His geeky *Star Wars* T-shirt wasn't a problem since I knew what lay beneath the worn material. Even his normally bothersome glasses looked sexy. I found myself mentally undressing him.

"Are we moving the card game out to the hallway?" In my momentary trance, I didn't notice Adam coming up behind me and throwing an arm around my neck. Trent's eyes narrowed behind his glasses and I could see him processing Adam's familiarity with me.

"Oh my, who is this?" Adam drawled, eyeing Trent appraisingly. "Love the shirt, by the way. Where have I seen that before?"

"Excuse me?" Trent asked, nervously pushing up his glasses.

"I've got it!" he said. "*The Big Bang Theory.* Sheldon wore that shirt on the show. Tim and I are avid fans," Adam said, indicating his partner, who joined us. Adam gave Trent another once-over, clearly liking what he saw.

Derek arrived with the food and beer before Trent could say another word. "Hey, it's Clark Kent," he said, clapping Trent on the back while basically pushing him away from the front door. "Too late to turn back now, buddy boy."

"Oh, I'm not going anywhere," Trent said, catching everyone's attention by eyeing me meaningfully.

"Aww, isn't that sweet. Sheldon here has a crush on our girl." Adam dabbed at his eye like he was wiping away a tear. "This is my kind of card game."

"Adam, you're impossible. Everyone, this is Trent," I said, making the introductions. "Trent, this is Adam, Tim, and, of course, Derek."

"Hello, Trent," the three of them answered in unison.

Oh God. Tonight was going to be like a trip to the seventh circle of hell. I should have bought marshmallows and wieners to roast in the pits of fire, although I was starting to think I would be the one roasted.

Trent remained unfazed as he shrugged out of his hooded jacket. This night might seriously be my undoing. It had been easier when I could place Trent in the "geeky" box, but lately I had realized there was more to him than that. He was smart, of course, and acted like a robot at times, but he was surprisingly sensitive and caring. It also didn't hurt that he was sporting a chiseled abdomen beneath all those clothes.

"Do you want some pizza?" I asked Trent, deciding I might as well play the good hostess. I tossed the three jackets I was holding on the couch. That was about as far as my hostess duties extended.

"Sure." He followed me to the table where the others had already sat down, leaving two remaining chairs right next to each other.

"Two seats left," Adam said, patting one of the chairs. "You two lovelies come on now. I am eager to get this game started."

Between the five of us, the pizzas Derek brought home didn't stand a chance. I divided out the poker chips and began shuffling the cards.

"You play a lot of poker?" Tim asked Trent oh so casually.

"I've played a few times. Haven't had a whole lot of opportunities for a sit-down game lately, though," Trent replied, arranging his chips in precise stacks. It was like an OCD wet dream.

Tim and Derek grinned at each other, deeming Trent an easy mark. I should have felt bad for him, but I had a feeling Trent would be able to hold his own.

"Hold 'em, right?" Derek asked as he dealt the first hand. I watched everyone's faces as each card was tossed in front of them. I liked to study their expressions as they discovered what they had received. I noticed Trent waited until all the cards were dealt before he checked his hand. He slightly lifted the corners of the two cards so no one could see what he was holding. He had also angled his chair so he was practically on top of me.

At first I thought maybe he was trying to sneak a look at

my cards, or maybe he was trying to keep Tim from catching a peek at *his* cards since he was sitting at the end of the table near Trent. Whatever the reason, Trent was definitely invading my personal space and the extra distraction wouldn't help me or my game.

The issue was his damn hot-as-sin cologne that swirled around me like some freaking erotic blanket. I wanted to bury my nose in the crook of his neck. One of my favorite spots on a guy was the soft part of his neck, just above the collarbone. It was a perfect spot to start kissing. After which, my mouth would take a slow journey down to his pecs, making sure to give proper attention to each nipple. Finally, my tongue would trace each and every groove of his eight perfectly sculpted abs, past his belly button until I reached his . . .

"Yoo-hoo, Tress," Derek said, waving his hand. "Are you going to bet, or are you waiting for an engraved invitation?" He was looking at me like he'd just read my thoughts. I kicked him under the table and smiled when he reached down to rub his leg.

Finally focusing on my cards, I discovered I'd been dealt pocket queens, which put me in a strong position. I made my face an unreadable mask and placed a bet that wasn't too aggressive so I wouldn't scare anyone into folding.

Trent was next. I angled my chair away from him to give myself a little more personal space. Watching him closely as he peeked at his cards again, I was unable to get a good read on him. He kept a small smile on his face like he was amused.

At first I thought I'd figured out his tell, but he killed that idea when he folded.

"Getting out while you can?" Adam commented. "Good, that gives us a chance to chat. I fold too."

"It's not even your turn," Tim said.

"Oh, I'm so bad. Tell you what, honey. You can spank me later."

"No whips, I hope?" I joked.

"Heavens no. My soft tush can't take it," Adam replied, rubbing his bottom.

I looked at Trent, who was smiling.

Adam turned his attention to Trent. "I guess you go to MSC also?"

"Yes. I'm finishing my master's and then Professor Nelson is going to help me with my doctoral thesis."

"And you're single and heterosexual?" Adam probed.

Derek spit out his swig of beer. Luckily, his head was turned away from the table.

"Really, Adam? You're going to make him leave," Tim said, taking Adam by the hand.

"It was just a question. For years everyone thought I was the only square peg in my family until my cousin Jake came out of the closet. He was a big-time football player. So you see, you never can tell."

"It's cool. Yes and yes," Trent answered as he placed an arm on the back of my chair. I would have glared at him, but I was in the process of taking Derek to the cleaners.

All the signs were there. Derek was so easy to read. I was

just about to lower the boom when Trent's fingers grazed a small patch of my shoulder. My breath left me and my hands jerked forward simultaneously, sending my chips flying and my cards to the table, faceup.

"I fold," Derek said after seeing the two queens I had been holding.

"That's cheating," I snapped at Trent, who had withdrawn his hand from my shoulder.

"What?" He feigned innocence.

The others cleaned up the mess on the table as they watched us like we were part of their favorite reality show. No one noticed what Trent had done, but they were enjoying my reaction immensely.

"Isn't this fun?" Adam asked with merriment. "I believe it's your deal, Tressa darling." I glared at him, tossing a card in Trent's direction.

"It was just a tap." I looked at Trent to see if he'd argue.

"That's right. Nothing but a love tap," he said. His look was unwavering. When did he become so self-assured?

"Love tap," Derek snorted. He moved his cards to cover his smile when I shot him a death glare.

"This one is a keeper, Tressa. No doubt about it," Adam commented. He was finding great joy in the situation.

Each of the guys received my death glare as I finished dealing the cards. With Adam's encouragement, Trent appeared oblivious to my mood. His arm remained on the back of my chair whenever he wasn't placing a bet. I could have made him move it, but that would only have enlisted more razzing from the guys. Every once in a while, his fingers would brush against the bare part of my neck, presumably by accident. I showed no reaction and managed to hold on to my cards those times.

As the night progressed, I found myself more and more comfortable with the feel of his touch. It was nothing but a stroke of his fingers, and never lasted longer than a couple seconds, but definitely made the hair on the back of my neck stand up. And caused goose bumps on my arms. Everything inside me hummed with awareness. I shifted in my chair, hoping to encounter his hand so it would remain on that small, lucky patch of skin that had every other part of me envious. Who knew it was possible to be jealous of your own skin? His hand always seemed to be just beyond my reach. If it had been anyone else, I would have said he was deliberately toying with me, but this was Trent. I'm sure he had no idea what he was doing.

Even though my concentration was shot to hell, I eventually cleaned everyone of their money, with the exception of Trent, who turned out to be a decent player. Derek, Adam, and Tim grumbled about being hustled and then scooted their chairs to the side so they could watch Trent and me face off against each other. Taking the game more seriously than I had all night, I moved my chair to the other side of the table, which Derek had just vacated.

No more innocent touches. I was in this to win.

Adam agreed to deal as Trent leaned forward on his side of the table. We'd decided this would be the winner-take-all hand. I insisted on five-card draw, so there would be no up cards to see.

"You ready for this, Geek Squad?" I asked, holding my cards close to my face. I was feeling pretty cocky. I was sure I had figured out his tell and this hand would prove it. "I'll have fun spending all the cash I win tonight," I taunted.

"You sure your mind is in the game?" His eyes glistened with confidence. My eyes narrowed as he smiled wickedly.

"Don't worry about me, Spock."

"Oh, I liked him in the new *Star Trek* movie. Very cute," Adam interjected.

"Not now," I said.

Trent's smile widened as the others giggled like hyenas. They all deserved a knee in the nuts or, better yet, something that involved honey and fire ants.

Ignoring the trio of grinning idiots, I turned my attention to the cards in my hands. I had the worst hand imaginable. What the hell was I going to do with a six of spades, a two and four of clubs, and a five and nine of diamonds? Talk about a colossal bank-busting hand. Deciding I had nothing to lose, I kept the two clubs. I placed my bet, accepting my three cards. I waited to look at them until Trent took his turn. That fact that I discarded three cards was a pretty good indication that I had a crap hand.

Trent looked me in the eyes. He indicated he needed no new cards, that butt licker. I was screwed. He looked away before placing his bet. That was his tell. Or so I thought. Of course, I could be way off and he could be holding four kings.

I looked down at the three cards in front of me that were still lying facedown on the table. Scooting them to the edge of the table, I slid them up without looking at them for a moment.

My eyes started to focus on them when I felt my leg being nudged under the table. "Really?"

He grinned at me. "It was worth a shot."

"I'm going to shoot you," I threatened, moving my leg away. I managed to stomp on his foot for good measure. He grunted but didn't say anything. "You okay?" I asked sweetly, finally glancing down at my cards. I looked at them in disbelief. It was as if angels themselves had picked my cards. I'm pretty sure I could hear cherubs singing above our heads. I went from having nothing to pulling a straight flush. I really wanted to get up and get my groove on, but I remained still.

Before placing my bet, my eyes moved to Trent's to gauge his reaction. His eyes flickered and he glanced away. He was totally bluffing me. I forced a look of uncertainty on my face before pushing all my chips in. I gnawed my lip for good measure.

"All in?" He looked worried for the first time.

I shrugged casually. "Last hand, right?"

"That's pretty rich," he commented.

I held my breath. If all went well, maybe he would think I was bluffing. After a long, drawn-out moment, he finally scooted his chips to the center of the table. I wanted to crow with delight, but controlled myself as the others leaned in close. "How about we up the stakes?" I offered coyly.

"What do you have in mind?" He looked at me with curiosity, pushing up his glasses.

"Just a little friendly wager," I said, feeling some of my wild persona returning.

He waited for me to continue. I could hear Adam's murmur of approval.

"Are you game?"

"That depends."

"On what?"

"I get to pick my side of the bet."

I felt the first stirrings of wariness. "Deal," I answered cautiously. "What do you want?"

"Let me hear yours first," he said.

"If I win, you have to show up at the next Bears game without one of your geek shirts on, or any other clothes for that matter."

Derek whistled his approval.

"Let me get this straight. You want me to go to a football game completely naked?"

"I want you to streak across the field," I said mischievously, wondering if he would fold. Bluffing with cash was one thing. Having your junk hanging out for the world to see was a different story.

"I'm not into football, but that's a game I might have to go to," Tim interjected, earning a playful swat from Adam.

"Completely naked?" Trent repeated like he was trying to find a loophole.

"As a newborn baby," I laughed with delight. I missed this part of me.

"It's not like you'll see me with your activities probation." His words took a little wind from my sails.

"I think it would be worth the risk."

Derek looked practically gleeful. He'd played enough cards with me to know I had this one in the bag.

Trent wavered for a moment, and I was sure he would fold. "Deal," he said. "But if I win, you have to go out with me."

"You have to do better than that," Adam interrupted. "You're risking being naked against a date? Come on, raise."

"Okay, I get a kiss too," Trent said.

"On the lips and open mouth," Adam added.

"Stay out of this, Kewpie doll," I teased Adam.

"No, he's right. A date and an openmouthed kiss on the lips. If the stakes are too high, I guess you'll just have to fold."

I weighed his words. I was almost positive I had the winning hand, but if I did lose, it would basically kill two birds with one stone. It would get Brittni off my back and maybe show Trent once and for all how wrong we were for each other. "Deal."

"Show me yours," he said. Heat flared through me like a firework. His statement was meant for my cards, but my mind went immediately to the gutter.

I fanned out my cards and sat back in my chair, smiling.

"A straight flush," he said approvingly.

"Yep, luck of the draw I guess you could say."

"Very impressive." He studied my cards. I felt the kiddie urge to clap my hands with glee. Victory was mine.

Derek laughed, clapping Trent on the back. "Don't feel bad, dude. She's taken us all to the cleaners before."

"She's definitely a fine player and very lucky, but—" Trent said as a grin spread across his face. He laid down his hand and the blood drained from my face as I eyed the ten, jack, queen, king, and ace of hearts—a royal flush. Who gets dealt a hand like that? I'd been hustled by fate.

13.

"Holy hell, he totally played you," Derek chimed in, sounding more impressed than necessary.

"Shut up," I muttered, looking at Trent. I expected him to at least look remorseful for conning me, but he looked downright pleased with himself. The bastard even had the nerve to wink at me.

"Dude, that was freaking epic. I don't think I've ever seen our girl here lose," Derek praised him.

"That's because I don't lose," I said through gritted teeth. "Not since I started playing my dad back when I was thirteen."

"There's a first for everything," Trent said, smiling. His meaning was clear—he would be collecting on all aspects of the bet.

Derek continued to jabber away about my loss like a kid

hyped up on caffeine. Without acknowledging him, I continued to straighten up, still not believing I'd fallen for Trent's bluff. The guys pitched in and within minutes our living room was back to its previous state.

Adam and Tim hugged me before turning to shake Trent's hand with gusto. Without even asking me if it was okay, they invited Trent to join us for the next game. I took it all in stride, not wanting to look like a sore loser. They said their good-byes, leaving Trent and me alone in the living room. Even traitor Derek had slipped away to the bedroom.

Trent shrugged into his jacket, but didn't make a move to leave. I had pretty much ignored him since the game ended, but now that we were alone, it was a bit awkward. He stood watching me like he had something he wanted to say. If I didn't know him better, I would almost think he felt guilty. If that was the case, good, it served him right to feel guilty. I didn't care if I was being a hypocrite. It wasn't my fault my plan to toast his ass at cards had backfired. That justification sounded better in my head.

"You played me," I said, breaking the silence.

"Yep." He looked downright pleased with himself, without the slightest hint of guilt. "I'd do it again if the opportunity presented itself."

"I'm learning more and more about you. You're not the good boy you pretend to be."

"Whoever said I was pretending to be good? I had an opportunity, and I took it."

"All for a date that's sure to be a disaster?" I reminded him.

"And a kiss," he added quickly.

"And a kiss," I repeated. "I figured maybe you'd let me slide on that one since, technically, it wasn't your idea. Anyway, I'm sure you won't be as excited by the time the date is over."

"Why do you think that?" He made the bold move of stepping closer to me. "And don't tell me it's because we're opposites." He moved even closer. He seemed to like invading my space, but I made no move to step away.

"I'm completely wrong for you," I answered.

"What if I say I think you're mistaken?" He leaned toward me, testing my boundaries.

"I may not have your brain, but I know this kind of stuff. You'll be bored with me within an hour."

"I don't think so," he said, reaching his hand toward me. I waited, holding my breath. His hand hovered by my cheek for a moment, stroking it with a featherlight touch before snaking around to caress my neck.

My breath began to wheeze out from the anticipation of what was coming. "I'd be bored within an hour," I threw out in a weak attempt to halt his progress.

"I don't think you will." He eyed my lips, slowly moving toward me. I could have stopped him. He was giving me that chance. His lips loomed close to mine. I was shocked and appalled at how badly I wanted them to touch mine.

The front door of my apartment flew open, effectively killing the moment. Cameo stomped inside in a fit of rage as Trent and I sprang apart like two preteens who'd gotten caught groping each other in one of their parents' basements.

I was surprised to see my usually cheerful roommate looking so upset. Considering everything that had happened the past few weeks, I immediately expected the worst.

"Cameo, what happened?" Suddenly, I no longer gave a damn that we were at odds with each other.

She looked frantic as tears leaked from the corners of her eyes. Her mascara was running, leaving a trail of midnight black down her cheeks. Whoever had upset her would answer to me.

In all the time I'd known Cameo, I'd only seen her cry once, and that was when her mom called to tell her that her cat, Sam, had died. This was so much worse. It was as if floodgates had been opened in her eyes as the tears poured out at an alarming rate. I reached my hand out to comfort her. She looked at it for a moment before gripping it tightly. I led her over to the couch, tugging her gently down beside me. By that time, Derek had appeared from the bedroom.

"Cameo, what happened?"

A broken sob bubbled out of her throat. "We-e-e broke up," she finally got out as sobs shook her petite frame.

"You and Chad?" I asked, not quite understanding. Cameo had gone through so many boyfriends since I met her a year ago. She had always handled the breakups with indifference, most times already scouting for a replacement before the previous boyfriend made it to the parking lot. Tears were never part of the equation until now.

"Yes," she wailed brokenly as more tears fell. Her nose began to run from all her crying. I'd no sooner processed the thought of getting her some tissues when a box was being pushed toward me. Looking up, I smiled gratefully at Derek, who was hovering beside us. I took the tissues and noticed Trent as he mouthed a good-bye at me. He held up his phone, wanting me to text him later. I nodded my head, then turned my attention back to Cameo.

It took nearly an hour to get the complete story out of her since she would dissolve into tears anytime she started to talk. Eventually, she ran out of tears and was able to get through the whole sordid breakup. It turned out Chad had broken up with her because he walked in on her while she was playing a drinking game with a bunch of frat boys. Cameo claimed they weren't doing anything wrong. Chad had taken it completely out of context when he walked into the basement and saw one of the guys with his arm around her shoulders.

Listening to her version, I could only imagine what it must have looked like to Chad. Cameo was an affectionate person and was always hugging, giving love taps or lingering kisses on everyone's cheeks. She was very touchy-feely. Seeing your girlfriend with some guy's arm around her would be an ego slayer for any guy. Still, I would have thought Chad would know Cameo by now. I wondered if maybe Chad was dealing with his own demons like I was. My life wasn't the only one affected by David's death.

I kept those thoughts to myself and provided Cameo the sympathy she needed as she told me everything. She soon ran out of steam and slumped back against the couch cushions completely spent. I placed a throw pillow on my lap and tugged her so she was lying down. Running my hand over her head, I soothed her like my mom used to do for me. After a few minutes and a few more suppressed sobs, she fell asleep, much like a child who had cried herself out. I waited until her breathing was even before I slid her head off my lap and placed it on the couch where I had been sitting. Pulling the heavy quilt off the back of the couch, I covered her up.

For the first time in two weeks, I felt like my roommate and I had a common bond. Switching the lights off in the living room, I tiptoed quietly to the bathroom so I could get ready for bed.

Derek was lying on my bed scrolling through Facebook when I silently crept into our room. He had walked away, thinking it was best for Cameo and me to be alone.

"Is she okay?" he whispered as I lay down next to him.

"She fell asleep, thank goodness."

"That's good. She was pretty upset. Sorry to bail, but I wasn't sure what I could do."

"It's all right. Believe me, I have experience with this," I said, making him feel better.

He nodded. "Cameo would have shut down if I was out there anyway. You know how she hates for people to see her cry. She's just like you."

He was right. In that regard, Cameo and I were mirror images of each other. Tears translated to weakness, and showing weakness wasn't an option.

Derek and I chatted late into the night. Both of us were floored that our roommate, who followed a no-attachments guideline when it came to guys, had fallen hard. I hoped Chad was equally miserable and would realize what he had witnessed was just a misunderstanding.

Shockingly, the next morning Cameo acted like nothing had happened. She was up before Derek and me and had showered away all the evidence of her meltdown. We woke to the sound of her vacuuming in the hallway outside my room. Derek and I staggered out, surprised to see her not only up out of bed, but also cleaning. Saturday chores were a thorn in all of our sides, and we had gotten into the habit of sleeping in late to avoid them just a little longer.

Cameo flashed us a smile that might have fooled someone who didn't know her as well as we did. Derek started to give her a hug and tell her it would work out, but she squirmed out of his arms, refusing to talk about it. He shot me a look, but I shrugged my shoulders. There was no reason to push her. Cameo would talk to us when she was ready.

None of us mentioned Chad the rest of the morning as we tackled cleaning the apartment. Cameo was like the Tasmanian Devil, buzzing around the apartment like a hundred-pound tornado. Derek waited until she left the apartment carrying a load of laundry down to the washer and dryer on the second floor before commenting that a crazy cleaning Cameo wasn't entirely a bad thing. I nodded my head in agreement. Not that I wanted my friend to have her heart ripped out. I'm just saying a nice clean apartment isn't a bad thing, especially since I had to work today.

Thanks to Cameo's early-morning-vacuuming wake-up call, I managed to arrive not only on time, but actually early to work. I sat in my Jeep trying to coax what little heat I could out of the vents while I waited for Larry to arrive and open the doors to Javalotta. I warily pulled my phone out of my pocket while I waited. My phone, which had been my life-force practically from the day my parents had gotten me one for my fifteenth birthday, was something I tried to avoid lately. I had yet to log on to my Instagram or Facebook accounts since the accident two weeks ago. I debated whether I was ready to face social media again or if I should text Trent. Neither were very appealing choices.

After a night of rest and with no booze flowing through my veins to cloud my judgment, I was hyperaware of what almost happened before Cameo stormed in. I tried to tell myself it was a fluke. I mean, from a guy's perspective, his timing was perfect. It had been ages since I had hooked up with anyone, and I had to admit, I was beginning to feel the urge. It could have been any guy standing there. Of course, what did that mean for our date? It would finally make my friends shut up, but I owed Trent a kiss too, and I've never welched on a dare or a bet. How the hell did I let this happen? It was like I was going on this date as a favor to Brittni and to pay off my bet to Trent. The only one not getting anything out of it was me.

Despite feeling like I'd somehow been hustled, I sent a text to Trent. He answered immediately, which was a little shocking since he never seemed to have his phone on him whenever I was with him. Our texting conversation went pretty much how I expected.

Hey

Hey. How's your roommate?

She's better.

That's good. I'll pick you up tonight? No beating around the bush. I swear, he could stand to take some texting etiquette classes.

I work until nine.

That's fine. How about I pick you up at your place at nine thirty?

Fine

See you then

And that was how we set up our date. Not in the mood to deal with social media, I stowed my phone in my pocket and turned up my radio to a near-deafening decibel. The bass vibrated through the metal floorboards of my Jeep, traveling up my legs until my entire body felt like it was a part of the song.

I was so lost in the music I didn't notice my boss Larry had arrived until he rapped against the window. Jumping, I turned to look out the window. I pulled my stomach out of my throat and turned off my car.

"You scared the crap out of me," I complained, opening my door. A blast of northern wind cut through my double layer of clothes, making me swear. It was mother-sucking cold. Why did I love Maine so much? I bet my friend Ashton was lying on the beach in Florida drinking margaritas while I froze my nips off.

"I'm surprised you heard me. Your music was so loud I could see your Jeep rocking from across the parking lot. Loud music is bad for your hearing," Larry said, pulling his keys out of his pocket so he could unlock the back door of the coffeehouse.

I shrugged my shoulders. "Isn't that just an old person's scare tactic because they're out of touch with the superior generation?" I scooted past him, chuckling. It was common knowledge that the owners of Javalotta considered themselves hip and in touch with the youth. Teasing them about being old was always a surefire way to keep things interesting at work.

Today was no exception. Larry turned up the volume on the coffeehouse speakers a couple notches louder than usual. I bit back a grin as I readied Javalotta for the day. He was almost too easy.

Reanna, another part-timer, came in ten minutes later, apologizing to Larry for being late. He gave her his classic warning, but let it go since she was technically only a few minutes late. Tardiness was frowned upon, but as long as you didn't make a habit of it, Larry was pretty cool about it.

Reanna joined me behind the counter where I was filling the industrial-sized coffee makers and espresso machines. She looked flustered as she tied her apron on.

"What's up?" I asked, nudging her with my hip.

"I hit another damn mailbox. My dad is going to have a fit."

I had to laugh at her. Reanna was singularly the worst driver I had ever met. During normal driving conditions, she was known to hit a few obstacles. Add in some bad weather and she was a total terror on the road. "Whose was it this time?"

"My nitpicking old bag of a neighbor. She's always complaining about something. Me hitting her mailbox will not go unnoticed when I get home."

"Did she see you hit it?"

"Yeah, go figure. She was outside picking up her paper, which is why I hit it in the first place. She distracted me and I didn't see the patch of ice. I turned the wheel a little too hard and wound up jumping the curb." Reanna gave me a pained look before continuing. "She was yelling and hollering that I had tried to run her over on purpose."

"Why would she think that?"

"Because she knows I've disliked her since she ratted on me senior year when Tommy Heckler and I were just about ready to do the deed in the front seat of his pickup truck. Nothing like trying to get everything in the right place only to look up and see some old lady's face squished against the window. Talk about things going flat."

I nodded my head knowingly. There was nothing like those moments when a parent or other adult walked in on you. Jackson and I had had our share of mishaps with his mom.

"Anyway, she went screaming over to my house that I was trying to kill her, so I did the only thing I could."

"You really did run her over?" I teased, still laughing. I bent over to check the mini fridges under the counter to make sure the whipped cream and milk jugs were filled. Saturdays were notoriously busy at Javalotta, and nothing sucked more than having to run to the stockroom for supplies midway through a rush. It was never good to make coffee lovers wait for their next caffeine fix.

"Funny. I should have run her ass over. No, I peeled off down the road like I had no idea what was going on."

"Okay, so it's your word against hers," I joked.

"Sadly, she has proof," she said, looking embarrassed as she filled the napkin dispensers.

"What did she do? Snap a picture?"

"Um, no. Her mailbox—well, it's sorta wedged under the back bumper of my car."

I looked at her, waiting for her to continue, while trying not to laugh since she looked so distressed.

"See, when I hit it at first, it sorta flew into the road from the momentum of the crash. I panicked because she was screaming like a lunatic, so I tried to speed away, and I ran it over on my way down the street. It somehow got wedged up under my car."

There was no way I could suppress my laughter anymore.

"The funny part was the god-awful noise it made as I was driving here," she said, joining in on my laughter over the story. I was wiping away tears when Carl, one of the other employees, joined us.

"What's so funny?" he asked, placing a till in one of the registers.

"She, sh-sh," I tried to explain, but I dissolved into more laughter. I held my side, trying to ease the stitch from laughing so hard.

Carl looked at Reanna to elaborate. "It's not as funny as she's making it," she said, trying not to laugh as she stacked cups in one of the dispensers.

Her comment made me laugh again. I left her to explain it to Carl while I went to Larry's office to retrieve my own till.

"What's going on out there? Sounds like someone let in a pack of hyenas."

"You'll have to ask Reanna. I'm not sure I could get through the story," I said, laughing again.

The story of Reanna's mishap ran through the entire coffeehouse as the day progressed. We began to make bets on which customers would comment on the car that had a mailbox stuck under it. I cleaned up. The informers were easy to spot. They were the ones who walked in the door backward since they were busy gaping at the mailbox like it was roadkill. In a way, it was.

At three o'clock, the next shift of employees showed up,

and Reanna left with a grinding noise as she drove off with the mailbox still attached. We all watched from the window to see the fountain of sparks coming up behind her car from the metal mailbox rubbing against the asphalt. The morning crew laughed before heading out, leaving the afternoon crew and me feeling bereft now that our source of entertainment was gone.

The steady stream of customers that was typical for a Saturday continued all afternoon and into the evening. The time was flying by, even though I found myself checking my phone more often than normal. I had to give credit to Liz and Larry for putting together a great crew. We ran like a well-oiled machine.

"You seem pretty antsy tonight," Heather observed as I pulled my phone out to check the clock for the umpteenth time in the last hour. "Is there some killer party I need to know about?"

"Not that I know of," I answered offhandedly, hoping she'd drop it. I stepped up to the counter so I could ring up the energy drink a pimply kid had plunked on the counter. I handed him back his change.

"Tressa, Queen of All Parties, doesn't know if there's anything going on tonight? Are you holding out on me?"

I sighed. That really was my reputation. How sad my college legacy would be. "I have a date," I said, trying to save face, even though I had intended to keep my date with Trent on the down low.

"Oh, even better. Spill." She leaned against the counter with sudden interest.

Seeing no out, I gave her an abridged version of my impending date. Her questions made it easy since she was all about the physical stuff. It was easy to describe Trent's physique in great detail. Heather sighed with pleasure as I talked about his abs and of course his eyes, which were his best feature. By the time I finished talking, I felt like everything in me was a puddle of liquid heat. Being sexually deprived was muddling my brain.

14.

Trent, who normally couldn't keep track of time to save his life, showed up at my apartment at nine thirty on the nose. I was in the middle of trying to squeeze into my favorite skinny jeans when he knocked on the front door. Derek and Cameo weren't home yet, which meant I had to bounce my way to the door to get my jeans pulled up over my hips, which have always been on the curvy side. After I managed to shimmy my jeans on and button them up, I smoothed my shirt down and opened the door.

"You're early. Come on in," I stated, backing up toward my room for my long socks and boots.

He looked at his watch as he stepped through the doorway. "I said I'd be here at nine thirty." I thought that was funny. It seemed like no one wore watches anymore. I remembered thinking I was cool when my older cousin, Jamie, had bought me a Relic watch when I was fourteen. I never touched it again after my parents gave me my cell phone.

"Yeah, but you're always late," I answered as I ducked into my room to get the rest of my stuff.

His answer was muddled but pretty much sounded like a denial. I pulled on my socks and boots and then headed to my bathroom to spray perfume and touch up my makeup. I wasn't sure where Trent planned to take me. Probably some comic book store.

I threw on my jacket and we headed out. I was wrong about the comic book store, but where we ended up wasn't much better.

"This is where you decided to take me?" I don't think I could have guessed the Halloween megastore if I had been given ten chances, but there we were nonetheless.

"Sure. I know you don't have a costume. Tonight's as good a night as any to get yours," he said, opening his car door.

"How do you know I don't have one?" I climbed from the car and into the cool night temperatures.

"You mentioned it Monday when we saw that kid wearing a wolf mask outside the library." He started walking toward the brightly lit Halloween store.

"So? I don't need one. I'm not going to any parties this year." I wasn't overly sad about missing the campus parties. Last year I had gotten completely wasted after the third party of the night. Waking up in the living room of some frat house with vomit that you're not entirely sure is yours is not the best feeling.

"I thought you said you were going to Woodfalls for the festival." He opened the door of the store and a blast of warm air enveloped us as we walked in.

I didn't answer him right away since I was awestruck. I'd never seen so many costumes. Aisles and aisles of them. I wondered why Cameo and I had felt the need to slave over making our own costumes when a store like this existed.

"You are going, right?"

"Huh?" I asked, running my fingers over a black wig that would have been perfect for my Cleopatra costume last year. Instead, I used temporary dye for my hair, which ended up dyeing my neck too.

Trent stepped in front of me, cutting off my view of the costume wonderland in front of me. "Halloween festival. Woodfalls?"

"I guess I'm going, but I didn't intend to dress up."

"You have to dress up," he said, grabbing me by the wrist and leading me down one of the endless rows of outfits. "How about this one?" He reached into the rack and pulled out a short beer maiden's costume.

"Did it two years ago, except my skirt was shorter."

"Uh, of course it was," he said, adjusting his glasses. I smirked at his reaction. His responses to some of my comments were flattering.

"How about this?" I asked, pulling on a mask from a popular slasher film franchise. Brittni and I had watched all the movies when we were freshmen. For months afterward, I would call her up and ask her in a creepy voice if she liked scary movies.

"The first movie wasn't bad, but the rest were pretty ridiculous," Trent said, handing me a fake butcher knife so I could get the full effect in a mirror at the end of our row.

"My mom probably wouldn't be thrilled if I showed up to the festival wearing this."

"No, but you'd get cool points from your brother."

"Maybe I should get it for the snot runt." I pulled the mask off and patted my hair back in place.

We rounded the corner into a new row that looked like Disney princesses had puked in it. "Wow, talk about princess fetishes." I'd somehow been lucky enough to escape the love affair every girl seemed to have with wanting to be a princess.

Trent held up a yellow monstrosity of a dress. "What, you never wanted to be Belle?"

"No, thanks," I answered disdainfully, leaving the aisle behind.

The next aisle was much more my speed. It was like a blast from cartoon heaven. Trent and I spent a good thirty minutes in the cartoon aisle trying on different masks and headgear. I couldn't resist pulling out my phone and snapping a picture for Brittni of Trent wearing a Johnny Bravo mask. Johnny Bravo held a special place in our hearts. I posted the picture on Instagram also. I ignored the message section that showed I had more than a thousand comments on pictures I had posted.

The next few aisles were kid costumes, so Trent and I skipped over them. I couldn't help giggling when he dragged me down a superhero aisle like a kid who had just spotted

Santa Claus. His major geek came out when he picked up a Green Lantern ring and quoted something that sounded like a pledge.

"Do I even want to know how you knew that entire thing?" My attitude changed when I spotted a Princess Leia costume, complete with a freaking cinnamon roll–looking wig. I wasn't much of a sci-fi nut, but I'd always been obsessed with Han Solo. Mom told me that when I was little they dug out my dad's collection of action figures from when he was a kid and I instantly zoned in on the Han Solo and Princess Leia figures. I was like three at the time. I recently saw a movie with the guy who played Han Solo and he's totally some old dude now. I can't believe I had crushed on him so hard.

I held up the costume, which was completely impractical for Maine since the belly was bare and all, but I wanted it. Bad.

"That's the costume you like?" Trent asked in a strangled voice.

I turned my attention away from the costume in my hand to eye him, wondering what the big deal was. "Yeah. Why?" His eyes were practically bugging out.

"You know that's from a major 'geek movie,' as you like to put it, right? Maybe you'd like one of the costumes over there," he said, pointing to a nurse costume.

"I know which movie this comes from," I said, clutching it to my chest. "What's your deal? You wanted me to pick a costume, and now you're going to get all judgmental? What, you don't like *Star Wars* or something?"

"Are you kidding? It's the biggest cinematic movie of its generation. It revolutionized how movies were being made."

"Okay, so what's your deal with Princess Leia? Let me guess, you hated that a woman got to kick some ass? That's a pretty sexist attitude," I said, stalking off to one of the mirrors so I could try on the wig.

"I don't have a problem with Princess Leia," he said as he came up behind me, looking embarrassed.

It took a minute for the pieces to click into place. "Ah, I see. You have a thing for Princess Leia. You don't think I'll make a good one?" I didn't know if I should be pissed or hurt.

"That's not it," he said, looking uncomfortable.

"Then what is it?" I pressed, stepping closer to him. He took a step back, hitting the rack behind him. A couple wigs fell at his feet, but he didn't notice.

"Well?" I asked, stepping even closer. This was the first time I had invaded his space and it felt oddly invigorating.

He mumbled under his breath, looking at a loss for words.

"I didn't catch that," I said, running my finger up his arm. There was a special place in hell for me for messing with him, but I couldn't seem to stop myself.

He turned the tables on me when he placed his hands on my hips, stopping me from stepping closer. His hands resting intimately on the curves of my hips evoked a feeling of want that was so strong I wanted to crush myself against him. I wanted to feel those hands guiding me with a whole lot less clothing on.

"My only objection with that costume is being able to keep my hands off you. I'm trying to take things slow so I don't scare you off. If you wear this costume, you'll be fulfilling every fantasy I've ever had."

"Oh," I said, getting a taste of what he'd just felt. I stood contemplating what he'd admitted. He'd all but told me he fantasized about me. This should have jerked me to my senses, caused me to ease off, but it did neither of those things. If anything, his words made the desire I'd been holding back rise to a near boiling point that throbbed through me as completely as the bass had in my car earlier that day.

His eyes were on mine. I watched as they darkened and I could practically see my own reflected in them. Did he sense I was entertaining thoughts of jumping his bones? Did he know I was imagining what those hands would feel like elsewhere?

A voice squawked across a loudspeaker telling us that the store would be closing in fifteen minutes.

"So you have a thing for Princess Leia," I finally said, stepping back so I could control my hormones.

"I hate to break it to you, but half the male population had a thing for Princess Leia," he replied.

"Really?" I asked, adjusting the wig. "Why?"

"That costume, right there," he said, pointing to my selection. "The gold bikini from *Return of the Jedi*. She looked, you know, sexy."

"Oh, well, now I have to get it," I declared, heading for the registers. I was pretty sure I heard Trent mumble something about how I'd been warned. I smiled.

There was a small line at the register and I nearly groaned when I spotted Chuck standing two customers ahead of us. I was tempted to dump the Princess Leia costume and leave before he could spot me. He had tried to call me a couple times after his asinine behavior at the frat party. I only answered once and that was to tell him to stop calling me.

Trent pulled two suckers out of his pocket. "Tootsie Pop?"

Dragging my eyes from the back of Chuck's head, I snorted, eyeing the candy Trent was offering me. It reminded me that Chuck had never offered me anything when we were together.

"Thanks," I said, accepting the sucker as the line moved forward. Chuck placed a hockey mask on the counter and pulled out his wallet. I tried to maneuver my body so that Trent was blocking me from view as Chuck finished his purchase and turned to leave. I knew before he even said my name he had spotted me.

"Tressa? What are you doing here? Girl, are you done breaking my balls and ready to go out with me again?" He stepped to me, not giving Trent a thought.

I rolled my eyes, unsure what I had seen in the asshole. He was nothing but a party buddy, which was an aspect of my life I was glad to leave behind. "You're joking, right?" I asked as the line moved forward.

A hard look crossed his face and I turned away. Chuck was nothing but a blowhard.

My amusement disappeared when Trent stepped between us. I placed a hand on his shoulder, not relishing the idea of scraping him off the floor after Chuck was done pounding him.

Chuck looked like he wanted to say something else, but with a small audience of customers, he thought better of it.

"Whatever," he said, shaking his head as he walked out of the store.

I let out a pent up breath and turned to Trent, ready to tell him we had dodged a bullet. I was surprised to see he was looking at me incredulously.

"What?" I asked, placing my costume on the counter.

He shook his head. "You seemed relieved that your pal left without saying anything else."

"One, he's not my pal. Two, I'm relieved that he didn't accept your silent, but unnecessary challenge. He would have wiped the ground with you." I took my bag from the cashier and walked toward the exit.

"I'm insulted," Trent said, following me.

"Don't be. Chuck is a big lug. He'd put most guys on their asses," I said, climbing into the car.

Trent closed my door and walked around to his own side. "How do you know I can't take care of myself, especially when defending my woman?"

I raised my eyebrows. It was sweet that he was willing to stick up for me, but I wasn't crazy about him thinking I was his girl. I chose to ignore him as I buckled my seat belt.

"So, is that it?" I asked as he started the car and backed out of the parking space. Sure, the date was unconventional and didn't exactly feel like any of the dates I'd ever gone on, but until we ran into Chuck I had been having fun, which had been sadly lacking in most of my dates.

"You don't seriously think the date's over, do you? I'm not letting you off that easily. I haven't even fed you yet."

"I hate to break it to you, geeky, but you're not going to find any restaurants open this late unless you're thinking fast food," I said, pulling out my phone to show him the time.

"That works perfectly." He looked unconcerned, pulling out of the parking lot.

"Taco Bell?" I teased, trying to come up with places that were open late. I had plenty of after-party experience with that.

He shook his head.

"Wendy's?"

"No way, I hate that place," he said.

"What?" I asked, completely scandalized. "How can you hate Frosties? I think that's classified as un-American. They're perfect to dip french fries in."

"They're overrated. Give me a chocolate shake any day. Gross on the fry thing, though," he said, turning down several side streets that were lined with warehouses.

"No way. Fries dipped in ice cream should be added as a food category." I peered out the window as he slowed the vehicle down and turned into a gravel parking lot behind a nondescript building. The exterior paint of the building was peeling so badly that the industrial steel beneath it gleamed in the moonlight. It had definitely seen better years, like twenty or thirty years ago.

I would have thought I was in an episode of *Dexter* and Trent was leading me to a plastic-draped room if not for the relatively full parking lot.

"Ready for phase two of our date?"

15.

"We're eating here? I'm not much into rats and bugs," I quipped, climbing from the vehicle. I eyed the building with interest. I was definitely intrigued. I didn't know of any raves in this area of town. I was doubtful it was anything like that considering it was Trent who had brought me here.

I mentally ran through a list of things that could possibly be hiding beyond the double doors he was leading me to, but my brain was blank. He pushed the door open for me, guiding me into a dark hallway. Maybe this was a haunted house. My friends and I had gone to one near here last year. It was strange there were no signs, but I prepared myself for someone to jump out at me at any moment. The hallway was dimly lit by industrial-looking outdoor lights like you might find on a construction site. They were attached to the walls with S hooks and connected by heavy-duty cords.

My haunted house theory went out the window when we'd walked the entire length of the hallway without a zombie, ax murderer, or mummy jumping out at us. I was a little disappointed since a haunted house would have been pretty awesome in this building.

We reached the end of the hall and turned right to face a large wooden door that had a small peep slot. Trent knocked on the door twice before the little window opened and a very round face with a nose that looked like a squished tomato peered out at us.

"Password?"

"Oh lord," I muttered. This was going to be some nerd convention where they trade those idiotic cards that were so popular when we were thirteen.

"Very funny, Peewee," Trent said, shooting me a look of reassurance.

This was what I got for caving and agreeing to a date with a nerd. Our tastes ran down totally different rivers. Finally, the burly guy behind the door swung it open.

He reached out a hand that was as plump as his face. "Dude, is this your girlfriend?" He eyed me appreciatively.

"That's the plan," Trent answered. I didn't know where the authority in his voice came from, but it was a side I might like to see more of.

"He wishes," I answered, holding out my hand. "I'm Tressa."

"Trent and Tressa. The double Ts. That's cool." He chuckled at his reference. "I'm Peewee. Ironic, right? It's okay. You can make fun of my physique. I do."

A laugh tickled my throat. I liked this guy.

"Not cool, man," Trent said, walking around him.

"Hey, don't want to give the lady the wrong impression. You can head in. Your usual table is open." Peewee sank back on a stool, waving as we walked away.

"What is this place?" I followed alongside Trent as he pushed open another door. I was floored by the space we had just entered. We were in some kind of restaurant/jazz club judging by the bearded saxophone player who had just stepped out onto the small stage. It looked to be a factory that had been converted to a club, but still maintained a very industrial vibe. Tables that looked like they had been rescued from thrift stores and garage sales were scattered around, and no two chairs were the same throughout the entire place. The cool thing about the tables was that they were covered in old ticket stubs, concert flyers, and papers with handwritten notes, and were lacquered over for protection.

The well-dressed patrons who took up most of the tables clashed with the club's décor. By the looks of the place, I would have expected to see poor college kids who were too cheap to pay to get into one of the trendier places near campus.

Trent seemed at home as he weaved his way between the tightly packed tables before stopping near the front of the stage. The small round table was barely big enough for two people. I'd call it a little less than cozy, but definitely intimate. Our knees knocked together as I slid my chair under the table. He didn't scoot his chair back like I might have expected him to. Instead, he spread his legs apart slightly so one of my knees slid between his.

It was a bold move and erotic as hell. Where had this debonair person come from? It was as if the building had morphed him into someone else. Maybe calling him Clark Kent was appropriate and this was where he'd turn into Superman. Or maybe I'd already spent too much time with Trent and I was the one morphing into someone else. Like the Geek Queen.

"What is this place?" I asked again, examining the relics underneath the clear hardened surface of the table.

"It's called the Secret Club," he answered, returning a nod from a couple sitting two tables from us.

"Seriously?" It was so hokey I figured he had to be messing with me.

"I'm serious. It's one of the best-kept secrets on the East Coast."

"And they couldn't come up with a more obvious name than that?"

"I know, but you wouldn't believe some of the talented musicians, poets, and even writers who got their start here. The place is only open on Fridays and Saturdays. Saturday is for musicians and Fridays are for poets and writers. I'll bring you back for that sometime. It's a different crowd than this—more serious and very scholarly."

"They should have called it Club Irony. A secret club called the Secret Club with a big guy named Peewee watching the door, and now you want to bring *me* back to hang out with a bunch of scholars. It's almost too funny."

"Kudos for the observation, other than the last part about you. You need to give yourself more credit," he said, watching the saxophone player onstage.

Not fair. I was trying to find reasons why Trent and I wouldn't work, and he was not helping by giving me the best compliment any guy had ever given me.

"How come I've never heard of this place?"

He leaned in close since the music was too loud for real conversation. "As funny as the name is, they really do manage to keep it a secret. This is the sort of place you can't just show up to and hope to get in. Peewee's mom, Shirley, started this place back in the sixties. It's rumored she was friends with some of the greats in rock music. You name some of the legends and chances are they sat at these tables. It was supposed to be a kind of safe haven for them. They knew if they came here, fans wouldn't mob them and the press would never find out. To even perform here you have to sign a confidentiality statement. To get in you have to either know Shirley directly or have friends with connections."

"So how did someone like you find out about this place?" The question came out harsher than I'd intended. "I mean, what's your connection?"

He didn't look insulted by my question. "One of my professors last year is Shirley's brother. That's how some of his lit majors find out about the Friday performances."

"You're not a lit major," I said, still confused.

"No, Shirley needed my help with something else. I refused to accept money, so she told me to consider this place my second home."

"What kind of help did she need?"

"Computer issues. Hackers had gotten into her personal and business accounts. I set her up with firewalls and made sure she had virus protection," he said as a waitress approached the table carrying a tray with two plates loaded with burgers and fries and two glasses of water.

I looked slightly confused at the plates after she plunked them on our table. She smiled at Trent and shot me a territorial look before walking away.

"The kitchen only serves burgers and fries. Shirley always says that's what she likes to eat, so that's all she'll serve. I can get you something other than water if you want." He picked up his burger and took a big bite.

I eyed the food warily. I was as hungry as a rhino, but it was a little unsettling not knowing where it came from.

"You don't like burgers?"

"Is it safe?"

"Really? You eat Wendy's."

He had a point. I lifted the bun of my burger to get a better look. It looked good. I sniffed it before I took a tentative bite. It tasted as good as it looked. I hadn't eaten all day, so I scarfed the food down quicker than normal. I would have liked the water to be a beer, but I didn't want to ask if he wasn't having one.

"Told you it was good," Trent teased once our plates were carried away. The conversation during our meal was surprisingly smooth. Maybe it was because we'd been together so much during tutoring. Whatever the reason, it wasn't as awkward as I'd imagined it would be. First dates were usually so hit-or-miss. Most times, the guy was a total freak show or an egomaniac. I could already tell Trent was different. He was smart, but didn't make me feel like an idiot. And the stuff he was into was harmless. It didn't make him a freak. I couldn't believe I was sitting here defending Trent to myself.

"So, you're telling me what you did for this Shirley woman was worth getting an all-access pass to all of this?" I asked, leaning back in my chair. The live music throughout our meal had changed genres multiple times. The sax player was replaced by a country singer whose guitar twanged as he sang about beer, horses, and no-good, cheating women. My favorite performer of the evening was an a cappella singer. I'd never heard anyone hit a high note like this guy. His performance had all the diners pausing midbite.

Trent shrugged modestly at my words. "A computer nerd who likes live music. I guess that makes you more cultured than me," I teased.

He retaliated by gently squeezing my knee between his. He leaned in close. "Face it, Tressa, you're beginning to find me pretty irresistible. You're kicking yourself for not giving me a chance before."

"Oh, I'm going to kick something. It just won't be me," I said, hitting him on the side of the leg with my free foot.

"Come on, why fight it? Can you honestly say tonight hasn't been fun?"

"It's been okay."

"Bullshit, you've had fun."

"Fine, I had fun. It's probably a fluke."

"Go out with me again and I'll prove it to you," he persisted.

I weighed his words before answering. It would be so easy to shoot him down and keep insisting we were too different for each other, but hell, my denial was even beginning to get on my nerves. What harm would it do to cave? If it didn't work, we could walk away. No harm, no foul. It's not like I was looking for some permanent thing.

"Fine," I finally answered. I bit the inside of my mouth to keep from laughing as he did a fist pump. You could dress up the geek, but you couldn't take the dork out of him.

"Halloween festival next week?" he asked, not missing a beat.

Holy hell. I'd decided to go out with him, but I wasn't ready to go all balls-to-the-wall, batshit crazy and show up in Woodfalls like we were a couple.

"Come on, you know we'll have fun. I'll go as Han Solo." His words brought a mental image to mind that took fantasy to a whole new level.

"What makes you think I'd like you to dress up as Han Solo? He was pretty buff and all," I teased.

"Trust me, I think you'll like the uniform."

"Are you telling me you already have the costume?" I wasn't sure if I should laugh or be horrified.

His look said it all. Oh lord. Was I really agreeing to go out with someone who liked to play dress-up? I couldn't even imagine what Cameo would say if she heard this little tidbit considering we'd totally mocked the loser who wanted to role-play with her in the bedroom. The funny thing was my disgust alarm wasn't going off. Truthfully, I found it a little cute. Not that I'd ever admit it to anyone. Least of all to Trent.

"Fine." I couldn't believe I had agreed, but it would satisfy my curiosity to see if he could really fill out the costume. Besides, agreeing to a second date would quiet my friends for good. They would never get to say that I didn't at least give Trent plenty of chances.

We stopped talking when an elderly woman stepped between the red velvet curtains on the small stage. She was dressed in jeans that looked like they'd been washed just enough times to make them fit exactly right. She wore a black rock band T-shirt advertising a tour that ended like thirty years ago. Her forearms were covered in tattoos, and her hair hung to the middle of her back in a curtain of gray. She had to be close to sixty I would think, but she was a classic definition of the old saying that age is only a number. She looked totally badass. She was definitely someone I could hang with.

"Shirley, I guess?" I asked Trent.

"That's her."

Her eyes scanned the crowd as she nodded or waved to

those she knew, which seemed to be pretty much everyone. When her eyes landed on our table, they swept over me. I felt I must have passed her examination when she winked at Trent before speaking into the microphone.

"Thank you, everyone, for coming out for another Saturday jam fest. The last group tonight is one we've all come to love. It's a bittersweet moment to have them on our stage one last time before they start their tour with their brand-new record label." She beamed with pride before continuing. "Put your hands together to welcome Die Hard to the stage one last time." The other patrons erupted into cheers.

Trent leaned in close so I could hear him. "Die Hard got their start performing here. They all go to MSC and were discovered by one of the big record labels."

I nodded my head. "That's awesome." I loved music and was pretty psyched to be watching a live show of a band that might hit it big. I thought it had to be a joke, though, when they walked out onstage. They were a group of five who looked like they had just time traveled from the nineteen twenties. There were three guys wearing button-up shirts with bow ties and baggy wide-legged trousers. The pants had no belt loops, so they wore suspenders, and they each wore matching oxford shoes. Two girls wore calf-length dresses that swished around when they moved, with old-fashioned boots that laced up to their ankles. Thick stockings peeked out in the small amount of space between where the dresses ended and the tops of their boots began.

I looked at Trent, wondering if their act was a parody or something to that effect. He merely grinned at me.

The group did a quick bow at the applause of greeting before picking up their instruments. All my doubts evaporated as they began playing. Their sound was alternative and sharp. The voices of the two lead singers were hypnotic. They melded together in a harmonious duet that made your heart clench with ache and indescribable wanting. The set shifted seamlessly from a ballad to hard-core rock that had all of us clapping and surging to our feet as one. My inner party girl roared to life as I moved to the music. I had missed this. Music had always been a big part of my life. It greeted me like an old friend.

I turned to Trent, wanting to share my excitement with him, but found him sitting in his chair, looking more uncomfortable than he had all night. "What's wrong?" I called out over the loud music.

He shook his head, indicating that I should keep dancing.

I moved closer to him, sensing the issue. "You don't know how to dance?" I asked, trying to keep the surprise out of my voice.

He shook his head and pushed his glasses back up on his nose. Reaching a hand down, I hauled him to his feet. "It's easy. You just have to let the music tell you what to do," I said loudly into his ear.

I placed my hands on his hips so I could guide them to the beat of the music. He watched as I moved effortlessly to the rhythmic music. His body was stiff in my hands, much like a robot that wasn't built to move certain ways. I grabbed his hands and placed them on my hips so he could get a feel of the movement. The intimacy of the action caught me by surprise. My eyes moved up to his. I watched as they darkened to a blue that matched the sky right before a storm moved in. Unconsciously, I swayed closer to him. My hands seemed to move up to his shoulders on their own. His hands clenched my hips, dragging me closer to him. I zeroed in on his full lips with a mental image of them trailing over my body.

I took a step back before I did something stupid like stick my tongue down his throat like I was dying to do. Trent prevented my retreat. His hands held me firmly in place as he closed the gap between us. "This dancing thing isn't all that bad," he said, pulling my body flush against his. The stiff robotic movements from moments ago were gone.

"This isn't dancing," I said, trying to control my breath.

"That's why I like it," he whispered in my ear. His left hand moved up to the nape of my neck and he began gently caressing my earlobes with his fingertips. I could feel my body responding to his touch as the heat of desire filled me.

His lips moved slowly toward mine as the music and the crowd around us seemed to fade away. We were hitting the point of no return. His puppy-love crush on me would be even harder to sideline, but I didn't care.

His lips met mine tentatively. They were unyielding and almost cold. Disappointment coursed through me from the lack of spark between us. I should have been happy. This justified everything I'd been trying to say. I could have pulled away. I should have, but the stubborn person inside me wouldn't allow it. "Is that really the best you got, Geek Boy?" I mocked. I used the tip of my tongue to tease his lips open. They parted, letting my tongue sweep in. His hand tightened on the back of my neck and he moaned against my mouth.Holy-set-my-panties-on-fire, his moan was my undoing. My tongue boldly stroked against his, teaching him how sensual a good kiss could be. He was a quick study, and it was my turn to moan as his own tongue tangled with mine. The lips that just moments ago had been unyielding crushed against mine. They devoured me.

We parted as the music around us glided to its final notes. Trent looked at me with a combination of disbelief and lust. I would be lying if I said I wasn't quaking with the same feelings. That had to be the best dare and payoff to a bet I had ever experienced. I couldn't help thinking of a few other things I would like to teach him, only they would require a horizontal position.

16.

Once Die Hard left the stage, Shirley came over to chat with Trent and me while the club began to clear out. Several people stopped at our table to thank Shirley for another great evening. One guy in particular came over and I swore he was someone famous, but I couldn't put my finger on it. Only after Shirley teased him about dragging himself out of his writing cave did the light bulb explode in my head.

Holy shit, I mouthed to Trent. "Stephen effing K—" Trent grabbed my hand and nodded quickly before I could embarrass myself. Shirley and you-know-who exchanged pleasantries before he walked away and she turned her attention back to Trent and me.

We chatted for several minutes. It didn't take an Einstein to figure out she was fond of Trent. She all but threatened that I better treat her boy right, which, by the way, sounded even more intimidating than she probably meant because of her raspy voice. I wasn't offended. It was sweet that she was so protective of him.

After reassuring her I'd toe the line with him, she hugged us both and we headed out. The drive to my apartment passed with Trent filling me in on everything he knew about Shirley. Talk about someone who lived her life to the fullest. Her stories and the things she'd witnessed could have filled several books. It was admirable, and I hoped I could say the same thing about my life someday. My worst fear was that I'd grow up and have nothing that ever amounted to anything. Deep down, I think that's why I submersed myself into the party atmosphere. If nothing else, I'd have some great stories to tell when I got older. Now reflecting back on the evening we'd just had, I never would have imagined a date with Trent would eclipse the memories of any party I'd ever been to.

Trent pulled into the parking lot of my apartment complex and climbed from the vehicle to walk me to my door. We walked in silence up the three flights of stairs. I tossed around the idea of inviting him to stay the night until I remembered I was sharing a room with Derek. It was probably for the best anyway. Our kiss may have left me wanting to climb him like a monkey, but I wasn't ready to fall into bed with him. Yet.

That didn't mean I wasn't seriously anticipating kissing him again, along with a few other things I'd like to show him. If we were lucky, Derek and Cameo would be out and we'd at least have the apartment to ourselves.

"You want to come inside?" I asked when we arrived at my door.

"Oh, uh, I have to go. Thanks, though," he answered, shocking the hell out of me. He claimed he had to finish working on a few things before meeting with Professor Nelson in the morning. With a squeeze of my hand, he was gone. Not a kiss. Not even one of those awkward ass-sticking-out-behind-you arm hugs, like you're afraid you might catch a disease if you get too close. No, I got a flipping hand squeeze. I was surprised he didn't pat me on the head.

I walked into my apartment grumbling under my breath and contemplating how I'd rip the heads off all his action figures the next time I was in his apartment. A little extreme maybe, but damn it, he'd left me as horny as a dog in heat. The only satisfaction I had now was in hoping he'd suffer the rest of the night with a serious case of blue balls.

As luck would have it, I didn't get a chance to behead any of his action figures like I'd wanted to. I spent Sunday morning working on my business project before I had to go to work. Trent and I were supposed to have another tutoring session on Monday, but he texted me saying he would be tied up all day at the lab. I got a similar text on Tuesday, which had me suspecting something was up. By Wednesday, I'd received the last form-letter text I was going to get this week. Rather than replying via text, I marched down to the science building to give him a piece of my mind.

The day was blustery as I walked across the campus. I paused beside a giant oak tree so it would buffer the wind while I buttoned up my jacket and wrapped my scarf more securely around my neck. My eyes watered from the cold wind that whipped around my face, but I didn't mind. I was fuming at the moment. I loved watching the leftover leaves that had fallen to the ground swirl around my feet as I walked. Those that weren't airborne crunched pleasantly under my boots. Ashton may get the sunshiny days all year long in Florida, but she didn't get to hear fall leaves crunching under her feet. She would be green with envy when I bragged about it next time I called her.

The science building was bustling with students when I arrived. I could practically feel my IQ quaking as I walked through the buzzing hallways. Just like math, science and technology weren't my strong suits either. My iPhone and iPad were about as tech savvy as I got. Thankfully, I had been smart enough to take my required science classes at community college before I transferred to MSC, saving me from embarrassing myself in this building.

I managed to find the lab where Trent was working without having my brain melted from some experimental laser, or without catching some disease from whatever they might be growing in the biology labs. These were just some of the things I imagined went on in this building. Trent was bent over a computer when I peered through the glass in the door. Actually, he was surrounded by five computers, along with several other electronic gizmos I didn't recognize. I pushed open the door to the lab and approached his workstation. It took him several minutes to realize I was there. Only when I coughed did he look up from the computer.

He looked at me startled and slightly confused. "Hey, didn't you get my text?"

"Yeah. I was just checking to make sure you weren't being held hostage or anything," I said, feeling like a complete ass for coming all the way across campus. It was obvious he really was busy.

"I wish." He scratched his head in aggravation. My eyes focused on his hair. One of these days I should tell him what a difference it made when his hair was messed up a little.

"Can I help?" I asked before I could even think about the words. I couldn't believe I'd really just volunteered for something that was sure to make my brain hurt. At least I was secure in the fact that he would turn down my offer.

"Really?" he asked enthusiastically. "You don't mind?"

Damn, let this be a lesson. "You actually have something *I* could help with?"

"Yes! I need a test study. I was using some freshmen earlier, but they had to leave."

"Of course they did. What do you need me to do?" I asked suspiciously. I didn't want something like electrodes hooked to my body or some metal contraption stuck on my head like in old science-fiction movies. He went into a long-winded explanation while I unbuttoned my jacket and draped it over one of the hard plastic chairs. Basically, he needed me to answer several questions while he added the data into the program he was working on.

"What exactly are you hoping to achieve with this?" I asked, wheeling over the heavily padded chair that sat behind a desk at the front of the room.

"It's going to be an app that will revolutionize the way users access everything they do on their smartphones or tablets. It will be an interactive application that will learn likes and dislikes and will change the way people use their devices." He sounded as excited as if Batman himself had swooped in and asked him to be the next Robin. Don't ask me how I knew that reference. Let's just say his enthusiasm was inspiring. I wished there was something I felt as passionate about, other than partying anyway.

His excitement was contagious, and soon I was peering over his shoulder as he entered my information into the computer. After fifty random questions, the program was able to suggest movies I would like to see and music that matched my tastes. The amazing part was that much of the music his program suggested I already had on my iPhone. It was pretty remarkable. Beyond the music and movies, the app suggested books and even pinpointed places on a map that I might want to visit. By clicking the site on the map, the program would provide information about the location and the surrounding area.

The afternoon melted away as Trent continued to navigate through the system, showing me its full potential. Only when my stomach began to growl did I remember I had forgotten to eat anything for lunch.

"Hungry?" he laughed.

"Nah, my stomach makes that noise when it's full."

"Fine, smart-ass. I was going to offer to buy you pizza, but if you're not hungry . . ."

"I'm not ready to go," I pouted, mad at my stomach for ruining my fun.

He laughed. "And you said you weren't a techie person."

"This isn't techie. It's cool like my iPhone or iPad."

"It's all cool. Everything on your iPhone started out just like this. See, you love techie stuff and didn't realize it. Here, have one of these while we wait for the pizza to get here," he said, handing me one of his Tootsie Pops.

"Do you have a red one?"

"Beggars can't be choosers," he said, reaching into his bag and pulling out a red lollipop. "Here."

I grinned at him. "Does this mean we're going steady?"

He blushed as he slowly unwrapped his sucker. I had to bite the inside of my mouth to keep from laughing out loud. He really was cute. An easy target, but cute.

"I was kidding, slick." I finally laughed. The laughter died in my throat as he looked up at me. His eyes moved to my mouth.

"I'd like to kiss you again," he said. It was like he was reading my mind. It was funny how he could get so easily embarrassed over some of my teasing, and yet still be so blunt about wanting to kiss me. My heart raced at his words. His declaration was made. It wasn't like he was asking permission, but rather telling me his intention. He pulled the armrests of my chair, wheeling me closer.

"Then do it," I dared him.

"You're awfully bossy," he said, maneuvering my chair so my legs were straddling his.

I shrugged my shoulders. I could own it. "Are you going to keep stalling?"

"I'm building the moment." His hand moved intimately to my side, sliding between the chair and my back.

"You're a cocky son of a bitch," I muttered. I thought about turning the tables on him to show him who was really the boss here.

He smiled at my words. "I've been giving a lot of thought to our first kiss. I'm not sure I gave the right impression."

"Really?" I asked, raising my eyebrows. "You mean you think you can do better?"

"I know I can." He slid his free hand under my right leg so it draped over his thigh. My chair rolled the last few inches until it rested against his. The sensation of his hand on my thigh made me want to slide my hips forward, allowing him access to the traitorous part of me that was already damp from arousal.

A second later, he crushed his lips to mine. I could tell instantly he'd learned under my guidance from our last kiss. His lips were soft but insistent as he took control. He made the first move with his tongue, gently nudging my mouth open. My hands moved to his chest as his tongue swept into my mouth, teasing and tantalizing my senses. My fist clenched his shirt as I dragged him closer to me. He lifted my other leg and pulled me so that I was straddling his lap. I could feel his erection against me. I shifted against him, trying to ease the ache between my legs. Just rubbing against him was enough to bring me to the edge of the big O.

He pulled his mouth from mine. "Wait," he said, noticeably adjusting his crotch.

"What's the matter?" I asked, suspecting I wasn't the only one close to finishing. "It's cool if you—you know." I didn't want to embarrass him.

"What? No, it's not that. I was just going to ask how I was doing."

"Oh, sorry," I laughed.

"That's not exactly the reaction I was going for," he said.

"No, I'm not laughing at you. I mean, I thought you had, you know," I said, indicating the still-evident bulge between his legs. "You just caught me off guard because I've never had anyone stop and ask how it was going. All right—and this is in all seriousness—did you load up on porn since the last time we kissed?" I teased.

A vibrant shade of red crept up his neck.

"You really did? Well, hot damn," I laughed.

He made a move to scoot his chair away until I locked my legs around his waist.

"Hey, don't be embarrassed. I find it cute," I said.

"It wasn't porn. I just watched a couple movies to see where I could improve."

My hand moved up to his cheek, which was still flushed with warmth. "Obviously you're a quick learner."

He looked at me skeptically. "Right," he finally said, waiting for the punch line.

"Believe me, I don't joke around when it comes to this. Besides, what better way to improve than to practice," I said, pulling him toward me. I wanted to pick up where we'd left off, but the rattling of the doorknob had us both scrambling backward like horny teenagers. He shoved at my chair, trying to put distance between us. I had to reach for the table to keep my balance as the chair threatened to topple over.

"Tressa, this is a surprise," Professor Nelson's voice boomed from behind me. I swiped a hand over my lips, wondering if they looked like they'd just been devoured.

"Professor N," I greeted him, pivoting my chair around so I could face him.

Trent cleared his throat while he adjusted his clothes. "Tressa has been helping me out by graciously agreeing to answer some questions for more data. I think we might have worked it out."

Professor N clapped his hands with glee. "Excellent, my boy, excellent. What do you think of young Trent's creation?" He wedged himself between the two of us so he could peer at the computer screen.

I winked at Trent over Professor N's head, grinning with pleasure as he flushed slightly. He might have studied up on kissing tips, but he was still easy to mess with. I pulled out my phone to order the pizza when the two of them started chattering away about another bug in the program that needed to be fixed. Once they started talking gigabytes and megabytes, my eyes glazed over with boredom.

They paused long enough to suck down the pizza once it arrived and the drinks I retrieved from the mini fridge in Professor N's office. I stayed long enough to eat with them, but when it became clear they were going to be working for quite a while longer, I headed out. Neither of them paid much attention to me as I left. They threw an absentminded good-bye my way as I walked out.

As I made the walk down the long corridor of the science building, I couldn't help feeling pissed and a little hurt at being ignored so completely. Add computer programs to the list of sports, other girls, or any other thing guys had dissed me for in the past. Feeling disgruntled, I contemplated that maybe my issues with men had everything to do with me and not them. Maybe I just wasn't interesting enough to hold a guy's attention.

I was pushing the door of the science building open when my phone dinged, alerting me to a text. Pulling my phone from my pocket, I read the message.

You forgot your Tootsie Pop.

I'm surprised you noticed.

I notice everything you do. Sorry about the interruption. Hopefully we can get this done by tomorrow.

Right. You can't deny you're in geek heaven.

This stuff is cool, but it's not my idea of heaven. That would require you.

I grinned like a mega cheesehead over his comment.

And what would your idea of heaven be?

Just put it this way: It doesn't involve Professor Nelson. I gotta go, though. I'll text later.

Fine. Have fun playing with Professor N and his toys.

Not funny.

TTYL

Trent ended up calling me late Thursday night. He apologized for not calling me sooner. He sounded exhausted but gleeful. I asked him if they killed all the bugs, which only confused him. He laughed, but I could tell his brain was not open for business. I instructed him to get some rest and told him I would see him the next day.

Smiling, I plugged my phone into the charger next to my bed.

Derek laid the book he'd been reading on his chest and looked at me. "Seems like you and Dreamy are getting along well."

I shrugged my shoulders, acting indifferent. "He's not as

bad as I thought. It's different going out with someone who is hung up on me. I'm sure soon enough he'll find out his illusions of me were distorted and then he'll probably drop me on my fat ass."

"Don't be a jerk. You're not fat. If he's hung up on you, it's because he realizes how fabulous you are."

"Right," I snorted. "We all know what a catch I am." My words were filled with sarcasm.

He shook his head. "Just because he treats you with respect and not like a doormat doesn't mean all those other douchecanoes were right. He's obviously smart enough to know what a catch you are."

I shrugged. Why argue? I knew my flaws and weaknesses, and if Trent could look past those, who was I to argue? "I guess if Leonard can date Penny, who am I to argue with whatever is going on between Trent and me? Or should I say Sheldon?" I joked, referencing our favorite TV show.

Derek chuckled. "Just ask Adam, right? He was way off, though. Sheldon on the show is nowhere near as dreamy as your Clark Trent."

I smirked. He definitely had a point.

17.

The next evening Trent arrived to pick me up for the Halloween festival in Woodfalls, and Derek's words from the night before couldn't have been truer. Trent had delivered on his promise and came dressed as Han Solo, a sexy-as-hell Han Solo. All I could do was gape. I wanted to use my own version of the Force on him.

"Damn." He whistled, reminding me he wasn't the only one in a sexy costume.

I grinned wickedly, happy I wasn't the only one turned on by a few scraps of material. "You like?" I sashayed around so he could get a full look at the barely there gold outfit. My midriff and back were both bare, and I had to admit, if nothing else, I most definitely had the chest to stand out in a crowd in this costume. Luckily for me, the Woodfalls Halloween festival was an indoor/outdoor kind of affair; otherwise, my heavy wool jacket would have hidden the best part of my Princess Leia costume.

Trent cleared his throat before answering, which earned a very non-Tressa-like kind of schoolgirl giggle. It was a heady experience to be looked at the way he was staring at me. "You look hot," he finally spit out.

"You don't look too shabby yourself. I have to admit, I had my doubts when you said you already had a Han Solo costume, but it's awesome."

"Told you," he said proudly, smoothing a hand down the front of his shirt.

I heard a familiar snort of laughter behind me. "What's so funny, chuckleheads?" Turning around, I spotted Derek and Cameo looking overly amused at my expense.

"No, it's not funny," Cameo said, trying to suppress her laughter. "I mean, you two definitely look—"

My aggravation level began to rise. "*Good* is the word you're searching for."

"She's just teasing," Derek said, pushing Cameo into her room. "You look hot. That's a pretty extravagant costume, Trent. You actually got that from one of those Halloween stores?"

"Nope. I bought this sucker for Comic-Con a couple years ago."

"Don't forget to use protection for your lightsaber," Cameo called out from her room, causing Derek to bust out laughing.

"Actually, Han Solo doesn't have a lightsaber. He's not a

Jedi," Trent replied, looking oblivious to the razzing he was receiving.

"We're out of here," I mumbled, grabbing my coat and purse. Taking Trent by the wrist, I tugged him toward the door before my roommates could say anything more that would cause me to do something I would regret.

"Tress, don't be mad. We're just goofing around. You guys seriously have fun," Derek said.

"You guys can suck it," I replied, slamming the door behind us. Sure, I liked to poke fun at Trent, but it didn't mean I was going to stand by and let him be the butt of my friends' jokes.

I stomped down the hallway and was halfway down the first flight of stairs before Trent spoke.

"Hey, where's the fire?" He lengthened his steps to keep up with me.

I glared at him, which he responded to with the same clueless look he always had. Why he was so oblivious to the world around him I didn't know, but he was seriously turning me into a two-faced twat. Anytime I was around him, my inner protective demon seemed to pop up. Well, protective from everyone other than me, considering at the moment I wanted to push him down the last remaining flight of stairs to make my point. Either that or hurl myself down the stairs.

By the time we reached the bottom step, I had gotten to the point that I was regretting even going to the festival with him. I could come up with some lame excuse and save us both some aggravation.

Trent halted at the first-floor landing and grasped my wrist loosely, but didn't say anything as I turned around. As clueless as I thought he was, he could tell when I was upset. Of course, I wasn't exactly a closed book when it came to expressing myself.

"I don't need you to fight my battles," he said quietly, sliding his hands inside my jacket, which was gaping open since I had pulled us out of the apartment in a rush. His warm hands slid intimately across my exposed midriff, leaving me breathless.

He tugged me in close, keeping his hands firmly hooked around my waist. "You make yourself an easy target," I muttered.

"Tressa, I am what I am. You don't have to apologize for me. Do you think I care what everyone thinks?"

"I care," I replied. My words were sharper than I'd intended.

He tugged me against his body. "Why?"

His closeness was so distracting I could barely string together coherent thoughts. It was like getting wasted at a party, but without all the side effects. The subtle hint of his cologne combined with the smell of orange Tootsie Pop, which had recently become so familiar, filled my nose.

"Why do you care?" he repeated, rubbing my back. His touch was sure and confident.

I wanted to tell him the reason, but up until this very second, I wasn't sure I wanted to believe it myself. I had been working so hard the past couple of weeks at denying my true feelings, even blaming Trent for my own hang-ups and insecurities. If I admitted now how I felt, I would be giving someone else control. "I care because I'm starting to like you, dumb-ass," I snapped. My admission was a leap of faith against my better judgment.

He smiled and the urge to punch it off his face was so strong I clenched my fist. "I like you too," he said smugly.

"No shit, Sherlock. We all know that. The issue is that *me*—Tressa the Party Girl—likes *you*." I pointed at him dramatically.

"Whoa, let me step out of the way to make room for your ego."

"It's not my ego I'm worried about, it's you. I told you from the beginning, we're so different. You're a genius and I'm, well, me. Eventually you'll realize I'm not good enough for you, and shame on me for letting you do that to me," I said, out of breath. I had nothing left to hide.

"Wow. First you insist that we are too different to be together. Then you admit you like me, and now you already know how the relationship—which hasn't really started yet—is going to end. Talk about a spoiler alert," he said, trying to make me laugh.

"It's not funny. I'm just trying to give you a chance to get away," I said, hitting him in the arm.

"Tressa, remember the speech you gave me about emotions? Well, I get that, but please listen this time, and trust me. Forget about your emotions, just for once, and focus on two facts: I like you and you like me. Plain and simple."

Here I'd made up my mind that he was a nerd-brained nitwit who knew nothing beyond what was on a computer screen, and what he just said about us made more sense than any of my preconceived notions. So what if we liked each other? If someone didn't like it, they could take a flying leap into mind-your-own-damn-business. Great, I had been taught a lesson in love from a robot. We were like an effing Lifetime movie—*The Party Girl and the Geek*. Tune in to see if the party girl can teach the geek to let loose.

"*Like*? You make it sound like we're ten years old," I joked. "This isn't grade school. We're not going to slip each other notes and chase each other around the slide and kiss under the monkey bars."

"You were kissing under the monkey bars when you were ten? Damn, I went to the wrong elementary school." His eyes sparkled with mirth.

"That's not the only thing I was doing under the monkey bars," I said, smashing my lips aggressively against his. I could tell he was shocked by my boldness when his hands slackened around my waist. Deciding to go big or go home, I slid my fingers through his hair, pulling him tightly against me. Just because I'd admitted I liked him didn't mean I wasn't still me. I had my ways of keeping the control in my favor.

I pulled back as abruptly as I had thrown myself at him. "Let's do this."

"Uh, do what?" His grip around me tightened.

I smirked. "Festival."

"Oh, right. I knew that's what you meant."

I reached up to pat his cheek. "Get your mind out of the gutter, big boy."

He dropped his hands from my waist abruptly, like I was electrified and had shocked him. He was pretty cute when he looked like a kid who had gotten caught with his hand in the cookie jar.

"Come on," I said, lacing my fingers through his. "It's time I show you how to corrupt a small town."

"Can you corrupt something more than once?" he taunted, opening my car door for me. Score another point for him. I'd always loved that move from a guy.

"I have so much to teach you about the Tressa handbook."

During the drive to Woodfalls, Trent asked about my group project that had been turned in today. I was feeling more confident about our chances for a decent grade ever since Trent offered his input. Once I got the other lunkheads in the group to see reason, we were able to work through our differences. If we scored well enough on the project, I could bring my grade in the class up to a low B. I was close to getting all my grades back to a respectable level. The professor in my Microsoft applications class had reopened all my missing assignments, and with all my free time lately, I had raised my grade to an A, which was a first for me. My statistics grade was still in the toilet, but once I made up the section-two exam, it should at least be a C. I owed it all to Trent, and made sure to tell him so. He took the praise modestly, giving me credit for my hard work.

The conversation moved from my classes to his thesis project. Now that I had a better understanding of what he was doing, I felt I could hold my own in the conversation and even sound halfway intelligent.

The forty-five-minute ride to Woodfalls flew by and before

I knew it, we were driving past the familiar *Welcome to Woodfalls* sign. Usually the drive home seemed endless. Being an antsy kind of person made riding in cars one of my least favorite pastimes. I always ended up dwelling on everything I could be doing if I wasn't cooped up in a vehicle. Driving with Trent kept the ants in my pants at bay.

Despite my previous love affair with partying and living on campus, Woodfalls was still my home. My heart always felt pangs of warmth anytime I was away for too long. Once I graduated, my plan was to come home to work with Dad at his law firm.

His receptionist/business manager, Lola, wanted to retire soon, and in the grand scheme of things, it was assumed I'd take over for her. I had no interest in law, but I'd always enjoyed working in his office during the summer. In eight months, I would take over for her completely. Brittni was afraid I was giving up my life for my family, but she'd never understood the closeness I shared with them. She and her mom had only just recently forged a close relationship. What she couldn't understand was that I didn't find working for my dad a hardship. Going away to MSC was my opportunity to be wild. Woodfalls would always be my home.

I gazed out my window as Trent drove slowly through downtown Woodfalls. Main Street was decorated as it was every year. The bakery had its cupcake display in the shape of a giant jack-o'-lantern, and Trent's grandfather's hardware store had its usual fake Freddy Krueger standing in the window. Years ago, he had replaced the finger knives for long nails from his store. Dad's office had its typical haystacks and scarecrows in front of the main atrium.

Fran's general store was always my favorite with its display of carved pumpkins. Fran carved a different pumpkin for each of the thirteen days leading up to Halloween. They were all very intricate. I could study them for hours.

Trent pulled into the dirt lot behind the general store. "I figured this is the most central location for the festival."

I nodded, climbing from the vehicle. A breeze blew through the large trees that grew in abundance throughout Woodfalls. I sniffed appreciatively, buttoning my jacket to ward off the cold temperatures. Woodfalls in the fall had a distinct smell. It was a combination of sawdust from the mill, woodsmoke from Penny's restaurant, hay from the big pumpkin patch at the Baptist church, and pumpkin from the endless array of carved jack-o'-lanterns around the town square.

"Tressa, where you been hiding?" Fran chastised me, stepping out of her store. She reached a hand back inside and flipped off the lights before closing the door behind her. "You too good for us country folk?" She drawled her words for emphasis.

"You got me. Now that I've been to the city, I'm too sophisticated for you simple folk." I laughed when she swiped at my arm.

"Don't be sassy, little miss. I'll put you to work scraping siding like I did when you were younger and you got busted putting firecrackers in my pumpkins."

Trent turned to look at me. "You did that?"

"I plead the Sixth," I answered, cracking a smile. Who

knew the pumpkins would blow up so spectacularly? I paid for it by scrubbing dried pumpkin guts off the front of the store for three days. The windows alone took two days to squeegee clean. It was tedious work and definitely taught me a lesson. If I was going to blow up pumpkins, it was wise to be away from the building, or at least make sure I was nowhere near the prying eyes of adults.

"I think you mean the Fifth," Trent corrected me. Fran laughed while I glared at him.

"Whatever. I plead that."

Fran looked at us appraisingly. "I didn't know you two were hooking up."

Trent turned away, but I laughed. Fran might be the only woman her age that used the term "hooking up." If I didn't know any better, I could have sworn on a stack of Bibles that she was my biological mom. She had my foul mouth and sassy attitude. I'd gravitated toward her when I was much younger, sensing a kindred spirit. Mom tried to curb my fascination with Fran when I was eight because she thought my colorful language came from hanging around Fran's store too much. It was no use, though. Fran and I were thick as thieves. Even when I was pranking her customers, she still kept me around.

"Trent is tutoring me," I replied, winking at Fran.

She cackled at my words. "Is that the new word for it? In that case, I remember tutoring when I was younger. My lips saw more action than my schoolbooks."

"Fran, you dirty dog. I knew you were a tramp."

"Watch your mouth, missy, or I'll be washing it out."

I snorted. She was a fine one to talk. "I learned from the master," I teased.

"I have no idea what you're referring to. I'm nothing but a poor old lonely woman." She looked at us innocently, but her eyes sparkled with mischief.

"My ass. What about Mr. James and his afternoon visits?" I said, looping my arm through hers.

"Bite your tongue. One thing you still need to learn, my dear, is that a lady never talks, especially when his kin is standing less than two feet away," she said, laughing at Trent, who looked like he wanted to be anywhere else.

"You were just trying to pry into my love life and now you want to hold back on your own dirty deets? How fair is that?"

"Honey, when you're as old as I am, you don't care about being fair."

"Obviously not," I laughed, rolling my eyes. "Now, tell me everything that's been going on. I feel like I've missed a whole season of my favorite show being away from here."

Fran needed no further prompting as we walked toward the town square. She launched into a full-scale account of everything that had been going on in the last few months while I'd been away at school. Trent trailed behind us silently. By the time we got to the square in front of the small city hall building, I felt like I'd been caught up on all the melodramas.

"Who's Mayor Fedderman dressed up like this year?" I asked, searching the crowd.

"Oh, I can't say. I wouldn't want to ruin the surprise. Just put it this way: You young people won't be disappointed."

Trent, who had been silent during the short walk, finally piped in. "It can't be any better than last year when he dressed up like Cleopatra."

"Oh, honey darlin', it makes Cleopatra look tame."

Trent and I exchanged a look. Mayor Fedderman's costumes were legendary. Much to the dismay of his wife of twenty-five years, Edith, Mayor Fedderman chose to dress up like a famous woman every year. Besides Cleopatra, some of his other memorable years included Jackie Kennedy, Amelia Earhart, and Oprah Winfrey.

The town square was crowded with festival booths that ranged from food stands to arts and crafts for sale. The Woodfalls annual Halloween festival was legendary and drew crowds from several counties. Woodfalls used it as a way to fund school functions for the entire year. That's why everyone in the community got behind it. During my senior year in high school, the festival raised enough money to send us to Washington, DC, for our senior trip.

Fran ditched us when she spotted Mr. James across the courtyard.

Her absence left an awkward gap between Trent and me for some reason. Maybe it was the knowing stares we were getting from the other residents. I knew I was going to have to eat crow when I showed up with Trent beside me. As much as I loved Woodfalls, 99.9 percent of the residents were total gossip whores. I felt a moment of panic. Was I really ready to admit to everyone I'd known all my life that I was dating the one guy I swore I'd never date? "You want to go say hi to your granddad?"

"I'll see him around. Besides, him and Fran flirting is not something I need a front-row seat for," he said, shuddering.

"Oh come on. It's sweet. Besides, old people can get nasty too."

"La-la-la-la. I'm not listening to you," he chanted, covering his ears with his hands.

I could barely talk from laughing so hard. "I bet she knows just what he likes," I said, yanking at his arms.

"Gah, stop it. That's so not cool."

More and more people stopped in the middle of their conversations and activities to stare at us. In a matter of minutes, we would be the talk of the entire festival. Maybe if I put a little space between us, everyone would think Trent and I had just run into each other.

Trent laced his fingers through mine, claiming ownership of our new relationship. So much for my plan. I guessed there was nothing I could do except follow along.

Trying to ignore the whispers and stares, I dragged Trent over to the long row of food tents on the east side of the square. My mouth started watering as I breathed in the aroma of greasy foods that were all a heart attack waiting to happen. Fried food may be the downfall of mankind, but damn if it didn't taste like a small slice of heaven. At least it would help take my mind off everyone watching us.

"Do you want to eat now?" Trent asked. "Or do you want to pull off the Band-Aid first?"

"Band-Aid?"

"You know, face the firing squad. Admit that you're dating Nerd Boy."

He had a point. I should be ashamed of myself for caring what any of the busybodies around here thought. It took a lot to embarrass me. Hell, I had done things in this town that would make Charlie Sheen blush. I needed to stop acting like such a wishy-washy wimp-ass.

Dropping Trent's hand, I turned to face him. His eyes held no judgment, but I would have deserved it if they had. Stepping closer to him, I could see the surprise in his eyes, despite the dim light as the sun dipped down in the horizon, when I looped my arms around his neck.

"There's no Band-Aid to pull off," I said, bringing my lips to his. It was time for me to go ahead and lay my claim. Go big or go home.

18.

Word of my impulsive display of affection spread through the festival like a match held close to an old brittle newspaper. I didn't feel boxed in like I had been expecting. Instead, I felt proud to be on Trent's arm as we chatted with friends from high school and eventually our own families when we ran into them.

Despite seeing me with Trent, my dad's only concern was my probation at MSC. He had already received an update from Professor N and was pleased with my improvement. He asked if the police officers from David's case had been in contact with me.

"Only to return my phone. The fraternity suffered a lot. His parents were gunning for someone to be held responsible for what happened."

Mom clucked her tongue. "I don't blame them. I couldn't

imagine being in their shoes, but I suspect my reaction would be similar to theirs if I ever lost your brother or you in a senseless accident."

I nodded. During the last month, I'd given everything that happened a lot of thought. I understood where David's parents were coming from, but deep down, I knew it was an accident. We were all stupid that night and every night before that, but I wasn't sure I agreed with some of the punishments that had been handed out to the fraternity. One thing was certain: The ripple effect of David's accident would be felt for a long time.

Dad changed the conversation after that, which I was thankful for. It was still upsetting to think about that night, and I had chosen to block it from my mind.

After a few minutes of idle chitchat about how long we'd been dating, Trent asked if I wanted to visit the haunted house at the library.

"Sure. It's always on my list, even though I hate when people jump out at me. I always feel like I need to punch them or something to defend myself."

"Please don't do that," my mom ordered. "Your brother is working in the haunted house this year, and I'd rather he didn't get a black eye from his big sister."

"Why? That punk totally deserves it for what he did to my Jeep this summer," I grumbled, remembering the blown-up condoms that had covered every square inch of my Jeep.

Both Dad and Trent laughed at the now-infamous condom incident.

"That wasn't one of my finer moments of being a parent to you two heathens," Mom mused.

"He was just expressing his displeasure over the sex ed class they forced him to take at school." Dad laughed again.

"Yeah, but that creep even tagged the picture on Facebook, so everyone in the world could see it."

Everyone laughed at my expense. That was fine with me. It would make my revenge that much sweeter on both him and his partner in crime, John. Giving Mom a kiss on the cheek, I told her if we didn't see them again at the festival, I would see them at home later. Trent and I had decided that if we were going to come home for the festival, we might as well stay for the weekend. Now that everyone knew about us, I was glad I had agreed.

The haunted house was the most popular part of the festival, so the line was always long. To make it spookier, they waited until the sun went down and only took in small groups of six people at a time. The haunted house weaved through the library, but also extended into the forest behind the building. It took a good twenty minutes to walk through it.

By the time Pam, who controlled the line, chauffeured our group in, I had already freaked myself out in anticipation over what waited for us. I was by no means a chicken, but I hated walking through dark places and found myself cowering against Trent as we entered the first room.

"You do know it's fake, right?" He slid an arm around me to pull me close as he whispered in my ear.

"Yes, but it doesn't make it any less scary," I answered, snuggling into the crook of his arm. He tightened his arm protectively around me when someone dressed like a mummy jumped out, making two tween-aged girls in our group shriek with fear. I found his protectiveness extremely sexy, and being wrapped in his arms in the dark, I could think of a few other things I would have liked to be doing in lieu of walking with a couple of squealing girls.

The scares continued throughout the rest of the haunted house. I had to admit, the performers were acting their parts with gusto this year. The two loudest members of our group chickened out just as we were about to enter the forest section, which left just Trent, me, and a couple I didn't recognize.

The soft hue of the moon provided just enough light to keep the forest from being blacked out. After walking for a few minutes past fake webs with overgrown spiders and a pack of mutinous werewolves, I spotted a break in the trees and pulled Trent off the path so we could be alone.

"Are we allowed to leave the tour like this?" He looked around like he expected someone to catch us.

"That's the fun part of being bad," I said. "I had something else in mind that we could do out here, but we can go back if you want." I pulled him toward me, pressing my lips to his. He was a willing participant and returned my kiss with so much vigor my legs were literally shaking by the time we separated. It was all I could do to resist the urge to push him on the ground and straddle him. The steady pulsing of desire was making every nerve ending feel like it had been charged with electricity.

He cupped my face between his hands. Even in the faint light, I could make out his features and the intensity behind his stare. "I'd always imagined you kissing me like that," he said, stroking a finger over my bottom lip.

I sucked his finger into my mouth, wanting his desire to match mine. I swirled my tongue around, smiling with triumph when he moaned with pleasure. My actions fueled his fire as he slid his free hand inside my jacket. His palm stroked across the bare skin of my abdomen before making its way to my lower back and then down to my ass. Pulling his finger from my mouth, he tugged me tightly against his hips, allowing me to feel his body's reaction to me. I let my hands wander, sliding them down between his legs. To say he was ready was an understatement. His hands shimmied underneath my costume, finding nothing but my bare-skinned ass. Our kiss had become a dance of seduction. I nearly lost the last shred of self-control I was holding when he gently sucked my tongue into his mouth and began grinding his hips against mine.

"I'd say get a room, but damn if this isn't hot," a snide familiar voice said, breaking through our haze of desire. "Once a slut, always a slut, I guess."

I could feel Trent stiffen. I pulled away from him and stepped back. Pivoting around, I stepped in front of Trent, hoping to shield him from what was sure to be a slew of insults. Jackson stood before us with his typical shit-eating grin. I wanted to pick up a stick and knock that smile off his face. Trent shocked me by wrapping his arms tightly around my waist. I found his actions endearing. Stupid, but endearing.

Compared to Trent, Jackson was a bear and would most likely sweep the forest with him.

"Jackson, are you lost? I'm surprised your mom let you go to a haunted house all by your little self, or is she waiting for you on the other side?" I made a point of looking around him like I was searching for her.

"Same old Tressa. Can't come up with any new material, so you insult my mom. What a surprise."

"Actually, that was meant for you, stupid, but ten bucks says I'm right." There had never been any love lost between his mom and me. Ultimately, I'd come to realize that Jackson was exactly like her.

"You're just upset because she saw the person you really are." His tone was mild, but I knew him well enough to know he was mad.

"What do you want, Jackson?" I sighed, deciding it wouldn't be worth it to allow things to escalate further.

"I heard you shacked up with fucktard here and I had to see if the rumors were true for myself. I can't believe you're that hard up you'd sleep with this pencil dick," he said, nodding at Trent. "If you're that hard up for cock, I can give you a freebie. If you ask me nicely," he said, cupping his hand behind his ear.

My fist clenched and I was on the verge of thrusting my knee at the cock he'd just offered me when another fist came up from behind me and clocked him in the mouth. The power behind the punch hit Jackson like a Mack truck and had him sinking to his knees with his head snapping back from the impact.

"In case you missed it, you lug nut, that's a no to your

offer," Trent said, grabbing my hand and dragging me around Jackson's body, which was now flat on the ground.

My jaw dropped at the sight of Jackson touching his now-busted lip. As Trent and I made our way out of the forest, I stumbled over downed tree branches with my mind stuck on what had just transpired. If I hadn't seen it with my own eyes, I would never have believed it.

This was the first time a guy I was dating had stood up for me. At that moment, nothing else mattered. I didn't care about how different we were or that we were a complete and utter contradiction. Trent had stolen my heart.

For the rest of the evening, it was I who clung to Trent's hand. I wanted everyone in Woodfalls to know he belonged to me. Hell, I wanted the word to spread that he had just kicked Jackson's ass, but I left it alone. Seeing it for myself was enough. The best part was that it hadn't ruined the evening. Trent acted like nothing even happened.

We couldn't tell which of us was having more fun as we moved from one game booth to the next, trying to win worthless prizes for my roommates. I was convinced I needed to win a goldfish for Cameo, even though I felt sorry for them in their little glass bowls.

Unfortunately, it turned out that both Trent and I were equally bad at bouncing a Ping-Pong ball into one of the glass bowls. My lack of skill was no surprise. At MSC, I always lost at beer pong. Since drinking was a perk of losing, I never felt my lack of skill was a downfall. Here at the festival, with no booze as a consolation prize, I was only losing my money.

I plunked another five-dollar bill on the counter to try again. "Cameo better appreciate this if I win."

Trent was so bad at the game, he had been banned from playing again. He had already spent ten bucks with nothing to show for it. Unless you counted dirty looks from the people running the game when he lost three Ping-Pong balls after they bounced off the sides of the bowls and were swallowed up by the darkness.

"Here, blow on this one." I held up my last ball in front of Trent's mouth so he could blow on it for good luck. "This is it. If this one doesn't make it, I'm out. I will not let this game make me its bitch." My comment was greeted with a gasp of disgust from behind me. Turning around, I watched a mom dragging her two young kids from the booth. "Oops," I said as she glared at me.

"Corrupting another generation?" my brother, Chris, asked after suddenly appearing at my side. "Is it not bad enough that you corrupted your own flesh and blood?"

"You wish. You were rotten before you even clawed your way out of the womb." I slung an arm affectionately around his shoulders. He was a total punk, but I was crazy about him.

"Come on, not in front of the guys, Tress," Chris said, looking over at his buddies with embarrassment. He tried to squirm away, but I tightened my arm around him. I was going to kiss his cheek, but ended up licking it instead.

The look of disgust on his face was priceless as his friends hooted with laughter.

"It's definitely on now," he threatened, squirming away.

"Don't even waste your time, junior. It's not going to happen in this lifetime." I socked his arm.

"Whatevs. One of these days, when you're least expecting it." I laughed at his words as his friends cackled with glee. He ignored us, pulling out his wallet. "Give me one," he said, plopping a dollar on the counter.

"One?" I scoffed. "I wouldn't put my wallet away, big spender." My words had barely left my mouth when his one solitary Ping-Pong ball fell cleanly into the narrow opening of one of the glass bowls. To add insult to injury, both his cronies made their shots too. Great, they had a bright future in beer ponging.

"Here," Chris said, handing me the fish he had just won.

"You don't want him?" I peered through the glass bowl at the big-eyed goldfish.

"Are you kidding? Mom would kill me if I brought home another pet. Besides, Baxter would try to eat him."

"True story." Baxter had followed Chris home from school when he was in first grade. With two dogs and a cat already at home, our parents had been adamant that Baxter would have to go. We hung multiple flyers around town, but no one stepped forward to claim the orange marmalade cat with his squished-in face. Mom and Dad finally admitted defeat and agreed to let Baxter stay. I felt like we'd been played when innocent-looking Baxter turned out to be part demon.

From the beginning, he loved Chris, but seemed to take great pleasure in tormenting the rest of us, including our two dogs. He was a sneaky bastard that would jump out at your feet when you walked by or dive-bomb you from shelves when you least expected it. The other pets in our house didn't stand a chance with him around. He was always stealing Bailey's and Troy's dog beds. Both were too chicken to challenge him, and would instead look at us with sad eyes until we forced Baxter from their beds. With Chris, Baxter was a completely different animal, playing the role of the sweet, innocent, purring kitty that would follow him around. The rest of us agreed that when Baxter died he wouldn't be chasing birds across golden clouds in kitty heaven. He would be roasting chickens in the fiery pits of hell.

"Maybe if we're lucky, Baxter would drown trying to get him out," I teased. I was sure that cat was Satan incarnate, but he was still part of the family.

"Not funny," Chris said, looking appalled. "You just don't know him like I do," he added, turning away from me. "Hey, Trent, did you get the new Batman game for Xbox?"

"The day it came out. I've already done the side missions to unlock Robin."

I tuned them out as soon as they started talking about different bat suits or something like that. I didn't speak gamer, so pretty much everything they said went over my head.

Eventually, my brother and his friends left when a group of girls snagged their attention. A crowd had gathered around the small stage in the middle of the town square where Mayor Fedderman had revealed who he had chosen for his costume this year.

"OMG. That might be the scariest sight I have ever seen," I proclaimed as we watched the mayor strutting around the stage, lip-syncing to "Poker Face" by Lady Gaga.

"Well, he nailed the makeup," Trent commented. "Is it weird that I'm turned on? I mean, I kinda have a thing for Lady Gaga."

"Hey, if that's what you're into, I can introduce you to Destiny from my apartment building. I'm sure you two would have a lot in common."

"Is she hotter than Mayor Fedderman?"

"You mean, is *he* hotter than Mayor Fedderman," I corrected him.

"Ooohhh, now I see—I think I'll stick with you," Trent answered, nudging my arm with his elbow.

"Gee, I'm so flattered. You really know how to make a girl feel special."

"Let's go," Trent laughed, slinging an arm around my shoulders. "I better quit now before you start doubting how I feel about you."

Trent and I decided to head over to the gym where the annual Halloween dance was being held. "My brother really seems to like you. I didn't know you two knew each other that well."

"He's a cool kid. I helped him with his Xbox over the summer. He was freaked-out when he thought the drive had crashed, but I got it fixed for him," he explained as he held the gym door open for me.

"Of course you did. What can't you fix? You've reached god status if you were able to save his most prized possession."

The heat of the gym greeted us as we shed our jackets for the first time that evening. I'd forgotten about my costume until Trent stopped midsentence. "What's wrong?" I asked, feigning innocence.

"I've been waiting to see this all night," he said, letting his eyes slide down my frame.

I was always a bit self-conscious about my body. The costume had me slightly stressed that my hips were too curvy for the low-slung bottoms or that my chest was a little too ample in the skimpy top. The look of desire in his eyes, though, made it clear he was quite pleased with the way the gold outfit fit me. “You saw me in it earlier,” I teased, dragging him toward the dance floor, where a slow song was playing.

“That doesn’t mean I can’t appreciate it again,” he answered, sliding his arms around my bare waist and locking them behind the small of my back.

“That works for me,” I murmured, lacing my arms around his neck. He pulled me closer and I leaned my head into the crook of his shoulder. Our heights were very compatible, almost like they’d been specifically designed for activities that involved closeness. We swayed slowly back and forth to the music. This kind of dancing was foreign to me. I was used to thumping music, urging me to dance harder and faster. If sweat wasn’t dripping off me, it wasn’t dancing. That was my motto up until now.

Even when the music changed and everyone around us moved to the loud rhythmic beat, we remained in each other’s arms, oblivious to everyone but ourselves. We were in our own separate bubble.

19.

The next day, Trent and I spent the entire time holed up in my parents' basement watching all the *Star Wars* movies back-to-back. Being in a dark basement with only the light of the TV seemed like the perfect excuse for us to pick up from where we'd left off in the forest the night before.

Unfortunately, my family derailed my plans. Watching movies snuggled together under a throw blanket wasn't nearly as fun since we were chaperoned pretty much the entire day. It was like they were taking turns babysitting us, which made copping a feel or stealing a kiss nearly impossible. I tried glaring at Chris when he joined us, but he ignored me and made himself comfortable on the other half of the sectional. Trent watched each movie with a boyish enthusiasm, like it was the first time he'd ever seen them. I came to the conclusion that I was the only horndog in the room. We paused long enough to eat dinner with Mom and Dad before heading back downstairs to continue our marathon. Much to my dismay, Chris followed us back downstairs. I couldn't help wondering if this was part of the revenge he'd threatened the night before. Eventually, I gave up hope of being alone with Trent and settled in to watching the movies.

Somewhere during the fifth movie, Chris headed up to his room to go to bed, finally leaving Trent and me alone. Too bad I was close to dozing off with my head on Trent's shoulder. Fooling around was the furthest thing from my mind until I felt his hand, which had been sitting on the sofa between us, move slowly to my knee. The simple gesture was enough to wake me completely, like I'd been zapped by a Taser.

I waited with bated breath for him to continue, but his hand remained stuck to my knee with no promise of movement. I wanted to reach under the blanket and guide it up my thigh, but I decided to let him take the lead this time. After several agonizing minutes, his hand slowly began to caress my knee. Every minute or so, his fingers would drift a fraction up my leg. My head was still on his shoulder, but my breath was coming in short gasps. Not since I was a teenager had a simple hand on my leg felt so enticing. I couldn't remember a time I'd been so turned on, and he wasn't even touching one of the important spots.

I chanced a look up at his face to see that he appeared to be watching the movie as intensely as he had been all day. I would have thought he was unaffected by the moment if not for the hard set of his jaw. Unable to fight temptation, I pressed my lips to the underside of his chin. His fingers gripped my leg, and I watched with satisfaction as he swallowed hard. I ran my tongue lightly along his jawline until my mouth found the lobe of his ear. I gave it a gentle tug with my teeth. This time it was his breathing that became labored. My hand moved to the hem of his shirt, sliding underneath as I continued tickling his ear with my tongue.

Darth Vader no longer stood a chance. Trent's eyes clashed with mine, filled with barely suppressed lust. The dampness between my legs matched my desire as his hand boldly moved to my thigh. I twisted around so I was sprawled across his lap, giving us both full access to explore.

I lifted his shirt, observing the lean muscles I'd witnessed before when he stood in his bath towel. He watched with fascination as I licked my finger before gently painting his nipple, making it harden instantly. I moved my mouth to his chest, showing each side the proper amount of attention.

His groan of approval rumbled through his body, encouraging me to continue. I sucked hard on his nipple as his hand tangled in my hair, pulling me closer.

"Damn, that feels incredible," he moaned.

"You can't be too loud." I shooshed him. It was hot as hell that he was enjoying himself, but I didn't want someone walking in before we could finish.

"Sorry," he apologized. I sat up from his chest as his hand moved the rest of the way up my thigh. He looked directly into my eyes, holding my stare while he moved his fingers underneath my shorts to the part of me that was practically drenched with need. My hips instinctively lifted slightly, urging him to touch me more.

My orgasm came out of nowhere, thundering through me like a roller coaster. If we hadn't been in my parents' basement, I would have screamed with pleasure. His tongue plunged deeper in my mouth as I came apart in his arms, and he continued to stroke me until I rode out the wave. I shuddered in his arms in a state of shock that I'd come so quickly and with clothes on. I was no stranger to orgasms, but while I dated Jackson, they had been few and far between, and usually took a lot of work to get me there. Jackson was such an asshole, claiming the effort to get me there was too much work.

Lying in Trent's arms, I didn't know if I should be embarrassed or if I should thank him. I knew I wanted to return the favor. Trailing my hand down his chest, I dipped my fingers into the waistband of his jeans. He surprised me by capturing my hand and bringing it up to his mouth. He placed a hot kiss against my palm as I looked up at him, confused.

"You don't like that?" For a moment, I thought maybe he wasn't turned on by what had happened, but shifting slightly, I could feel him pressed hard against my side.

He chuckled at my words. "Trust me when I tell you that was the hottest thing I've ever seen."

"Then why won't you let me touch you?" I tugged on my hand so I could finish my exploration.

"Because, tonight wasn't about that," he said, firmly holding my hand. "Tonight was about you."

"That doesn't sound fair. Why can't it be about both of us?"

He laced his fingers through mine before dropping a kiss on my knuckles. "Because I've been dreaming for years about the moment I finally make you mine. When we do everything, it won't be in your parents' basement."

I wanted to argue more, but the thumping above our heads reminded me we weren't alone.

"Are you sure? I could easily slide under the blanket and . . ."

He placed a finger against my lips. "Soon we'll be all alone and I can do everything I've always fantasized about."

"Hmmmm, so you're admitting that you've had fantasies about me?"

He looked at me balefully. "I might be ashamed to tell you some of the things I fantasized about with you."

"That's something I'd like to hear sometime," I purred, as a fresh wave of heat percolated inside me. The idea that he had thought of me intimately was intoxicating.

"On that note, I better head out," he said, giving me one last kiss that was filled with promise and made me wish we were anywhere but my parents' house. I would have liked nothing more than to spend the night wrapped in his arms and making his fantasies a reality.

After he left, I straightened up the rec room before heading up to my bedroom. I changed into my pajamas, never bothering to turn on the light. This room was as familiar to me as the back of my hand. Crawling into my bed, I reflected on everything that had changed in the last two days. I had fallen for Trent, no doubt about it now. The ache in my heart after he left was proof of that. I had vowed not to get serious with anyone after Jackson. At least not until after I graduated, but somehow Trent had managed to weasel his way into my heart.

I fell asleep still wanting him. My dreams were filled with vivid pictures of what we would do when we were finally alone.

I woke the next morning to my own version of a wet dream. Feeling inadequately satisfied from the images that had tantalized me all night, I jumped in the shower, hoping to tamp down some of the heat that was simmering through me.

The shower seemed to help a little. I was able to focus on something other than sex when I caught the smell of frying bacon and Mom's famous apple spice pancakes.

20.

I found both Mom and Dad in the kitchen after I followed my nose to the source of the intoxicating aroma.

"Morning, sweetheart. Did you sleep well?" Mom asked, flipping a row of pancakes on the griddle.

I flushed slightly. I couldn't imagine what she would think if she were privy to my dreams. "I did," I answered. "It's always kind of nice to sleep in my old room. Plus, it was peaceful without Derek's snoring," I added, opening the cabinet to pull out a coffee mug.

Dad looked up from his Sunday paper. "He's still staying with you two?"

I nodded, filling my cup to the brim. "He'll probably be with us until graduation. The new roommates he got stuck with this year are total douchecanoes."

"Language, Tressa," Mom chastised me, looking pointedly at Chris, who had just entered the kitchen.

Chris smirked. "Mom, I hear a whole lot worse than that at school. You know I'm in high school, right?" He winked at Dad and me.

"What you hear at school and what we say in this house are two different things," she said, pointing the spatula at him for emphasis. "Besides, do either of you even know what a douchecanoe is?"

"I don't think that matters. It just sounds like a good insult," I teased. "Don't act innocent, Mom. We've all heard you drop your share of f-bombs over the years."

We all laughed when she looked scandalized at my accusation as she placed a platter stacked high with pancakes and bacon on the table.

"She's got you there, dear," Dad said, giving her a peck on the cheek before grabbing the pitcher of freshly squeezed orange juice off the counter. He placed it on the table before sliding Mom's chair out so she could sit down. I smiled watching their interaction. Dad was old-school when it came to treating a woman right. I loved that after twenty-five years of marriage he still held the door open for her and brought her flowers every Friday. She always claimed they were a waste of money, but all of us had witnessed her love for them over the years.

"I do not drop f-bombs," she defended herself as Dad slid her chair up to the table.

Chris and I both snorted loudly. Mom was a lady in most senses of the word. She took care of her appearance when she was going out. It would be a cold day in hell before she would pass gas in front of anyone. That one we teased her about, telling her that holding it in was not good for her system. She was polite to a fault and was the most loyal friend anyone could ever ask for. All that being said, it was common knowledge that she had a trucker's mouth when she was frustrated.

"What?" she said innocently as she loaded up her plate.

"Need I remind you of the blender episode last year?" I added helpfully, taking a bite of my crisp bacon.

Chris and Dad both cracked up at the memory. Chris had made the mistake of attempting to make a smoothie, but the doofus forgot to put the lid on the blender before he turned it on. His mixture of strawberries, bananas, and yogurt splattered everywhere. It covered the floor and dripped from cabinet doors. He even managed to reach the ceiling. Mom cursed like there was no tomorrow as she took in the mess that covered her usually pristine kitchen. We'd all pitched in cleaning up the mess, teasing her about her outburst the entire time. She'd claimed I'd gotten my mouth from hanging out with Fran, but this was a prime example that the apple didn't fall far from the tree.

"That was a special circumstance," she defended herself, patting the corner of her mouth with her napkin before cracking a smile.

The conversation after that switched to my grandma, who was in the hospital with pneumonia. She and Grandpa had retired to Florida a couple years ago. Her prognosis was good, but it didn't take the worry from Mom's eyes as she talked. She knew the mild temperatures in Florida were better for both of them, but she missed having them close by. We all did.

"Maybe you and Dad should go see them over the holidays. You guys haven't been down there since they moved. Grandma probably won't be able to make the trip up here this year," I pointed out. "I'll be on break, so I can come home to babysit the squirt here."

"I don't need a babysitter," Chris replied, looking insulted.

"Don't get your Underoos in a bunch. There's no way Mom and Dad would have let me stay home by myself when I was your age," I said, ducking when he threw a piece of bacon at me.

"We can't leave you guys during Christmas," Mom scoffed, like it was a ridiculous statement.

"I'm talking about you guys leaving the day after Christmas. Chris doesn't go back to school until early January, and I don't have to be back at MSC until like a week after that. You guys can fly down on the twenty-sixth and spend a couple weeks in sunny Florida while we freeze our asses off here."

Mom chastised me for swearing, but looked intrigued at my suggestion. Dad piped in, pointing out that they hadn't taken a vacation alone together in years. He told her they could even drive down to the Keys for a few days. With endorsements from all three of us, Mom eventually ran out of objections.

My parents were still discussing the trip when Trent arrived to take me back to school an hour later. Dad carried my bag out to Trent's car while I gave Mom and Chris a hug good-bye. I promised I'd see them later in the month for Thanksgiving.

Chris tried to give me a wet willy before I left, but he was an amateur. I deflected it easily and gave him one of my own. I laughed as he grimaced, and told him to stay out of trouble while I was gone.

The three of them stood on the front porch as we drove away, waving until the car was out of sight. I felt the usual pinch of sadness I always got when I left home. It was so easy to fall into the family routine when we were together. I even missed Baxter, the devil cat, every time I left.

Once we made it past the town limits, my attention shifted to Trent. I felt like a sap as I gazed at him happily. I studied his features as he drove, wondering how I'd missed how handsome he really was. All the things that used to bug me about him now turned me on. I adored the way his glasses slid down his nose, and could clearly picture plucking them off his face as he positioned himself over me. I shifted in my seat slightly, getting hot and bothered just at the thought.

Trent continued to drive, unaware of my observations. We both remained relatively silent most of the way, except for some occasional small talk about the weather. Even after what we had shared last night, I was afraid to talk about us, as in *us*, the couple. He had admitted having fantasies about me, but what if that was all they were? Maybe all he wanted was a friend-with-benefits kind of relationship. I hated myself for feeling this way, but it was my own fault for falling for him. I couldn't help thinking that if I brought it up, I would somehow jinx us when I was the one who now wanted more.

With each mile that passed, I became more worried and

apprehensive. My month of mandatory tutoring ended on Wednesday, and that would be it for us. For the first time since our sessions started, I wasn't ready for them to come to an end.

As Trent pulled down the street leading to my apartment, I reminded him about my tutoring sessions ending soon. I tried to sound conversational and like I wasn't probing for an indication that we were now more than just an obligation. That was me, after all. Never show any weakness. That was my mantra.

"It's not like we won't see each other every day," Trent said as we pulled into my apartment complex.

"Does that mean you plan on stalking me?" I joked, trying to make light of how I was feeling, which was pretty damn confused at the moment.

"You better believe it," he said, turning off the car. Neither of us made a move to get out, even though the atmosphere in the vehicle had taken a sharp turn into Awkward-as-hell-ville.
"Looks like snow," he commented, breaking the silence. He peered out the windshield, looking up at the sky.

"Probably. I'm surprised we haven't gotten a heavy snow yet," I said, not quite believing we were talking about the weather again.

"So, do you want to stay the night at my apartment?" His voice shook a little. Damn, he was so freaking cute. I could eat him up.

"Hell yes," I answered.

He didn't miss a beat. He threw the car in reverse and

pulled out of my parking lot before I had a chance to change my mind. Little did he know there was no chance of that.

I laughed at the melodrama that had gone on in my head earlier. Thankfully, I wasn't the only one obsessing about our new relationship. Well, not thankfully, but I was glad he was stressing also. Let's just say I was relieved that I hadn't put myself out there for nothing. Within minutes, Trent was pulling into a parking spot behind his building. "You sure?" he asked. "Maybe it's too soon for this. It's probably too soon for this, right?"

His nervous energy was sexy, and I wanted him to see just how badly I wanted him. I snagged his hand, bringing it up to my lips. "It's not too soon, and believe me when I say I couldn't be more sure if I tried," I reassured him.

My words were all the prompting he needed. We got out of his car and carried our bags into his apartment.

"So, are you hungry?"

"Uh, sure," I answered. He was clearly nervous.

"Oh, okay. We can order a pizza or something," he said, taking a step back.

I snatched his hand before he could walk away and tugged him toward the bedroom."How about if we work up more of an appetite first?" I'd never really taken the dominant role in an intimate situation, but I sensed he needed a little coaxing. I found the role reversal to be a pretty heady experience.

The late-afternoon sunlight streamed through the curtains as I stepped into his bedroom for the first time. I took a moment to take in the furnishings that matched, just like the rest of his apartment. His OCD was something I'd come to appreciate. The fascinating part was the king-sized bed in the middle of the room.

"King-sized?"

"I like to spread out," he said, placing his hands on my waist. "That's why I have my own apartment. I realized freshman year I wasn't suited for roommates. By midyear, my roommate was ready to kill me . . ." His voice trailed off as I began to unbutton his shirt.

"Are we going to talk about furniture, or are we going to use it?" I asked, helping him slide out of his shirt.

He answered by pulling me into his arms. My hands splayed across his back as his lips found mine. We stood in the middle of his room discovering each other. I can't even say for sure how it happened, but somehow our clothes managed to end up in a pile on the floor.

I usually preferred the lights off and the room to be pitch-black to hide my flaws. I tried to edge us toward the bed so I could at least hide beneath a blanket, but Trent held me in place as his lips trailed down my neck and over my shoulder.

"Where are you going?"

"I thought we'd be more comfortable on the bed," I said, inching us closer. "Under the covers," I added.

"Are you cold?" He looked concerned but went with the flow, allowing me to lead us to his large bed.

I could have lied. I almost did, but the truth leaked out before I could tamp it back. "I'm not cold. I just prefer to do this part in the dark or under the covers."

He looked confused. “Why?”

“Because, I don’t like people to see my flaws,” I admitted, exasperated.

“Flaws? You’re kidding, right?” He took a step back to admire my body.

I felt like I was on display and had to fight the urge to snatch the comforter from his bed to hide behind. “You don’t have to flatter me, Trent. I’m not going anywhere.” My voice cracked slightly. I knew my body wasn’t perfect. Jackson had reminded me countless times while we dated.

“Tressa, come on. You’re smarter than that.”

I cut him off. “Are you calling me stupid?”

“If you think there’s anything wrong with your body, then yes, I am,” he said, circling his hands around my arms. His eyes scanned my body from head to toe. “Because from where I’m standing, everything looks damn perfect.”

He unexpectedly swept me off my feet and carried me to the bed. We tumbled down together, laughing until he began to trace the curves of my body with his fingers. I closed my eyes and allowed my body to completely relax while he switched to using his mouth. He started at my shoulders, kissing his way across my neck. I raised my hands to his chest, but he pushed them back down. “Just relax and let me play,” he said.

He continued to kiss his way down to my breasts while his free hand moved between my thighs. I couldn’t stop my body from reacting to his touch. Just lying there without being able to use my hands on him was torture.

"I want you now," I insisted. He climbed on top of me, using his knee to spread my legs apart. By the time he leveled his body over mine, I felt like I would die if he didn't ease the throbbing inside me. My hands looped around his neck, pulling his mouth to mine as he entered me. Our bodies moved in a synchronized rhythm as we both sought release. I felt my orgasm approaching, but I fought to hold it off, not wanting the moment to end. I could tell Trent was close as his movements became faster and more forceful.

"Together," I whispered, looking into his eyes. Neither of us was able to hold back any longer.

He answered by plunging deep inside me one last time, sending us both over the edge. He kissed me tenderly before collapsing on top of me. Deep shudders rippled through him. I stroked a hand down his back, marveling at how good he felt against me. I felt completely sated and could have purred like a pleased feline. Sure, it'd been a long time for me, but I couldn't remember it ever being like this.

It took several minutes for both of us to catch our breath. Trent headed to the bathroom while I snuggled under the blankets, too lethargic to move. I was more asleep than awake when he left the bathroom. He climbed into bed and slid his arms around me before we both drifted off in each other's arms. Another first for me. Wait until Brittni found out. There was no way she would believe it.

21.

The weeks following the Halloween festival passed so quickly I barely had time to catch my breath. My academic probation ended without any hoopla. I barely noticed. Trent continued to tutor me since the majority of my days were spent with him anyway. After our first night together, I pretty much spent every night at his apartment. Being with him was a new experience. He was attentive in and out of the bedroom and had a way of making me feel treasured. I was pleased that the passion that had consumed us so completely the first night didn't fade like it had in some of my previous relationships.

During the day, we fell into an easy routine. Trent did a lot of freelance work from home, but most of the time he saved it until I went to work. If something important did come up that he had to finish, it gave me an excuse to stay caught up on my own classwork.

Every few days I would return to my apartment to grab new clothes and other necessities. Derek seemed cool with my absence, but Cameo had returned to ignoring me like she had after David's accident. Ever since her breakup with Chad, it was like she didn't care about anything. I knew from texts and chats with Derek that she was partying hard. I'd tried to get her to come over and hang out with Trent and me, but she blew me off, saying my "married-couple social life" wasn't for her. Her words rubbed me like salt in an open wound. I thought we were the kind of friends that could be happy for each other. Regardless of whatever Cameo's problem was, I wasn't about to let it burst my happy bubble.

Before I knew it, Thanksgiving had snuck up on us, and Trent and I were heading back to Woodfalls. We both had mixed emotions about the trip home since we obviously wouldn't be sleeping together while we were there. We'd grown so accustomed to being together at this point that neither of us was looking forward to four nights in separate beds. I teased him that he was going to have to sneak through my window every night.

As it turned out, we only spent two days in Woodfalls. Larry called from Javalotta, asking if I could cover two double shifts over the weekend since two of the girls had come down with the flu. At least I'd gotten to eat Thanksgiving dinner at home. It would have sucked to miss my mom's famous stuffing. She was also nice enough to load me up with a bag of leftovers to take with me. Since Trent and I had driven to Woodfalls together, he ended up returning to MSC also. I felt bad about pulling him away from his family during the holiday, but he assured me that he'd much rather be with me. I couldn't have agreed with him more.

December started with a blizzard that closed the campus for two days. Several dorms lost power, but the utility trucks seemed to be working around the clock to remedy the situation. Derek and Cameo showed up at Trent's apartment the first night of the blizzard when our apartment became a casualty of the power loss.

Cameo's attitude thawed out long enough for us to have a mini snowed-in party. We stayed up late eating junk food and watching comedies from the eighties. It almost felt like old times—minus the frat house and coolers full of booze. We ended up sleeping in late while the storm continued to rage outside.

By midday, the storm lost steam, and Cameo and Derek found out from a neighbor that power had been restored to our apartment. They decided to head out, thanking Trent for letting them crash.

Life after the storm returned to normal, or at least what was our new normal lately. Trent was working longer hours in the lab, and I stayed busy working at Javalotta and studying for finals, which were coming up before the Christmas holiday. Statistics was still a thorn in my side, and Trent tried to help me study as best as he could, but he was having his own issues in the lab. I was sort of living back and forth between Trent's apartment and my own place with Derek and Cameo.

By the second week of December, all the studying and working with no playing was beginning to make me a dull girl. It didn't help that everyone seemed to be talking about some holiday party every time I turned around. My resentment over missing all the fun started making me edgy, and I found myself snapping at everyone.

Trent was a trouper through my mood swings. He kept assuring me that once my finals were over, I'd feel less pressure. I hoped he was right. Of course, if I failed my statistics final, I would probably go postal after what a pain in the ass that class had been.

In the end, I felt like all my finals went off without a hitch. I'd done everything I could, and the only thing left to do now was wait for my grades. Well, that and celebrate a little, which Trent and I did by going to Shirley's Secret Club.

"Still not sick of this Boy Scout?" Peewee asked, letting us in. "I could show you a good time," he added, winking outrageously.

"Hmm, let me mull that over," I answered.

"Get your own girl," Trent intervened, pulling me tightly against him.

Peewee and I laughed. "I guess that's a no," I said, blowing him a kiss as Trent propelled me to the main room.

His jealousy was funny. It was nice to matter so much to someone. The feeling was mutual, and I found myself struggling with my own jealousy when the waitress who dropped off our food started flirting with him. I handled the situation in my own mature way by accidentally knocking into her hand while she held a pitcher of water. The clear liquid drenched the front of her shirt, making her shriek in surprise. It took all my self-control to not laugh out loud.

Trent handed her napkins while I apologized insincerely.

"You did that on purpose," he stated once she left our table.

I didn't even try to pretend as I dipped a fry in ketchup. "So?"

"Why would you do that?" He looked intrigued.

"Because she was flirting with you, and I didn't like it," I whispered as a guy with a goatee stepped onstage through the parted curtain. He delivered a long-winded poem that completely lost me. Once he mentioned something about rubber ducks and finding your inner peace with chain-link fences, I didn't see the connection and tuned him out.

"So, anyway, are you jealous?" Trent asked once the reading was over. His tone sounded like he couldn't understand why I would feel that way.

I looked at him balefully. He really was slow on the uptake sometimes. "Of course," I replied. "Do you have a problem with that, Geek Boy?"

"Hell no." He sat back in his chair, looking like a toddler who'd just been handed a giant cookie. I should reel him in. He was on the verge of developing a major ego. Of course, it was hard to blame him when my feelings were becoming pretty damn obvious. It was no secret to our friends and family that I was seriously crushing on him. Mom even dared to mention the L-word on Thanksgiving, but I told her to stuff that. We were far from using that word.

"Don't let it go to your head, stud. I'm naturally a jealous person," I said, wanting to save face.

"No, you're not," he said, turning serious. He laced his fingers through mine, looking to make his point. "Matter of fact, you're a lot like a Tootsie Pop."

"You're comparing me to a candy?" I had no idea where he was going with this, so I didn't know whether to be insulted or complimented.

"Yes, you have a hard exterior with a soft, delectable interior, like a Tootsie Pop."

"Um, thanks. I'll try not to let your compliment go to my head."

He looked pensive for a moment. "Yeah, it sounded more romantic in my head. Would it help if I said you're like the orange-flavored ones to me?"

"Because you love the orange ones?"

"Exactly. See, I knew we could figure this out," he said, turning back to the stage as a young girl stepped up to recite a poem about lost love that floated away like a kite caught in a gust of wind. I watched her blankly, which I'm sure looked like I was into her reading, but really I was trying to sort through Trent's words. Had he just told me he loved me in his own goofy way?

The young girl finished her poem and swiped away a stray tear from the corner of her eye. Trent regained my attention by squeezing my hand. “You’re freaking out, right?” he asked, looking pleased with himself.

“Well, it’s not every day my boyfriend compares me to his favorite candy,” I said, skirting around the subtle elephant that he had let in the room.

I could almost see the words in his eyes before he opened his mouth to speak. “Tress, I love you.”

“Well, goody for you,” I said, acting unconcerned. My heart was racing and felt like it was trying to jump out of my chest. I knew what my feelings were for Trent, and now I knew where he stood. I just didn’t know we were going to blurt it out tonight. It’s not like it would be the first time I’d said the words. Jackson and I had said we loved each other. Of course, we were teenagers. When you’re in high school, you fall in and out of love every other week. That was my relationship with Jackson. Fight and break up. Apologize and make up. It happened over and over again for nearly four years. Eventually, even after getting back together, we sort of stopped saying we loved each other. I’m not sure how or when it happened, but it did. After that, love became sacred for me. I promised myself I’d never say it again unless I was absolutely sure it would mean something. For a while, I doubted whether I’d get the chance. I’d seen real love firsthand with my parents and most recently with my two best friends, so I knew it existed.

“Are you scared?” Trent asked, drawing circles on my palm.

“Only that you’ll confuse me with your lollipop in your

sleep and try to lick me to death." The joke was lame, and he didn't even crack a smile.

"I'm sorry to drop it on you without warning, and I know you're not there yet, but I needed you to know where I stood."

I bristled at his words. Why would he assume I wasn't there yet? I could be in love with him now. I could even tell him if I wanted to. I felt like I was wading into ice-cold water. I closed my eyes and took a deep breath—in and out.

"I love you too," I said, opening my eyes. "There, I said it. Are you satisfied?" As soon as the words were out, I felt relieved because I knew they were true. I loved every damn thing about him. Even his superhero collection had grown on me. Openly declaring my feelings for him did odd things to my body. I had a sudden desire to be alone with him, preferably with no clothes on.

"Do you want to get out of here?" he asked, leaving some money to cover the dinner we'd barely touched.

I answered by standing up to walk out without looking back. We threw a good-bye at Peewee, and before we could get outside, Trent was pressing me against the wall of the long hallway. He roamed my body with his hands and buried his mouth in my neck. "Say it again," he moaned.

"I love you," I answered, giving him what he wanted. My eyes met his, and I was a goner.

The ride home was an exercise in frustration. We tormented each other with roaming hands that only fueled our heat, which was already near a boiling point. The entire car seemed to blaze with sexual tension.

When we arrived at the apartment, Trent practically jerked the steering wheel of the car while trying to park. We all but jumped out and hurried toward the apartment. I fumbled through my purse for the spare key Trent had given me after Thanksgiving, not even considering that he had his keys in his hand. I wrestled with my own fingers, trying to slide the key into the lock. Trent was no help. He stood behind me, kissing the sensitive skin on the back of my neck. My head slumped forward and rested on the door as he ground his body against me. It was the sweetest kind of torture.

Finally, despite Trent's distractions, I managed to get the keys to cooperate, and we pushed the door open together. Trent slammed the door behind us and grabbed me in a bear hug, lifting me off the ground.

We never made it to the bedroom. We sealed our new professed status on the living room couch in a tangled weave of arms and legs. We leaned against each other in a heap of satisfaction.

"Why was me saying 'I love you' so significant?" I asked, trailing my hand over his bare chest.

He waited a moment to answer. His voice was low, but filled with intensity. "I'm not sure. Let's be honest. We've all known that I've been in love with you, well, forever, but that was superficial, right? I mean, I always thought you were pretty amazing, but over the last few months, I've gotten to see that even back then I never realized just how special you are. You're the funniest, most sarcastic person I know, and I love everything about you. When you said you loved me too, it sort of lifted this heavy weight off my shoulders. The words consumed me. Well, obviously, since I practically mauled you when we walked in the door." He turned his head to look at me. "Did my response scare you?"

I chuckled at his question. "I'm not sure you could ever do anything to scare me. And what we just shared is probably the furthest thing from scary I've ever experienced. The only scary part is how badly I already want you again." My lips trailed across his chest, moving toward his lips and rekindling our fire.

22.

My final exam grades came in three days before we were supposed to head to Woodfalls for Christmas break. The three As in my business classes were a nice surprise, but it was the A in statistics that completely floored me. That test was hard as hell. Considering all the erasing and reworking of problems, I was convinced I had failed miserably.

I rushed home to share the good news with Trent, but found the apartment empty.

Hey where u at?

Had to help Professor N. Did u get your grades?

Yep

So?

So what?

????!!!

I smiled. I could picture his exasperation as he waited for me to tell him.

All A's, baby!!! I'll be ending the term with 2 A's and 2 B's.

I knew u could do it. Will celebrate later.

By sexting?

That would be a little hard since I'm not alone.

Oh, it'll be hard, all right.

You're a bad girl. I'll call you later.

Party pooper.

Don't pout.

Fine.

Love you.

No, you don't. If you loved me, you would sext with me.

Be good.

Fine. I love you too.

I was grinning when I tossed the phone on the couch and headed to the kitchen to fix something to eat. Trent refused any sexting. He was convinced that nothing on cell phones was safe from hackers. I tried to make my case by saying I didn't care if some pimply-faced kid hacked my phone, to which he responded that it would suck if he ended up knowing the pimply-faced kid. You gotta love dating a tech-hard.

I made myself a sandwich and chips, which was the extent of my culinary talents. I didn't want to overdo it since I didn't know what our celebrating would entail. Staying at home so much was starting to get a little old, so I was looking forward to going out. I ate standing at the kitchen counter, debating whether I could talk Trent into going to the new restaurant that had opened on South Street. It was a restaurant/bar that I heard had a small dance floor. It was time to show Trent what real dancing looked like.

Once I finished my lunch, I straightened up the kitchen before heading to the living room to veg. Now that finals were over, I could do nothing but relax and not feel guilty about it. I had one more shift at Javalotta before we left for Woodfalls; otherwise, I had absolutely nothing hanging over my head.

Grabbing the remote, I flipped on Trent's massive TV, which

I'd grown quite attached to. If I ever started staying at my apartment more than a few hours at a time, I'd totally miss it. I'd been spending less and less time at my old place with Derek and Cameo. My things were slowly starting to trickle here from my apartment and never finding their way back. I now had a small section in his closet and a drawer in his dresser for my clothes. Trent had been trying to convince me to make it official and just move in with him, but I wasn't quite ready to give up my apartment and the illusion of freedom it gave me.

At the moment, though, as I pulled a blanket up over me and snuggled into the corner of the couch, I had no idea why I kept fighting him about it. This apartment felt more like home than my apartment ever had. Superheroes included.

I dozed the afternoon away, waking when Trent came home with takeout and a couple movies. I had to admit I was disappointed that our celebration would be at home again. Sure, the celebratory sex was good, but I wanted to go out.

The next night I went to a small Christmas party my roommates were throwing at our apartment. Trent stayed at the lab going over his project one last time since he would be turning it in the next day. We both knew it was perfect, but in order to stay sane, he needed to go over his checklist one last time. He felt bad for missing the party, but I lied to him and told him it was no big deal. Truthfully, it was starting to bother me that he always came up with an excuse to avoid social situations.

By the time I arrived at my apartment, I had gotten over my sour attitude. It had been ages since I'd hung out with my roommates, and I was excited to catch up on things.

"Tress, you're here," Derek greeted me, giving me a bear hug.

"I told you I'd be here, silly." I unbuttoned my jacket and pulled it off.

"Like that matters," Cameo said under her breath, walking by.

"What's that supposed to mean?" I turned to face her.

Derek laughed uneasily. "She's just joking," he said, handing me a beer.

"No, I don't think she is. She's had a problem with me this whole year, and I'm sick of her shit." My voice was loud as I took out my frustration from the last few days on her.

Cameo stomped toward me, not caring that I towered over her and could squish her like a bug. "That's because you act like your shit doesn't stink. Somebody dies and suddenly you turn into a fucking nun."

"Cameo, come on," Derek pleaded, looking like he wanted to be anywhere but here.

"So I'm a nun because I was put on academic probation? How does that make any sense?"

"Don't give me that bullshit. Even before your probation, you had thrown our friendship away."

"Are you high? I never threw our friendship away. That's on you." We were both yelling. Derek had given up trying to intervene and was now sitting on the couch, out of the line of fire.

Cameo's face was red from anger. "Nothing is on me. You

stopped living the day that David kid died. You didn't kill him, but you act like you did."

Her words hit me like a smack in the face. Talking about David was still a sore subject for me. I never talked about him and very rarely did I allow myself to think about him. Cameo had no idea what she was talking about. Yes, I wasn't directly connected to his death, but I was involved. We all were. "You fucking whore, you have no idea what you're talking about!" I said, lunging at her.

Derek jumped up off the couch to intervene before I could get my hands on her.

With Derek as a shield, Cameo wasn't finished. "As if that wasn't bad enough, you throw yourself at a guy completely wrong for you, obviously trying to remake yourself into someone better. We all see through your act. You're still the same, Tressa. The sad thing is, you don't even know who you are anymore. You can try all you want, but you're no better than me." Her shrill words were like knives to the heart, but in the end, it was Cameo who was insecure. She couldn't take it that people can change, and obviously, she was incapable of doing so.

"Fucking let go of me, Derek," I said, jerking my arm away. I pushed past Cameo before I pulverized her like she deserved. I slammed my full beer into the sink, feeling somewhat vindicated when it exploded all over the kitchen. Grabbing my jacket off the couch, I stalked out of the apartment. Derek tried to call me back, but I didn't stop. I jumped into my Jeep and tore out of the parking lot, shaking from rage and hurt to the core.

I had no idea where to go as I pulled onto the road. I didn't want to go to Trent's empty apartment, and in my current state of mind, I was in no mood to see him. I needed to let loose, to prove to myself that I was still me. I turned into a parking lot and pulled out my cell phone. Hitting my Facebook icon, I went to the MSC chat group one of the seniors had set up so we could keep track of when and where the parties were being held. Finding one that seemed appropriate for my current state of mind, I stowed my phone in my purse and left the parking lot.

It took ten minutes to drive to the other side of town. It was obvious I'd found the right apartment complex by the loud music and the crowd of students hanging around outside. I managed to squeeze my way inside.

"Tressa? Damn, where you been?" a loud voice boomed seconds before strong arms encircled me. My feet left the ground as I was twirled around.

"Ted, you lug, set me down." I laughed, feeling a small part of myself return.

Ted was a junior defensive tackle for the MSC football team, and he was built like a Mack truck. Word was he even stood a decent chance of being drafted into the NFL.

"I've missed your crazy ass cheering while I'm on the field. Where you been hiding?"

"I've been on academic and extracurricular probation," I said, giving him a pained look.

"No shit? That blows big ass."

"Tell me about it." I grabbed a beer out of a cooler.

"I heard you've been shacking up with some tool from the

science lab. What's up with that?" he asked, grabbing three beers for himself. He twisted off the cap of one of the bottles and downed the contents before I could even answer his question.

I shrugged my shoulders, deciding not to comment. It didn't take an Einstein to know who had told him about Trent and me. Cameo and Ted had been friends since freshman year. I downed my own beer and reached for another one, contemplating what I would do to Cameo if she were here.

"Damn, girl, I guess you're here to party," he said with admiration, grabbing the cooler. "Why don't we go hang out on the deck? It feels stuffy in here." He shouldered the cooler like it weighed nothing. I polished off my second beer before we even hit the deck, along with a couple Jell-O shots I had snagged off the kitchen counter on our way out. A nice buzz filled my head, camouflaging the hateful words Cameo and I had shared earlier. The deck out back was crowded, but Ted and I managed to snag a bench near the fire pit. Ted placed the cooler on the ground in front of us so we could prop our feet on it.

"I heard you kicked ass during the last game," I said, accepting another beer. I was well on my way to getting completely toasted, which was exactly what I needed.

"I slaughtered the other team. Their quarterback spent more time flat on his back than he did on his feet, which is how I like my women," he said, slinging an arm across my shoulder.

"You're a pig," I said, sliding his arm off my shoulder. I may be a lot of things, like Cameo pointed out, but I wasn't a cheater.

"Whoa, what's up? I thought maybe we could hook up."

"Ted, you've been trying with me for years. Besides, I'm seeing someone."

He looked intrigued. "You serious about this tool? Cam made it sound like it was some kind of guilt fling."

"Cameo's delusional about a few things."

"Man, don't tell me you two are still fighting."

"Hey, are we playing Dr. Phil, or are we drinking?" I asked, holding up my beer for emphasis.

"Girl, we be drinking. Screw Dr. Phil." He clinked his bottle with mine.

"Damn straight."

Several hours later, my mind was fairly numb and I had enough liquor in my belly to float a battleship. Ted had abandoned me after the first hour. I circulated the crowd, catching up with people I hadn't seen in months. Most of them claimed they'd thought I'd fallen off the face of the earth. They all said how much they missed my Instagram pictures. I think I gave vague answers on why I had given it all up, but honestly, I couldn't recall everything I'd said. The entire evening was beginning to become fuzzy. I began to feel an odd sense of loneliness I'd never experienced before as I circulated the party. Everyone was nice enough, but after the first few minutes of the same general "Hey, what's up, where you been?" bullshit was out of the way, I realized I had nothing more to say. Awkward silence followed me around like a dark cloud of gloom. I couldn't understand why.

The truth hit me like a kick in the teeth. Cameo had been right. Somewhere along the way, I had lost me. I hardly recognized the person I was pretending to be. I stumbled from the party in a haze of shock. The liquor I had so greedily consumed like I had a thirst that had to be quenched was now threatening mutiny as I left the noisy crowd behind.

I knew I was in no condition to drive home. I made my way to my Jeep and pulled out my phone and called Trent.

He answered just as I thought I was about to get his voice mail.

"Hey," he said, sounding distracted. Great, I was interrupting him. I should have called someone else, but then I remembered I had no one to call.

"Hey," I said, trying to keep my words from slurring. I didn't feel that smashed.

"You're drunk," he stated. I knew he was a smart guy.

"Thank you, Captain Obvenous—Obviless. Shit, you know what I mean," I retorted.

I could hear him sigh over the phone. He was aggravated. I started giggling because the fact that he was the one who was aggravated was hilarious. I was the one who couldn't remember who I was.

"I'll come get you. Are you still at your apartment?"

"Nope."

"You're not? Where are you?"

"Um, I's not sure. Lemme sheck." I walked to the corner to check the cross streets.

"Don't go anywhere. I'll be there soon."

I nodded, even though he couldn't see me, and headed back to my Jeep. I was beginning to feel cold and wanted to lie down. Crawling into the backseat of my Jeep, I curled up in a ball on the small, narrow bench seat that was built for someone with an elf's stature. I pulled my jacket up over my icy cheeks, trying to warm them.

I woke the next morning feeling like a cement truck had parked on top of my head. Squinting in the sunlight streaming through the window, I cursed the liquor gods for not only tempting me the night before, but for punishing me this morning. My tongue tasted like a goat had taken a shit in my mouth.

My head felt like it was in a vise as I turned to find that Trent's side of the bed was empty. I racked my throbbing brain, trying to remember how I'd gotten here. I vaguely remembered calling Trent last night, but for the life of me, I couldn't recall what the conversation had entailed. The memories of my fight with Cameo were as clear as day. They bounced around in my head like a frog on crack. Along with the desolate feelings I'd had from the party.

The urge to pull the blanket over my head and slip into a sleep-induced coma was strong. If it wasn't for my stubborn bladder that was insisting I visit the bathroom, I wouldn't have moved. I gingerly climbed from the bed, but the room swayed slightly. I couldn't believe I'd allowed myself to get so wasted. It was a total rookie move.

After a shower and half a bottle of mouthwash, I felt like

death wasn't as imminent as I first thought when I woke up. I left the bedroom to find Trent sitting in the living room. I figured I probably had a few things to apologize for, besides the fact that he had to lug my stupid ass home.

I stopped in my tracks at the unusual sight of Trent sitting on the couch doing nothing. I say *unusual* because Trent never just sat. Normally, he was busy on his computer and the TV was always on. The living room seemed like a morgue without the distraction of background noise. I must have been more of a mess last night than I thought.

"Trent," I said tentatively, edging closer to him.

He looked up blankly. Something else was wrong. This wasn't brought on by drunk-ass me last night.

"Is everything okay?" The question was asinine. Of course everything wasn't okay, but how else would I get to whatever was bothering him?

He looked at me for a moment. His mouth opened to answer, but nothing came out. He snapped it closed before dropping his face into his hands. Now I really felt reason to panic. Something was terribly wrong. I hurried to his side, ignoring the side effects of my hangover. All I cared about was finding out who had wronged the person I loved. I would make whoever it was pay for doing this to him.

Sitting down on the coffee table in front of him, I grabbed his hands, silently imploring him to tell me what was wrong. His hands lay in mine like dead fish. "Trent, what is going on?" I asked, trying to keep the hysterical edge out of my voice.

"Have you ever wondered what I did in my old school that got me in so much trouble?" he finally asked in a flat voice.

His words momentarily confused me. "You mean before you moved to Woodfalls?"

He nodded his head.

"Well, yeah, I guess, why?" We all had. In a town the size of Woodfalls, that kind of secret was practically against the law.

"I was kicked out for hacking into the school computer."

I wasn't surprised. I'd always suspected it was something like that. What I didn't understand was why he was mentioning it now.

"What do you know about hacking?"

I shrugged my shoulders. I really didn't know anything other than it sucked major ass when someone hacked my Instagram or Facebook accounts. It happened to me once and resulted in my entire friend base getting spammed with erectile dysfunction ads. "Someone hacked my Facebook account once. That sucked," I answered.

"Right," he said. It was strange to see so many conflicting emotions on his face.

"Okay, so you're a hacker. You didn't steal someone's identity and ruin their life or something, right?" I thought I was making a joke, but mentally I was crossing my fingers. I didn't know how I would handle it if he confirmed that fear.

I could see him mentally weighing his words before he answered. "I was a hacker, and no, I never did anything that bad."

"You were a hacker, but not anymore? I guess I still don't understand what the problem is."

"At my old high school, I set up my own little enterprise. I'd hack into the school computers in our district and change grades for a fee."

"Oh lord. No, you didn't," I laughed. Straight-as-an-arrow, Trent had done something illegal. I had myself a bad boy after all and didn't even realize it. "And you got busted," I stated as all the pieces clicked into place.

"It wasn't funny, and I got busted all right. Shit hit the fan with the school district and my parents. I was expelled from school and they threatened to fine my parents and even send me to juvie. Luckily, I was a minor, so there wasn't much they could do. Plus, it was my first offense. It is on my permanent record in the state of Missouri, so after that, it seemed I would never get a fair shake at any school there. My parents made the huge decision to move us out of state so I could start over with a clean slate. That's how we ended up in Woodfalls. I promised I'd keep my nose clean and wouldn't hack again," he finished. His voice broke like there was more he wanted to say, but he wouldn't look at me. I wondered again what I was missing.

"Okay, so obviously you wouldn't do it again, right?" It scared me that the look in his eyes was already answering my question. "I mean, why would you do it if that was the case? What could possibly be worth risking your future?" I asked the questions, somehow expecting that this was some sort of prank. He was just getting back at me for last night. The expression on his face spoke volumes. I looked at him blankly.

"Trent, what does this have to do with me?"

"I wasn't necessarily going to do anything; I was just checking."

"Checking what? I don't understand what you're saying."

"I wanted to make sure you passed your finals. I knew how worried you were."

"You checked my final grades?" It was hard to keep the hurt from my voice. "Please tell me you're not saying what I think you are," I pleaded.

His silence was the only answer I needed. My chest felt like it was being squeezed. "You changed my grades?" Embarrassment and shame filled me. After all my hard work, I was still nothing but a loser? "I don't deserve to be here," I said, standing on shaky legs.

The dead look left his eyes. "Wait, Tressa, no! You misunderstood me." He jumped to his feet. "I didn't have to change them. You got those grades on your own."

I shook my head in denial. "You're lying." I paced in front of the coffee table, jerking away as he tried to stop me. I felt so confused by the mixed feelings crashing around my head like balls on a pool table. What did this mean for Trent, or for me? Would I be implicated in this too? Did I work my ass off for nothing, and now I'd be kicked out anyway? In a way, this was my fault. If Trent had never gotten involved with me, this never would have happened. "I ruin everything I touch. I'm like poison."

Trent stood in front of me and placed his hands on my shoulders. "Don't say that. I'm not lying. You earned those grades fair and square. I should have made that clear. I'm the one who was wrong here. Not you." His voice was louder than I had ever heard it.

"I want to believe you," I said with a quiver in my voice.

"Then believe it. You will find out anyway when you see your actual tests." I felt slightly relieved until I reminded myself of what had started our conversation in the first place. "If you didn't change my grade, what is the big deal?"

"I tripped a flag when I hacked into the school's mainframe. I should have known they'd have several safeguards in place. I underestimated their security. Obviously, I'm not a great hacker since I've been caught twice."

"Do they think I had something to do with this too?"

"No, no, believe me. I made that crystal clear. It's me who's in trouble," he assured me.

"How much trouble could you be in if you didn't change my grades?"

His face turned grim. "That's the problem. I hacked into a computer with the intent to change something. I didn't destroy or harm anything, so it's not a felony, but it's still a class B misdemeanor."

"What does that mean for you?" I asked, gnawing on my lip.

"Most likely a fine, and if a judge wanted to be a hard-ass, I could actually get up to six months in jail. I think a lot of it has to do with how far the school wants to take it," he said.

"Holy shit, you could go to jail? What about the school? What are they doing?" I asked, flabbergasted. "Wait, I can call Professor N or my dad. Do you need an attorney?"

He sat back down on the couch, defeated. "Actually, Professor Nelson is helping me through this. Because of him, I'm fairly certain the school is going to drop the charges, but there are consequences. I'm out. They expelled me."

"What?" I shrieked. "They can't do that. What about your thesis?" Could they really make him walk away from all the hard work he had put in? The injustice of it all made me want to scream. What he did was nothing. I'd done pranks that were worse than this.

"They can do what they want, and they did. It could have been worse."

How could it have been any worse than to lose everything he'd been working toward? I began to feel sick. If we weren't together, he never would have done something so reckless, so careless.

"They could have pressed charges. Jail would have been a real possibility. They're not doing that. Yeah, I'm no longer a Maine State College student, but at least they didn't ruin my entire life. The fact that you aced your finals saved me. If I would have had to change your grades, things would have been a great deal worse for me. Any role they may have thought you had in this was quickly dismissed because there was a paper trail and all your teachers stepped forward to say how hard you've been working. So, you see? I should actually be thanking you," he said, smiling like there was a silver lining on this black cloud.

"Oh, give me a break," I stated indignantly. "You are seriously going to sit there and thank me? What kind of twisted-ass thinking is that? You were willing to give up everything for me. Was it stupid? Hell yeah. Am I furious that you would do something so incredibly dumb? Absolutely, but you are not going to act like a martyr and thank me for it." I punched him in the arm for good measure. A small part of me was sort of relieved that he had proven to be human and capable of doing stupid shit. I was beginning to feel like I was the only one making all the mistakes.

"God, you asshole. I could puke right now that you lost everything you were working for." My voice trailed off as I considered what this meant for our future. "What are you going to do?"

"I'm not sure yet. I'm still trying to wrap my brain around everything. I was sure you'd hate me and we'd be through," he admitted, leaning his head against the back of the couch and closing his eyes. I couldn't help noticing how exhausted he looked.

"When did you find all this out?"

"Well, yesterday is when I found out I'd been dropped from school," he answered, not opening his eyes.

I couldn't have felt any more like pond scum. I'd been out acting like a selfish bitch, trying to drink away my bullshit concerns, when Trent's whole life had been unraveling at the seams. "Why didn't you tell me sooner?"

"I didn't want to ruin your party. I knew how much you'd been looking forward to it. I was tied up in disciplinary meetings all afternoon anyway. Professor Nelson really went to bat for me. I owe him. He did everything he could, but the school just couldn't allow me to stay."

"I'm so sorry," I said, sitting next to him on the couch. "What can I do?"

He reached for my hand. "You're already doing it. Just having you here with me helps. I thought you would be gone for sure."

"Never, I'll always be here." I meant the words. All my doubts and insecurities from the night before no longer seemed relevant.

We sat in silence and eventually Trent drifted off to sleep. I sat beside him, stroking his hand and wondering where we would go from here. One thing was certain—I needed to mend some fences. I pulled a blanket around Trent, leaving him to sleep while I left to handle some business.

I drove to my old apartment, mulling over what I needed to say. Cameo and Derek were in the middle of cleaning up the mess from their party the previous night when I pushed the door open.

"Tress." The relief in Derek's voice was tangible. He left his stack of discarded red Solo cups on the table and gave me a tight hug. "I was worried about you," he whispered in my ear.

"Thanks. Do you mind if I talk to Cameo alone for a few minutes?"

"Sure," he answered, releasing me before heading toward our room.

Cameo and I faced off, both too stubborn to be the one to speak first. In that way, we were like two peas in a pod. It was our similarities that had brought us together in the first place.

Ironically, in a situation like this, they were also what wedged us apart.

For once in my life, I decided to swallow my pride and act first. "Cam, I know you don't understand what's going on with me. Hell, even I don't understand it most of the time. All I can do is try to explain, so maybe you'll get it a little." The stubborn set of her shoulders eased a bit, which told me she was at least willing to listen.

The words poured out of me like a floodgate had been opened. I confessed everything I'd been feeling the last few months. My embarrassment over my grades and the staggering guilt I still felt over David's death. Finally, I explained my struggle coming to grips with my feelings for Trent. I left out the bomb he'd dropped on me earlier.

"I know I'm different. I see it every day. It scares the hell out of me sometimes, but I don't think I'm ever going to be the old me again. I tried last night, but that girl is gone. David's death made me look at things differently, changed who I thought I was. And Trent helped me believe in myself. This is the new me."

Cameo was silent for a moment. "You're still a whore," she said grudgingly. At least she was smiling now.

"And you're still a slut."

"Does that mean you're never going to go out with me again?"

"Not at all. Just more in moderation, but you'll have to start doing stuff this new me likes to do."

"Like what?" she asked, grimacing dramatically. "Don't

you dare say going to the comic book store, or I swear I'll strangle myself."

I laughed. "Let's not go nuts. I meant like vegging out, watching movies, or playing cards with us on Friday night sometime."

"Friday is party night . . ." Her voice trailed off. "Fine," she grumbled.

I reached over and gave her a hug. "I've missed you, slut face."

"I've missed you too, whore bag," she replied, returning my hug tightly.

We talked for a while longer and she confided her own fears and hurt over her breakup with Chad. She still wasn't over him. I nodded sympathetically. I'd suspected all along that was the case.

"Maybe you guys will work it out, you know? He did have a lot of shit going on with the fraternity being shut down."

"I don't think so. He's dating someone else," she said in a small voice that was totally out of character for her.

"Oh, Cam, I'm so sorry. He's a donkey ass face," I said, hugging her.

"Did you two kiss and make up?" Derek asked, joining us.

"Sure did," I answered, giving him a hug. "I'm going to grab a few things and head out before Trent wakes up."

"So, we're guessing you'll be moving in with him," Cameo stated, standing.

"I'm not sure what I'm doing yet. Trent and I have a few things to work out first."

"Everything okay?" Cameo asked, trailing behind me as I entered my room.

"I hope so. I'll fill you in later," I said, shoving the majority of my clothes in my two big suitcases from the closet.

"You better," she threatened. I zipped up the suitcases and together we dragged them down the hall.

"I'll talk to you soon," I said as I gave her another tight hug. It was a relief to have finally gotten past everything.

Trent was awake when I wheeled my two suitcases into his apartment fifteen minutes later. He jumped up like he'd been worried I wouldn't come back. "Going somewhere?" he asked, eyeing my suitcases.

I nodded, walking toward him. "I'm going here," I said, sliding my arms around his waist. I rested my cheek against his chest.

"I was worried you'd left me when I woke up and you were gone."

"Why would you think that?"

"Oh, I don't know. Maybe the way I totally effed things up. I thought you came to your senses and bailed."

"Are you kidding? You wouldn't even be in this position if it wasn't for me. I'm not going anywhere. I'm standing by you through all this."

"You don't have to feel obligated to do that," he said quietly, tilting my chin so he could look into my eyes.

"The only obligation I feel is to show you how much you mean to me every single day."

"What did I do to deserve this?"

"Silly Clark Trent. I may not be the smartest cookie in the jar, but I know enough to hold on to a superhero if I'm lucky enough to snag one."

"Does this mean you'll dress up like Lois Lane?"

"Only if you're willing to be Superman," I answered, tugging his head down so my lips could claim his.

"I'm yours as long as you'll have me," he said.

"I hope you're ready for a long ride," I whispered as his lips settled on mine.

I sighed happily, settling into the kiss. Who would have thought two people who contradicted each other on paper would turn out to be a perfect match in reality?

Epilogue

"Are you sure you want to be outside tonight?" I asked skeptically. Everything about our evening had been kept a secret from me. Trent pulled a two-person sleeping bag and a tarp from the trunk of his car. He handed over the bag of goodies he had stopped and bought at Fran's market on the way. I eyed everything suspiciously, wondering if he planned for us to sleep outside. I hated to break it to him but camping wasn't my thing.

He grinned, looking into the narrow beam of the flashlight I clutched in my gloved hand. "Why, are you afraid Michael Myers is going to step out from behind a tree with a knife?"

"Please, he's too busy chasing dippy sex-crazed teenagers," I said, following behind as we left his car in the small clearing. "Hey, wait a minute. Are you Michael Myers? You are taking me into the woods."

His smile looked downright devilish in the beam of my flashlight. "You never know." He dropped his voice a notch and took a menacing step toward me.

"And here I thought you were the hero," I said, with mock outrage, taking a halfstep backward. My foot got stuck in a drift of snow and I tried using my arms to regain my balance, but it was a lost cause. My momentum was propelling me backward. Trent dropped the sleeping bag and reached out a hand at the last possible moment, capturing my wrist. He tugged on it just enough to settle me against his rock-hard chest. I smoothed my hands up over the planes of his pecs. "Hmm, maybe you are my hero," I murmured, kissing the corner of his mouth.

"You better believe it." His lips captured mine briefly before pulling away. "Stop tempting me, woman. We're going to be late."

"Late for what?" I whined, trailing after him as he trudged through the snow.

He didn't bother to turn around. "It's a secret."

I would have complained more, but he was too damn cute. He'd been planning this surprise for a while and wouldn't let me in on it no matter how I tried to persuade him. The Princess Leia costume had even come out of retirement to help convince him, but he remained close-lipped. At least we had fun while I tried.

"You know, we'd probably have more fun trekking through the forest if we had a little daylight," I pointed out.

I wasn't surprised when he didn't answer. I'd been using ploys like that for a week to get it out of him.

We trudged silently through the woods for at least five minutes. I was beginning to think maybe he was lost. He was more of an indoor kind of guy.

"Almost there," he finally said, reaching for my hand.

Linking my gloved fingers through his, I stepped out through the thin line of trees, gasping in surprise. We were on a slight elevation, overlooking a large clearing that gave the illusion we were standing atop the world. Far off in the distance I could see the faint lights of Woodfalls. Combined with the bright shining stars in the night sky, the view was absolutely picturesque. I watched in awe as a light that looked like a fast-moving plane streaked across the sky. "Whoa, was that a UFO?" I was kidding, of course, but wondered if he had seen it too. Before he could answer, another light streaked across the black sky, followed by another.

"Nope. They're meteors," he said, sliding his arms around my waist to pull me in close. "It's the Quadrantid meteor shower."

I tilted my head up to look at him. "Seriously? That's amazing."

"Have you ever seen one?"

I shook my head as he rested his head on my shoulder. The quick, streaking lights were like fireworks without all the noise.

After a few minutes he released me and unfolded the tarp, spreading it out over the blanket of snow at our feet. He placed the heavy-duty sleeping bag on top and smoothed out the wrinkles. "I saw a meteor shower one other time before we moved here, but the city lights dulled the experience," he said, plunking us down on the cushy sleeping bag.

He tugged off his shoes and placed them on the empty space on the tarp. I watched in amusement as he also pulled off my shoes and lined them up next to his before climbing into the sleeping bag.

"Are you planning on sleeping here?" We weren't exactly in some campground surrounded by other people. There were wild animals in these woods and we were by ourselves.

"Oh, we won't be sleeping." He tugged on my hand so I was lying on top of him.

"You expect to get lucky when it's colder than a witch's tit out here?"

Our lips were inches apart. His hands moved to my head, removing my stocking hat. "You'll be warm in here," he said, pressing his cool lips to mine.

I opened under his persistence, instantly responding to the way his tongue moved possessively against mine. "So you drag me to the middle of nowhere to have your way with me?" I teased breathlessly when we separated. Our warm breath was visible in the cool air. I snuggled closer in his arms, looking up at the occasional flashes of lights that would streak across the sky.

He chuckled, planting a kiss atop my head. "I didn't know it would take so little effort. Who knew you were so easy?"

I nudged him with my elbow. "Do you want me to start playing hard to get?"

His arm tightened around me. "Hell no. This is much better than having fantasies about you."

"Fantasies? Care to share?"

"Not on your life," he laughed, sitting up. He pulled a thermos from the bag and handed it to me. "Want some hot chocolate?"

"You're cute. You know that?"

"Cute? I thought we had elevated me to stud status." He tucked the sleeping bag snugly across our laps and removed the cup from the thermos in my hands.

The delicious scent of chocolate-infused steam rose from the container when he unscrewed the lid. I winked at him as he filled the cup. "You're definitely my stud," I answered, taking a sip of the rich beverage.

"Good," he growled, giving me another kiss. "Mmm, chocolate kiss."

We lay back in the sleeping bag, content in silence as we continued to watch the natural night show. "This is pretty amazing," I finally said. He tightened his hold around me, pulling me tightly in place. It felt secure. "Thank you for sharing this with me."

"I couldn't imagine sharing it with anyone else," he murmured against my ear, making me sigh with pleasure.

"It's like we're the only ones in the world." My throat felt tight as tears prickled at the backs of my eyes. For the first time in as long as I could remember, I felt truly happy. It seemed like Trent and I had taken a long road to get where we were. It was a shame it took a tragic event to bring us together, but David's senseless death had given me a new outlook on life and Trent was a part of that. Cameo finally understood all the demons I had been fighting. We even worked together, along with David's parents, in setting up a memorial scholarship in his name.

The official unveiling would commence in a ceremony the school had planned for when we returned for the spring semester. I had been asked to give a speech. I already knew what I would say and hoped my words would give his parents and friends some peace. I had to put aside my feelings about how MSC had treated Trent. It felt like a double-edged sword to work with them since they had stuck to their decision regarding his expulsion, despite Professor N and several other professors speaking on his behalf. It was Trent who encouraged me to put my misgivings aside, convincing me it was for the best. He was currently continuing the work on his project at Professor N's house. Trent seemed perfectly content with the way things had turned out, which was all I could ask for.

"You're the only person that matters in my world," he whispered.

I sighed happily as his lips tenderly captured mine. Without breaking contact, I pulled the sleeping bag over our heads. We made love beneath the sky full of stars and streaking meteors, never taking our eyes from each other.

READ ON FOR A SPECIAL PREVIEW OF

TIFFANY KING'S NEXT BOOK

A Shattered Moment

THE FIRST IN THE NEW FRACTURED LIVES SERIES

COMING SOON FROM BERKLEY!

Graduation night 2012

The breeze blowing through the open windows of the SUV was hot and sticky thanks to the blanket of humidity that was normal for this time of year. Not that my friends and I cared. Even with sweat running down our backs and our hair plastered to the napes of our necks. We were too amped-up to worry about something as pesky as the weather. Today we were free. This was the moment we had discussed at length. The moment we had planned for and dreamed about. We didn't need drugs or alcohol to experience our current state of euphoria. We were high on life and the anticipation of what the future held.

Laughter filled the interior of the Suburban, drowning out the roar from the oversized off-road tires as we cruised down the highway. It was the sound of exhilaration and triumph fifteen years in the making. Fifteen years of friendship that had stood the test of time. Through the muck of adolescent squabbles, preteen dramas, and the turbulent years of high school, we had made it to the other side of graduation. Our friendship was unbreakable. We made a pact many years ago over mud pies and juice boxes. We swore we would always be friends. No matter what the obstacles, we managed to stay inseparable. Our parents, who had also become close over the years, had coined us the "Brat Pack." They would laugh every time they said it, like it was some inside joke only they were privy to. I guess you had to be older than forty to get it.

I swept my eyes around the vehicle, listening to the loud music blaring from the radio as the wind played with my hair. With the exception of my family, anyone who had ever meant anything to me was here.

Zach was always our driver. His parents gave him the keys to the Suburban when he turned sixteen, knowing it was the perfect vehicle for our group. We were used to doing everything together, so it only made sense that the first of us to obtain a coveted driver's license would receive a vehicle big enough to carry everyone. The Suburban was a year older than we were and had its fair share of dings and rust spots, but it was trusty and reliable.

If he minded becoming our designated chauffeur, he never complained. That was Zach in a nutshell. He was the guy everyone liked, and for good reason. He was the first to lend a hand or volunteer his services, or just listen if you needed someone to talk to. He had been the captain of the football team and class president junior and senior year. Zach was a born leader, which is why he was bound for FSU in the fall on full scholarship. He had also always been my stand-in boyfriend. It was an on-again/off-again routine we had fallen into. I knew I could always count on him. My plan was to avoid a serious relationship before college. Zach had provided the perfect buffer. All along, we had planned to spend this final summer together before we headed off to separate schools. If Zach promised, I knew I could bank on it, or so I thought.

I pulled my thoughts away from their current path. There was no reason to muck up the evening we'd been planning forever. Instead, I moved my eyes to Dan and Kathleen sitting in the third row with their heads pressed together. They had been a thing since we were kids. Not a thing like Zach and me, but a real couple. Their love had been forged over shared cookies and building sandcastles. It had always been Dan and Kat/Kat and Dan. In the beginning, their parents tried to rein in their kids' feelings for each other, but that was like telling the sun not to shine. They were the image of soul mates. The pending separation of our group would be hardest on them. Kat's parents insisted on the idea of her and Dan attending separate colleges, at least for the first couple of years. They wanted her to be sure that Dan would be more than a childhood romance. Kat confided to us that she only planned on giving it a year, if that long. This is why I'd always kept things casual. As close as we all were as friends, the idea of planning your college career around a guy seemed extreme to me.

"Class of 2012, bitches!" Jessica yelled from the second row where she sat with my best friend, Tracey. Filled with exuberance, and more adventurous than the rest of our Brat Pack, they were usually also the loudest. They were ready to take on the world and would stretch their wings wider than any of the rest of us in the group. I actually felt a little jealous, wishing I had an ounce of their fearlessness. Tracey's eyes met mine briefly before darting away. I grimaced without saying a word. Nothing would mar today. That is the vow I made to myself. Tomorrow would be soon enough to analyze what I had discovered.

I shifted back around in my seat as Zach drove over the causeway. We all whooped with our hands in the air as we reached the top. In the remaining light of dusk, we could see the dark, never-ending expanse of water in the distance. We were close to our first destination of the evening.

Zach slowed to a crawl, maneuvering the Suburban around an old Lincoln Town Car going twenty-five miles per hour, even though the speed limit was almost double that. I had respect for my elders, but anyone who says teenagers are the worst drivers has obviously never lived in Florida.

Of course, Zach didn't mind. He was patient and cautious, even after jerking the wheel to avoid a moped that darted in front of us. The bikini-clad girl perched on the back didn't even bother looking at us as she flipped us off.

"Stupid asses, huh?" Zach laughed, shooting me a smile I thought I'd returned until I saw his face fall slightly before he looked back to the road. Sighing, I turned my head to look out my window. Of all the days for me to discover what had probably been going on under my nose for some time, why did it have to be today?

Seeing Zach's smile drop beside me, I realized I wasn't fooling anyone. I could put on a facade that everything was okay, but deep down, three of us in this vehicle knew differently.

Minutes later we arrived at the public parking lot at New Smyrna Beach. We piled out of the Suburban, breathing in the salty sea air. Kat linked her arms with mine and Tracey's while Jessica linked my other arm. Our human chain was complete when the guys bookended us on either side and we raced down the grassy slope to the long expanse of sand. We kicked our shoes off the instant our feet touched the sand, which had already started to cool now that the sun had gone down.

Laughter rang through the air as we raced toward the dark water without slowing. Our graduation robes flared out behind us like capes. With the wind whipping them around, we almost felt like we could fly as we splashed into the incoming waves. Nothing could hold us back. We were invincible.

We never made it to our second destination that night. Sadly, we weren't invincible.

I would later be asked countless times what happened, forced to recall what I remembered about the accident that changed everything. Clarity of the events was never an issue. I breathed it—had nightmares about it. It would haunt me for the rest of my life.

Zach had just merged onto the interstate, heading toward Orlando. Everything happened so quickly and unexpectedly. My mind was still focused on what had transpired as we left the beach. Not on the careless driver on the highway who acted like we were never there.

It was Jessica screaming after the semitruck slammed into the side of the Suburban that will be forever burned into my mind like a bad song that refuses to go away. The oversized advertisement for fresh strawberries that ran the length of the trailer was the last thing that appeared upright after Zach jerked the wheel to avoid another collision. I would later learn that our momentum combined with the impact from the trailer were the culprits for what happened next.

With the horrific grinding sound of metal against metal and the sickening smell of burning rubber, the wheels on the right side of the Suburban left the road, sending us airborne. I had heard once that when you're in an accident everything passes in a blur of slow motion. That is total bullshit. It's instant chaos. Fast and scary are more accurate—and loud. So loud you feel like your ears will burst. So hectic you can't tell where sounds are coming from. It's a jumbled mess of groaning metal beat out of its original shape, shattering glass, blaring horns, and, worst of all, screams of pain from your friends. And yet, through it all, I remember every detail with painstaking lucidity.

"How could you possibly know how many times the vehicle rolled?" That is always the first question asked when I recount the series of events for someone. It was a question that haunted me as well. It was as if I were being cosmically punished for some wrong I had committed. If I knew what it was, I would take it all back. I would trade places with any of my friends over being forever tormented by vivid memories that I could never escape. Each roll of the vehicle was significant for what it did to my friends. The first roll sent Tracey's head against her window with a thud. The second roll abruptly silenced Dan, who had been swearing from the moment Jessica started screaming. Kat shrieked Dan's name in anguish, overpowering Jessica's screams during the third bone-crunching roll of the vehicle. On the fourth roll, Jessica's screams stopped like someone had flipped a switch. I panicked, believing at any moment my last breath would be snuffed out like the flame of a candle.

We stopped on the fifth roll, finally coming to a rest mid-turn, leaving us upside down. The bench seat Zach and I shared tore away from the metal bolts that attached it to the floorboard and tumbled forward, pinning me to the dash-board. My head exploded with pain as it bounced off the windshield. I vaguely remember wondering why an airbag hadn't opened. It turned out the old Suburban Zach had been given by his parents was a year away from that upgrade. A steady hum filled my ears. It was as if I had been swaddled in a cocoon of cotton. I felt absolutely nothing.